Broadcasting Chaos

Thomas Brant

Copyright © 2025 Thomas Brant.

All rights reserved.

No part of this book can be reproduced in any form or by written, electronic or mechanical, including photocopying, recording, or by any information retrieval system without written permission in writing by the author.

Published by T Brant Publishing

Printed in Great Britain

Unless otherwise indicated, all the names, characters, businesses, places, events and incidents in this book are either the product of the author's imagination or used in a fictitious manner. Any resemblance to actual persons, living or dead, or actual events is purely coincidental.

Although every precaution has been taken in the preparation of this book, the publisher and author assume no responsibility for errors or omissions. Neither is any liability assumed for damages resulting from the use of information contained herein.

ISBN 978-1-0683106-1-4

CHAPTER 1 - Reflections
Tuesday 15th April 2025

James Smith knew that the past 4 months had been hard. Having been kicked out by his father, having fell deeper into the web of hedonistic chaos that had consumed his life, James now stood at a crossroads. The bright lights of his Ibiza Headbangers days had been replaced by voice tracking shows with Kylie for the new Manic Urban station, a station focused on a younger, edgier audience with a penchant for grime, UK drill, and the latest chart-toppers. The glossy excitement of his early Manic days had dulled into a blur of late-night recordings and an endless churn of "bangers only" branding. The station lacked the raw allure of Ibiza Headbangers but demanded the same energy—a relentless pursuit of virality, youth culture, and staying relevant.

Having dropped out of Wolverhampton University, the lure of cocaine and the slate of production line standard shows left James feeling like a shell of his former self. His relationship with Kylie Morgan was a shadow of what it had once been, their once electric chemistry now reduced to tense silences and arguments over dwindling opportunities. That he had become a pure submissive towards her, allowing her to use him and treat him as a tool to maintain her own relevance, gnawed at his pride. Yet, James couldn't bring himself to walk away. Kylie's dominance in their professional partnership—and his personal life—seemed unshakable. She was the driving force behind their rebranding, their calculated edginess for Manic Urban, and their social media personas that screamed curated chaos. For all his resentment, James felt trapped, unsure whether it was loyalty, fear, or sheer inertia that kept him tethered to her.

Standing in the dimly lit recording booth in the new One Snow Hill hub in Birmingham, James fiddled with the faders on the soundboard, waiting for Kylie to arrive. The stale smell of energy drinks and sweat filled the air, a stark reminder of the countless hours spent churning out content. Manic Urban had a relentless schedule, and James's once-aspirational career now felt like an assembly line of shallow hype tracks and contrived banter.

Suddenly the door opened, and James sighed, as he knew it was either Kylie or their producer, a 24-year-old male named Shane who, like James and Kylie, was hooked on cocaine and so tightly wound by the drug's grip that his once-sharp producer instincts had dulled into manic bursts of energy and erratic behaviour.

"I warned you, James," a voice from behind him said, and James knew instantly that it was Kylie. She swept into the room like a storm, her presence as commanding as ever. Dressed in a sleek, oversized jacket over a crop top and joggers that screamed high-fashion streetwear, she carried herself with the confidence of someone who knew the world revolved around her—at least in her mind. Her dyed platinum blonde hair framed her face, where sharp eyeliner and a hint of glitter contrasted with the darkness of the room.

"You're late," James muttered without turning around, fiddling aimlessly with the controls.

"Don't start," Kylie snapped. "I've got an hour until my Manic Vibe drive show, and you, slut, are to eat me out before I go to the Vibes studios upstairs and do my first Midlands drive show."

James got on his knees and waited for permission to continue, only for Kylie to slap him.

"Do you think I'd let you actually continue being a part of my world after everything you've done? You're lucky I even keep you around," Kylie hissed, her voice cold but calculated. She loomed over him, her sharp nails tracing along his jawline. "Now, its payday, and your money is not in my account. Your pay should always come to my account, not yours. Why?"

James flinched at the slap, his face burning from both the sting and the humiliation. He swallowed hard, forcing himself to remain composed, though every fibre of his being screamed at him to push back. Yet, he didn't. He couldn't. The tangled mess of power dynamics and emotional manipulation Kylie had woven around him held him in place like a web.

"You know what... don't answer. Now, Nott has been sniffing around, wondering why you aren't making an appearance in the public areas. That bitch is close to finding out about you being the office cum dump."

James's stomach churned at Kylie's words, the crude dismissal of his humanity cutting deeper than the slap. He stared at the scuffed floor of the recording booth, trying to suppress the overwhelming sense of shame that welled up inside him. Every part of his life, it seemed, was owned—his voice, his pay, his image, even his dignity.

Lyra Nott's name lingered in his mind. She had always been an enigmatic presence within Manic, a presenter who, unlike the others, seemed to hold onto some semblance of integrity. The thought of her discovering the depths of his entanglement with Kylie filled him with equal parts dread and hope. Perhaps someone knowing would force a change. Perhaps she could help him. Or perhaps it would only serve to cement his downfall further.

The fact that she was close friends with his dad, and had, three months earlier, moved into the Smith family home in Pensnett after her and her boyfriend, Si, a wrestler who had suffered a career-ending injury, had broken up, made everything even worse. Lyra wasn't just any presenter—she was practically family, someone his father trusted deeply. If she discovered what his life had become, the repercussions would ripple far beyond the walls of Manic Urban. The thought of Pete Smith knowing about this degradation made James's chest tighten.

Kylie's fingers snapped in front of his face, pulling him out of his spiralling thoughts. "Are you even listening, you idiot?" she barked, her tone dripping with disdain. "I don't have time for your sulking. Fix your face and look at me."

James forced his head up, meeting Kylie's sharp glare. "Yes, Kylie," he murmured, his voice hollow.

"Good," she said, her lips curving into a smirk that didn't reach her eyes. "You'll need to be on your best behaviour tonight. Shane's planning some big stunt for the 9 PM slot—something about going viral on TikTok. He's expecting you to be all in."

James nodded automatically, though he felt a pit forming in his stomach. Shane's idea of "going viral" often involved reckless, borderline illegal antics designed to grab fleeting attention. It was the epitome of what Manic Urban had become—style over substance, shock over sincerity.

"And for God's sake," Kylie added, her voice turning sharp again, "don't embarrass me. If Lyra catches wind of anything... well, let's just say you won't like what happens. Now, Lane is next on your list to service, and he wants your arse. Make sure that he puts the cock ring, anal plug and nipple clamps back on you as last time you forgot to remind him, he had to pay me extra as an apology. Now, he's outside, so when I go out, you will make sure to accept his cum, to accept his abuse, and to do so without a single complaint, or else we're done. And remember... Reevesy... I'm still within the time to get an abortion if you don't comply."

James knew that last bit stung, as Kylie was pregnant with his child—a fact that should have been a source of hope or at least grounding. Instead, it had become another weapon in Kylie's arsenal of manipulation. The mention of abortion twisted his insides, not because of his own feelings about parenthood, but because of how coldly and calculatedly Kylie wielded it as leverage.

"Understood," James whispered, the words barely audible. Each syllable felt like another brick in the wall of his growing resentment, but he knew better than to push back. Kylie thrived on dominance, and resistance only fuelled her cruelty.

She stared at him for a moment longer, her eyes narrowing as if searching for a crack in his compliance. Satisfied, she turned on her heel and swept out of the booth, her trainers squeaking slightly on the polished floor. James's head dropped again; his gaze fixed on the control panel in front of him. The room fell silent except for the faint hum of equipment, a sound that had once been comforting but now felt suffocating.

A soft knock on the door broke his trance, and James knew without looking who it was. Cody Lane, his brother-in-law, the man who his sister, Chloe, had recently married and entrapped with her own pregnancy. The fact that, unlike James, Cody, being a newsreader within Manic and a willing participant in James's degradation, had a life that appeared stable and put-together made the situation all the more humiliating for James. Cody was a rising star in Manic's newsroom, someone who seemed to navigate the same corporate swamp with ease and confidence that James had long since lost. The power dynamic between them had shifted drastically over the past few months, and Cody exploited it without hesitation.

The door creaked open, and Cody stepped in, a smug grin plastered across his face. His Linkin Park t-shirt, ripped denim shorts and expensive trainers, part of the unofficial uniform that male Manic staff wore to blend with the edgy branding, seemed to mock James's dishevelled appearance. Cody leaned casually against the doorframe, his eyes scanning James with a predatory gleam.

"Alright, Reevesy," Cody drawled, his voice dripping with faux camaraderie that barely masked his cruelty. "Kylie said you'd be ready for me. Let's not waste time, yeah? I've got to prep for the 4pm bulletin, so get those jeans down, get that arse plug out of your arse and lube my cock up with your mouth."

The scene felt unreal, surreal even. James sat frozen for a moment, staring at the console in front of him, the blinking lights of the equipment providing no solace. He could barely stomach Cody's smug voice, and the bile rising in his throat was only partly due to the humiliation.

Cody stepped further into the booth, closing the door behind him with a deliberate slowness that only added to James's dread. His grin widened as he leaned back against the door, arms crossed. "What's the hold-up, mate? Don't tell me you're losing your edge now. You're the one who wanted to be a star, yeah? This is part of the package."

James clenched his jaw, fighting back the surge of anger and shame that threatened to overwhelm him. He knew better than to protest. Any resistance would only bring more cruelty, more degradation. Manic wasn't just a station; it was a machine that consumed people like him, grinding them down to nothing more than tools for the brand. And Cody, despite his polished exterior, was just another cog in the machine—one who enjoyed his role a little too much.

****

Fifteen minutes later, James felt Cody's sperm from the third time the 24-year-old newsreader had climaxed drip down his thighs, staining the cheap studio carpet. His body felt numb, both from the physical exhaustion and the emotional void he had fallen into. The sterile studio lights hummed faintly above him, and for a moment, he wondered if this was all he would ever be—a puppet dancing to the whims of others, with no agency or dignity left.

"Now, bitch, clean my cock," Cody growled, and James was about to turn around and, as he knew that Cody hadn't used any protection such as a condom, meaning that the slightly elder twentysomething would be making James taste his own degradation.

As James started to work on this assignment, the door opened, and Lyra walked in, a frown on her face.

"What the fuck is going on?"

Lyra's voice cut through the oppressive silence like a whip. The sharp edge in her tone jolted both James and Cody, freezing them in place. For a moment, the sterile recording booth felt smaller, the air heavier, as Lyra's gaze moved between the two of them.

Cody, ever the chameleon, straightened up with a forced grin, pulling up his jeans as though nothing had happened. "Lyra! Didn't know you'd be dropping by. Reevesy wanted to give me a blowjob, so I happily complied," he said, his voice laced with a veneer of nonchalance that failed to mask the underlying tension.

James's heart pounded in his chest, his shame suffocating. He kept his eyes fixed on the floor, unable to meet the gaze of the Manic Vibes presenter.

"Didn't you, Reevesy?" Cody then said a bit more forcefully, hinting to James that if he didn't comply, he'd make things even worse for him later. James swallowed hard; his throat dry as sandpaper. His body stiffened, a mixture of fear and disgust coursing through him.

"That... that's right, Cody. It's because I love having your cock in my mouth," James choked out, his voice barely above a whisper, each word laced with humiliation. He couldn't bring himself to look at Lyra, knowing her sharp eyes were dissecting the scene in front of her. "After all, you're more of a man than I am. Can you... fuck me again?"

Lyra's eyes narrowed, her disgust evident. The confidence Cody usually exuded faltered for a brief moment under her icy stare. She crossed her arms, her stance unyielding, and exhaled slowly, as if trying to rein in her fury.

"This stops now," she said coldly, her voice cutting through the tense silence.

Cody smirked, though it was less convincing than usual. "Come on, Lyra, don't be such a buzzkill. It's just a bit of fun—consenting adults and all that. Isn't that right, Reevesy?" He threw a glance at James, whose face was a mask of shame and resignation.

James didn't respond, his silence speaking louder than any words could.

Lyra stepped forward, her presence commanding the room. She stood between James and Cody, her eyes locked on the latter. "Fun? This looks more like exploitation to me. You think I'm blind, Cody? Or stupid? Do you know who you're messing with?" Her tone was low but dangerous, her words laced with barely restrained anger.

Cody raised his hands in mock surrender, attempting a chuckle that fell flat. "Relax, Lyra. No need to get all heroic. Reevesy and I have an understanding."

Lyra's glare hardened. "The only thing I understand is that you're a predator who's gotten too comfortable in this toxic pit of a station. Get out of here before I make a call that will end your cushy little job in the newsroom."

Cody chuckled at that. "Really, Nott? Reevesy's my brother-in-law, and he's fully consenting, so if I want to let him suck me off or fuck his arse because he's a needy bitch who lives for this kind of humiliation, I will. Anyway, why are you so uptight? Is it because you're still a virgin? Reevesy, fuck this stuck-up bitch, and I'll tell Kylie that you might even be eligible for redemption."

Lyra didn't flinch, her piercing glare firmly locked onto Cody. The words he spewed, drenched in malice and arrogance, seemed to roll off her as she stood her ground, unshaken.

"That's enough," she said sharply, her voice carrying an edge that silenced Cody's smug retorts. "You think you can keep hiding behind this station's toxicity? Not on my watch."

James finally risked a glance at Lyra. Her usual poise, a mix of sharp wit and quiet strength, was now entirely focused on Cody. For the first time in months, James felt a faint flicker of something unfamiliar—hope.

Cody's bravado faltered, his grin shrinking into a thin line as he realised Lyra wasn't going to back down. "Fine," he muttered, adjusting his jeans and heading for the door. He turned briefly, his expression a mix of irritation and defiance. "Reevesy, don't forget who keeps you relevant around here." With that, he disappeared into the hallway, leaving an oppressive silence in his wake.

Lyra turned to James, her eyes softening as she took in the sight of him—dishevelled, humiliated, and visibly trembling. She crouched slightly to meet his gaze, her voice now gentle. "James... what's going on? What's really happening here?"

James opened his mouth to respond, but the words caught in his throat. How could he explain everything—the degradation, the manipulation, the sense of entrapment that had consumed him since he'd fallen under Kylie's control? His lips quivered as he struggled to find a way to express the mess his life had become.

"I..." he started, but his voice cracked, and tears threatened to spill. Suddenly, the next thing James knew, he felt Lyra's hand on his cock, and the cock ring that, for the past 4 months, Kylie had forced him to wear, being took off.

"F....fuck, Ly, I'm gonna cum if you take that off," James said, as he felt her soft hand wrapped around his most vulnerable part, seeing that she was taking off the torturous device that had become a symbol of his subjugation. His words trembled, barely audible, as he realised what Lyra was doing—not out of cruelty or dominance but with deliberate care. The gesture wasn't about desire or shame; it was about breaking the chain, both literal and figurative, that had held him captive.

"I'm not here to hurt you, James," Lyra said softly, her tone firm yet reassuring. Her hand remained steady, carefully working to remove the device that had been a physical manifestation of Kylie's control over him. "You're better than this. You don't deserve to be treated like some disposable plaything."

James's breath hitched as the sensation overwhelmed him, not just from the physical relief but from the emotional weight of someone showing him genuine compassion for the first time in what felt like forever. Tears slipped silently down his cheeks, and he bit his lip, struggling to keep himself composed.

As the cock ring came off, James came, ropes of semen spilling onto the cold studio floor, mingling with the humiliation and shame that clung to him like a second skin. He turned away, covering his face with trembling hands, his entire body shuddering as sobs overtook him. This wasn't release—it was a floodgate bursting open, weeks of degradation and despair finally breaking through.

"No, Kylie'll kill me if I don't have it on... and Cody forgot to put the anal plug back in. Please, Ly, put it back. That... or fuck me... make it look like you've finally put this whore in his place. If you don't... they'll... Kylie'll abort my daughter."

Lyra froze, the weight of James's words sinking in like lead. The dim light of the studio cast harsh shadows across his trembling form, the rawness of his despair cutting through her usual veneer of composure. She crouched next to him, placing a firm yet gentle hand on his shoulder.

"James," she said quietly, her voice steady but laced with urgency. "Look at me."

He didn't move, his face still buried in his hands as he shook his head. The shame was too much, the fear of what would happen if Kylie found out unbearable. Lyra's grip on his shoulder tightened slightly, grounding him.

"James," she repeated, more firmly this time. "I'm not going to hurt you. And I'm not going to let anyone else hurt you either. But you must let me help you."

Slowly, reluctantly, James lowered his hands. His bloodshot eyes met Lyra's, and for the first time in months, he saw something he hadn't expected—kindness. Not pity or judgement, but a fierce, protective determination.

"You don't have to live like this," Lyra continued, her tone resolute. "Whatever Kylie has over you, whatever she's threatened you with, it doesn't define you. You're not her property, James. You're a person. A human being."

The two kissed, a sudden, unexpected kiss, one that James knew from when he and Kylie had first done two years earlier, when they had been free of the chains that now bound them both in a web of manipulation and despair. But this kiss wasn't like those intoxicating moments with Kylie; it wasn't laced with ulterior motives or power plays. It was a kiss that spoke of genuine connection, of an attempt to break through the fog of shame and self-loathing that had enveloped James.

James pulled back suddenly, his face flushed, his emotions a whirlwind of confusion and vulnerability. "Lyra... I—" he stammered, his voice trembling as he struggled to make sense of what had just happened.

Lyra placed a finger gently over his lips, silencing him. "You don't need to explain," she said softly, her voice steady yet tinged with a hint of sadness. "I just need you to know that you're not alone in this. Whatever's going on, whatever Kylie or Cody or anyone else is doing to you—you don't have to face it by yourself."

James's eyes filled with tears again, but this time they weren't just from shame or humiliation. They were tears of something he hadn't felt in a long time: hope. Lyra's presence was a lifeline, a chance to pull himself out of the abyss he'd been spiralling into for months.

****

The clock showed ten past 4, and James and Lyra were on the studio floor, Lyra impaled on James's member, the two, for some, unknown, completely out of the blue reason having had sex. James knew that his sperm was potent, and that Kylie wasn't the only person in the last 6 months that he had been a Manic employee that he had got pregnant, and that he and Lyra had had active, consensual, intimate relations was something he couldn't fully process in the haze of his current state. He lay back against the cold floor of the studio, his mind swirling with the consequences of what had just happened. For all the tension and chaos that had preceded this moment, it felt surreal, like stepping into a story that wasn't his own.

Lyra sat up, adjusting her clothes and running a hand through her dishevelled hair, the weight of what they had done etched onto her face. She turned to James, her expression a mix of concern and regret. "This... wasn't planned," she said softly, her voice tinged with unease. "But it doesn't change what I said earlier. You're not alone in this, James."

James sat up slowly, his body aching from more than just the physical toll of the last few hours. "Lyra... I don't know what's happening to me," he admitted, his voice barely above a whisper. "I feel like I've lost control of everything—my career, my relationships, my life. I don't even know who I am anymore."

Lyra reached out, placing a steady hand on his shoulder. "You're James Smith. Not 'Reevesy,' not a pawn in Kylie's games, not anyone's tool or toy. You're Pete's son, and more than that, you're someone who deserves better than this. But you need to make a choice, James. Do you want to keep living like this, or do you want to fight for something better?"

James looked at her, her words cutting through the fog of self-loathing and confusion that had clouded his mind for so long. He thought about his father, about the man who had always stood for authenticity and integrity in an industry that seemed determined to strip those values away. He thought about Lyra, about her courage and her willingness to step into his mess and offer a way out, then he noticed the time - ten past 4, and he knew Lyra should be in her studio on the floor above, presenting the Manic

Vibes Stoke & Cheshire regional drivetime show. Panic flickered across his face as reality crashed back in.

"Lyra, your show—aren't you supposed to be live right now?" James stammered, scrambling to his feet and grabbing for his discarded clothes. The stark realisation of their actions and the potential fallout from them hit him like a freight train.

Lyra's eyes widened as she glanced at the clock on the wall. "Shit," she muttered, quickly straightening her shirt and grabbing her bag. "James, get dressed and come up to my studio with me... and afterwards I'm taking you home."

James froze, unsure of what to make of Lyra's sudden decisiveness. "Taking me home? What about Kylie? And Cody? They'll—" he started, but Lyra cut him off with a sharp look.

"Kylie and Cody don't own you, James," she said firmly, her voice brooking no argument. "Whatever they think they have over you, it ends now. I don't care how messy this gets. You're coming with me, and we'll figure it out together."

Her words hung in the air like a lifeline, but James hesitated. The fear of repercussions loomed large, a storm cloud of doubts and what-ifs. Yet, as he watched Lyra gather herself with the calm confidence that he'd always admired, something inside him shifted. The chaos and degradation of his recent months with Kylie and Manic Urban suddenly felt unbearable, a weight he could no longer carry.

"Alright," he murmured, pulling on his jeans and hastily stuffing his shirt into his waistband. "Let's go."

They left the recording booth together, the silence between them charged with unspoken emotions. The corridors of the One Snow Hill hub buzzed faintly with the sounds of production—the low murmur of presenters in their studios, the distant hum of music bleeding through soundproof walls. Lyra's pace was brisk, her determination cutting through James's lingering hesitation.

As they reached the lift, Lyra pressed the button for the fourth floor, where her regional studio for Manic Vibes was located. James shifted awkwardly beside her, the weight of everything that had happened pressing down on him like an iron cloak.

"You really don't have to do this," he said quietly, his voice almost drowned out by the ding of the lift doors opening.

Lyra turned to him, her eyes soft but resolute. "Yes, I do," she replied. "Because no one else will. And because you deserve to see that there's more to life than... this."

The lift ride was short, and as they stepped out onto the fourth floor, Lyra's producer, Zoe Marsh, was already waiting outside the studio door, her face a mask of confusion and irritation.

"Lyra, you're late! Thank goodness... wait, what's the office cum dump doing up here. He should be downstairs in the Urban studio recording links for some shit 'banger-heavy' playlist."

James knew Zoe was one of Kylie's friends, and that she had often made him eat her out, or have sex with the 29 year old. The fact that Zoe was one of the people that he had possibly impregnated gave him a new wave of anxiety as her words cut through him like shards of glass. His mouth opened slightly, but no words came out. Lyra, however, didn't flinch.

"Zoe, enough," Lyra said sharply, stepping forward to place herself between James and the producer. Her tone carried a weight of authority James had never heard from her before. "James is here with me, and what he does—or doesn't do—outside of your little clique downstairs is no longer your concern."

Zoe raised an eyebrow, a smug grin creeping onto her face as she crossed her arms. "Oh, is that so? And what makes you think you can waltz in here and change the rules? Don't forget, Lyra, you're just a regional presenter. You don't call the shots around here."

Lyra chuckled. "Really? You do realise that I'm leaving at the end of the month for Hits, right? Oh, and James and I are going down the cop shop after my shift has finished too."

The tension in the corridor thickened like smoke, suffocating the lingering noise of production beyond the studio doors. Zoe's smirk faltered at Lyra's sharp retort, the weight of her words sinking in with palpable force.

"Hits? You're leaving for Hits?" Zoe asked, incredulous. Her smugness cracked, replaced by disbelief laced with bitterness. "And what, you think you can just burn the place down on your way out? You think they'll let you waltz off with Reevesy and whatever twisted vendetta you're cooking up? And Reevesy, remember what Kylie said... one wrong move, and your baby is gone."

James flinched at Zoe's words, the pit in his stomach twisting tighter. He glanced at Lyra, her face a mask of calm resolve, and then back at Zoe, who loomed like a vulture ready to pick apart what little was left of his dignity.

"I don't care about your threats, Zoe," Lyra said evenly, stepping forward, her presence commanding the space. "If you think Kylie's going to keep running this circus unchecked, you're wrong. James isn't her pawn anymore. And neither are you. Now, did you start the show off and do the initial links?"

"Obviously, you uptight cow," Zoe retorted, her tone dripping with disdain. "Don't act like you're some hero swooping in to save the day. You're just as much a part of this mess as the rest of us."

Lyra's eyes narrowed, but her calm didn't falter. "Think what you want, Zoe. But the truth is, this station is rotting from the inside out, and everyone knows it. I'm done standing by while people like you and Kylie exploit others for your own gain. Now, get out of my way. I have a show to do."

Zoe hesitated for a moment, her bravado flickering as she registered Lyra's resolve. With a final sneer, she stepped aside, muttering under her breath as she disappeared down the corridor. James watched her go, his heart pounding in his chest. He wasn't sure whether to feel relieved or terrified by the confrontation.

Lyra turned back to him, her expression softening. "Are you okay?" she asked quietly.

James nodded, though his hands trembled slightly. "I think so," he murmured, his voice barely audible. "I just... I don't know how this ends."

Lyra gave him a small, reassuring smile. "It ends with you taking back control," she said firmly. "But for now, let's get through this shift. Afterwards, we'll figure out the rest."

****

CHAPTER 2 - Goldies Goes Live
Tuesday 15th April 2025

Pete Smith leaned back in his chair, taking in the unfamiliar surroundings of the Manic Goldies West Midlands studio. The sleek, modern glass panels of One Snow Hill in Birmingham contrasted sharply with the comfortable, if outdated, feel of the Waterfront studios in Brierley Hill, where he had spent the last five years hosting Midlands Manic's drive-time show. Yesterday, he had been introducing Dua Lipa and Harry Styles; today, it was ELO and Fleetwood Mac. A new audience, a new station, and, as Pete saw it, a chance for redemption—or at least a breather.

Six months earlier, Bauer's abrupt withdrawal of Greatest Hits Radio from regional programming had left a vacuum in the West Midlands, one Manic Goldies was all too eager to fill. Pete's move to the station felt like a bittersweet demotion, sold to him as a "lateral shift" but still carrying the sting of being shuffled away from the flagship CHR network. Now, instead of navigating TikTok trends and scripted "banter," he found himself in a quieter world of classic hits and loyal listeners.

The new studio was immaculate, polished to the same high sheen as the Manic corporate brand. The equipment gleamed with a cutting-edge precision that felt almost clinical, a far cry from the worn but beloved desks of the Waterfront. Pete's producer for the new show, a cheerful thirty-something named Rachel Powell, had just left to grab coffees, leaving Pete alone with his thoughts—and the empty studio.

The irony was that he had, for the previous 30 years, been part of Dudley FM, which had been the original tenant of the studios at The Waterfront, then Midlands Manic, and now Manic Goldies. The move had brought him full circle in a way that felt oddly poetic, even if it wasn't on his terms. He was back in the same city, talking to an audience that felt closer to home than the fast-paced CHR world of Manic Vibes. But as Pete scanned the immaculate studio and the playlist of '70s and '80s staples on the screen before him, he couldn't shake the feeling that this wasn't entirely his world either.

The Goldies brand promised nostalgia, authenticity, and a refuge from the relentless branding of modern stations like Manic Vibes. And yet, the corporate fingerprints were all over it. The jingles might be softer, the branding less in-your-face, but it was still Manic at its core—a finely tuned machine built to optimise listener figures and ad revenue. Even the playlists were algorithmically generated, with only a little leeway for presenters like Pete to inject their personal touch. He missed the days when a local presenter's personality shaped the sound of a station.

A soft knock at the door broke Pete from his reverie. It was Rachel, holding two steaming cups of coffee and balancing a tablet under one arm. Her easy smile was a welcome reprieve from the sharp-edged, high-stakes energy Pete had grown used to at Manic Vibes.

"Here you go," she said, setting one cup down on the desk. "Thought you could use this before your first show. You've got about ten minutes until we're live."

Pete smiled gratefully, taking a sip. "Thanks, Rachel. I'll admit, it feels strange being here. A bit... quieter."

Rachel chuckled. "That's Goldies for you. No viral TikTok challenges here, just good old-fashioned music and a lot of love from the listeners. I used to do the National Drive up until last week, based at the network hub at Speke, but I requested a transfer when this regional slot came up. I prefer working on something with a bit more heart, you know?"

Pete nodded, appreciating her candour. "It's refreshing to hear. Honestly, I was starting to feel like a cog in the machine back at Manic Vibes. Don't get me wrong, I enjoyed the energy—at least, I used to—but there's only so many scripted gags and pop star soundbites you can churn out before it starts to feel hollow."

Rachel perched on the edge of the desk, cradling her coffee. "Well, if it's any consolation, I think you're going to love it here. The audience for Goldies is loyal. They know what they like, and they're not shy about letting you know when they like you. We've already had a few texts come through saying how excited people are to hear you on the station. You know we're above the Vibes West Midlands studio?"

Pete knew that the floor below was the Manic Vibes floor, where that brand, along with some of the local IT and HR departments, operated, with the floor below that the one for Manic's other brands, such as Manic Rock, Manic Urban, which was formed when Manic brought Drill FM back in December, Manic Metal and Manic Soul, some of the other brands that Lite Group, which Manic Radio Group had become back in 2022 following the merger with the original Lite Group, operated. Pete had taken the lift up past those stations on his way to the Goldies floor, where the atmosphere was noticeably calmer and more focused. The buzz of energy drinks, Instagram posts, and TikTok brainstorming sessions gave way to the soft hum of a station built on nostalgia and genuine connection.

As Rachel tapped through some notes on her tablet, Pete's thoughts drifted. He wondered if James, down in the Manic Urban studio, was faring any better in his chaotic world of grime and drill. His son had barely spoken to him since Christmas, their relationship strained under the weight of the choices James had made—and the ones Pete hadn't been able to stop him from making.

"Right," Rachel said, pulling Pete back to the present. "You do know that, live Vibes, our playlist is controlled from HQ in Speke, right?"

Pete nodded thoughtfully, the mention of Speke and the automated playlists a reminder of how tightly controlled the radio landscape had become. Even though Manic Goldies promised freedom and nostalgia, it was still part of the overarching corporate system.

"Yeah, I figured as much," Pete replied, setting down his coffee. "But I'm hoping I can bring a bit of my own flavour to the show. Maybe sneak in the odd local connection or a listener's memory to keep things human. It's not just about playing the hits—it's about making them mean something."

Rachel smiled, a flicker of admiration in her eyes. "That's exactly why you're here, Pete. The listeners want someone who gets them, someone who feels like they're part of their world, not just another voice pushing algorithms. And trust me, with the texts coming through, they're ready to welcome you with open arms."

Pete glanced at the clock. Five minutes to go. He leaned forward, adjusting the headphones on the desk and familiarising himself with the console. It wasn't that different from the setups he'd used before, though the crispness of the tech reminded him just how far the industry had come since his early days at Dudley FM.

Rachel straightened up, checking her tablet. "You're leading with Fleetwood Mac's Don't Stop—seemed fitting for a fresh start. Then it's a bit of Elton John and maybe some Phil Collins. We've got the first hour set, but there's room for you to take requests after that if anything good comes through."

Pete nodded, grateful for the balance between structure and freedom. "Sounds perfect. Let's see if we can make someone's day with a bit of nostalgia. It's not every day you get to bring people back to the best moments of their lives."

Rachel chuckled. "Spoken like a true Goldies presenter. I'll be in the producer's booth if you need anything. You're going to smash it, Pete."

As Rachel left the room, Pete slid on his headphones and leaned into the mic. The familiar red ON AIR light flickered to life, and the comforting intro jingle for Manic Goldies West Midlands played in his ear. The sense of familiarity, combined with the excitement of something new, brought a small smile to his face.

"Good afternoon, West Midlands!" Pete began, his voice warm and confident, years of experience bringing an effortless charm. "It's Pete Smith here, and I'm absolutely thrilled to be joining you on Manic Goldies. Whether you're driving home from work, pottering around the house, or just taking a moment for yourself, we're here to bring you the songs you love and the memories they carry. First up, it's the news with Alana Kettlehurst."

The music faded, and the polished voice of Alana Kettlehurst came through the speakers, delivering the regional news with a calm professionalism that reminded Pete of the days when radio was a trusted companion for the community. He listened to the familiar rhythms of her report, his thoughts momentarily drifting to his son, James, and the stark contrast between their worlds. While Pete was easing into the nostalgic embrace of Manic Goldies, James was likely entangled in the high-stakes drama of Manic Urban, grappling with a career that seemed more about chaos than connection.

As the news wrapped up, Pete straightened in his chair, adjusting the microphone and glancing at the clock. It was time to officially begin his first show on Manic Goldies. The jingles played again, the cheerful tones announcing his presence to the West Midlands audience.

"And we're back," Pete said smoothly, his voice filling the airwaves. "Welcome to the very first Pete Smith Drive Time here on Manic Goldies West Midlands. It's great to be here with you, bringing you the songs that have stood the test of time—songs that make you smile, sing along, or maybe even dance like no one's watching. Now, if you're listening in Birmingham and the Black Country and wondering why 87.7FM isn't playing Midlands Manic... well, that's on DAB, online and on the Manic Prime app now."

Pete knew that, at 6am this morning, the frequencies of the former Midlands Manic and Warwickshire Stars stations had been changed, with Warwickshire Stars flipping to Manic Vibes WM, and the frequency he had been broadcasting on for years moving from CHR to classic hits, carrying the Manic Goldies name. It was a move designed to bolster the Goldies brand in key markets, particularly as Bauer's restructuring had left listeners searching for alternatives to GHR. Pete understood the strategy, but he also recognised the challenge: winning over an audience who had become accustomed to something entirely different.

He continued smoothly, addressing the transition with the seasoned professionalism that had carried him through decades in radio. "So, for those of you tuning in and wondering where Dua Lipa's gone, don't worry—Manic Vibes WM on DAB, on the app and on manicvibes.com have all the Dua Lipa, Harry Styles, and all the current hits you're looking for. But if you're staying with us here on 87.7 FM, you're in for a treat. We've got the best classic hits from the '70s, '80s, and '90s, and we're here to take you on a trip down memory lane. Let's start this journey with a track that reminds us to keep moving forward, no matter what—here's Fleetwood Mac with Don't Stop."

The iconic opening chords filled the studio, and Pete leaned back in his chair, letting the music wash over him. It was a moment of respite, a chance to breathe and centre himself in this new chapter of his career. The song felt symbolic—not just for the audience but for him personally. A reminder that, while the road ahead might be different, it was still worth travelling.

As the track played out, texts began lighting up the studio's display screen. Rachel had been right—the Goldies audience was loyal and vocal. Messages poured in, welcoming Pete to the station, sharing memories tied to the music, and even a few nostalgic nods to his days at Dudley FM.

"I used to listen to you on Dudley FM when I was pregnant with our Kyle," one text read, "and now he's driving me home from work, listening to you again! Thank you for being part of our journey, Pete!" Another message chimed in, "Pete, so happy to hear you on Goldies! Your voice feels like coming home after a long day." Pete smiled as he read through them, the warmth of the audience's response reminding him why he'd stayed in radio all these years.

There were some, however, which bemoaned the sudden switch from CHR to classic hits on 87.7 FM. A few texts expressed confusion, while others voiced disappointment:

"Where's Harry Styles? I had Midlands Manic on every day in the car!" one listener wrote. Another chimed in, "Not sure about this change—my kids miss the current stuff. Feels like a step back."

Pete nodded to himself as he read the messages. Change in radio was never easy, especially when it involved such a drastic shift in format. He'd seen it before—stations rebranding, presenters being shuffled around, audiences having to adapt. It wasn't always smooth, but it was part of the business.

The fact that it had been announced over the past 5 months that the stations were changing, and so listeners had some time to adjust, didn't mean everyone was happy about it. Pete had anticipated this, and he was ready to address it with the grace and professionalism that had become his trademark.

As Fleetwood Mac's Don't Stop faded out, Pete leaned into the microphone, his tone warm and understanding. "I know some of you might be tuning in today and wondering about the changes on 87.7 FM. It's a big shift, moving from Midlands Manic to Manic Goldies, and I get it—it's not always easy to say goodbye to something you've loved. But I'm here to tell you that while the music might be different, the heart of this station remains the same. It's about you, the listeners, and the moments that music can create. I've had a text from Angie in Leominster, who says that she's glad to hear the new local show, and that she was delighted to hear Fleetwood Mac starting things off. Angie, thank you for the warm welcome—this show is as much yours as it is mine, and I hope you'll stick around for the journey."

Pete paused, letting his words settle before segueing into the next segment. "Now, here's something I want you guys, the listeners, to do. I want you to text in with your first day at a new job or a new chapter in your life—what song got you through it, or what song reminds you of that time? Let's celebrate those fresh starts together. I'll try and get a few of your choices on the air later in the show. For now, here's a classic to keep us going—it's Elton

John with I'm Still Standing. You're listening to Manic Goldies West Midlands—let's keep those memories rolling."

As the opening piano riff of Elton John's hit filled the studio, Pete leaned back, watching the text line begin to flicker again. The response was instant—messages pouring in from listeners sharing their stories. Some talked about their first jobs in the '80s, others about life changes they'd faced with the help of music. A man named Dave from Kidderminster wrote about starting as an apprentice mechanic back in 1984, saying how Take On Me by A-ha had been a constant on the workshop radio. Another listener, Sheila from Walsall, mentioned moving into her first flat and dancing around to Walking on Sunshine by Katrina and the Waves.

It was then that Pete had an email on the internal email system.

From: *lyra.nott@vibes.manicradio.co.uk*

To: *pete.smith@goldies.manicradio.co.uk*

Subject: *Quick Chat?*

Hi Pete,

Any chance we could have a chat after our shows have finished? There's something important I need to discuss with you that can't wait.

Take care,

Lyra

****

The email from Lyra lingered in Pete's mind as he navigated through the rest of his first show. The flow of classic hits and listener interactions was a welcome distraction, but the message's timing and tone gnawed at him. What could be so urgent? Lyra wasn't prone to overreacting, but the phrasing suggested something serious.

As the final chords of Africa by Toto played out, Pete leaned into the mic for his sign-off.

"And that's it for my first show here on Manic Goldies West Midlands. Thank you to everyone who's texted in, shared your stories, or just tuned in to keep me company. It's been an absolute pleasure, and I can't wait to do it all again tomorrow. Coming up next, it's Goldies' Evening Playlist with Sarah Duncan. Until next time, take care and keep those memories alive."

Pete knew that that show, a network show which, despite most of them being from Speke, was being presented from the Exeter hub of Manic's where the South West based Manic Vibes and Manic Goldies branded shows were produced. Pete slid off his headphones and exhaled deeply, satisfied with how the first show had gone. The listeners' warmth and enthusiasm had made it feel less like a daunting new start and more like a homecoming. Still, the email from Lyra lingered in the back of his mind. Something about its tone had unsettled him.

Rachel popped her head into the studio, her tablet tucked under one arm and a broad smile on her face. "Brilliant first show, Pete. The text line's been buzzing nonstop.

You've already got people asking for dedications tomorrow."

Pete grinned. "That's great to hear. It's good to know the Goldies audience is as loyal as ever. Thanks for your support today, Rachel. Couldn't have done it without you."

Rachel waved him off. "You're a pro, Pete. Honestly, I just got to sit back and enjoy the show. Anyway, I've uploaded all the responses from today to your folder for tomorrow's prep. Anything else you need before I head out?"

"Not right now, thanks. You've been a star," Pete replied, his tone genuinely appreciative. As Rachel disappeared down the hallway, Pete took a moment to check his phone. There were a few congratulatory messages from friends and former colleagues, but nothing from James. He sighed, his thoughts turning briefly to his son and the widening gulf between them.

Looking at the time, a few minutes past seven, Pete knew that Lyra would be downstairs, packing up her gear after her regional drivetime show for Manic Vibes Stoke & Cheshire. He decided it would be best to catch her before she left the building rather than let the email gnaw at him overnight.

As he made his way to the lift, Pete couldn't help but reflect on Lyra's career. She had been one of the few presenters at Manic Vibes who seemed to hold on to a sense of integrity, even as the corporate machine swallowed creativity and authenticity. Pete respected her immensely—not just for her professionalism, but for the way she had navigated the turbulent waters of modern radio without losing herself.

The lift doors opened to the Manic Vibes floor, where the energy was still palpable despite the end of the afternoon's regional shows. Screens displaying brightly coloured branding flickered with promo videos, and the faint thump of a playlist echoed from a nearby production studio. Pete spotted Lyra in the Stoke & Cheshire studio, Studio B4, which meant that it was the 4th studio on the Manic Vibes floor. She was gathering her notes and headphones, her expression focused but tinged with an edge of weariness.

Then he saw James sitting next to her, his fingers twitching and his posture slouched in a way that spoke of exhaustion—or something worse. Pete froze for a moment, his mind racing as he took in the scene. What was James doing here, on the Manic Vibes floor? The last he'd heard, his son was tied up with Manic Urban's chaotic grind. Seeing him in Lyra's studio, looking like a shadow of his former self, sent a pang of worry through Pete's chest.

Then he saw James rubbing at his backside, as if he was in discomfort. Pete's concern deepened. The sight of his son looking so vulnerable was a stark contrast to the confident, ambitious young man he once knew. Something was clearly wrong, and Pete's protective instincts kicked in. He knocked lightly on the glass window of the studio door to announce his presence.

Lyra glanced up first, her face breaking into a relieved smile as she waved him in. James, however, barely looked up, his gaze fixed on the desk in front of him. Pete pushed the door open, his eyes darting between the two.

"Lyra," Pete began, his voice steady but tinged with curiosity, "I got your email. What's going on?"

Lyra set her notes down, taking a step closer to Pete and lowering her voice. "Thanks for coming down, Pete. I wasn't sure if I'd catch you tonight. Look, you know I don't go to the parties and that that some of the others my age here run, right?"

Pete nodded, his eyes narrowing slightly as he listened. "I've always respected that about you, Lyra. You've never been one to get swept up in the chaos here. But what's this about? And why is James here?"

Lyra's expression softened, but there was a seriousness in her eyes that made Pete's chest tighten. She glanced briefly at James, who remained slouched in the chair, avoiding his father's gaze.

"Pete," Lyra began carefully, "It turns out that... well, do you remember Zara Love, left after Christmas, did the Stoke and Cheshire breakfast?"

Pete frowned, his brow furrowing as he tried to recall. "Yeah, I remember Zara. She was the bubbly one, always seemed to have the energy of ten people. Left for Bauer, didn't she? Something about a better work-life balance?"

Lyra nodded, her lips pressing into a thin line. "That's what we were told, but there's more to it than that. Zara didn't just leave for a better deal—she left because of the parties. Or, more specifically, what was happening at those parties."

"Basically, Dad, she was the 'Hub Cum Dump'," James said without meeting his father's eyes, his voice a fragile mixture of shame and bitterness. "It's a position that the person most out of favour of the clique gets put in by the others when they've fucked up... like I did on New Years Eve when Kylie and I did the network countdown on the main station. Basically, they get used by everyone who's in on the sex and drug parties as the lowest rung of the ladder. It's sort of like a free-use kind of role," James continued, his voice breaking slightly, "where everyone just... takes what they want. And if you resist, you're out. They make sure you're out of the station, out of the industry—everything."

Pete's face hardened, his fists clenching by his sides as he struggled to keep his composure. "What are you saying, James? That you've been dragged into this... this nightmare?"

James gave a short, humourless laugh, finally looking up at his father. His eyes were bloodshot, his face pale and drawn. "Dragged? When Zara was here, I... I fucked her a couple of times... and now, because I'm the out of favour one, I'm the "Hub Cum Dump'. That's not all, Dad... there's another thing that happens... do you know why the maternity leave is high among female presenters?"

Pete froze, the air in the studio seeming to grow heavier as James's words hung between them. His son's expression was a mixture of defiance and despair, and Pete could feel the weight of everything unsaid pressing down on him. The tension in the room was palpable, and even Lyra, who had always been composed in the face of chaos, looked deeply unsettled.

"Maternity leave?" Pete repeated, his voice low and cautious, as though he were afraid of what the answer might be. "What are you saying, James?"

James looked away again, his shoulders slumping further. Lyra stepped in, her voice steady but tinged with sadness. "Pete, there's an unofficial HR policy. When a female presenter who's dating a male presenter gets pregnant, then Manic cover a ton of expenses. Maternity leave, childcare assistance, even a media-friendly 'family announcement package'... and an extra £2k a year extra in your pay for every year the child is alive until they're 18. It's a powerful incentive for keeping things quiet, presenting a 'family-friendly' image, and ensuring no scandal leaks out about how these pregnancies often happen in the first place."

Pete's jaw tightened, his fists clenching instinctively as he processed Lyra's words. "So, you're saying Manic... incentivises relationships and pregnancies? What about consent? Relationships built on manipulation and power dynamics?"

James flinched at the sharpness of his father's tone. "It's worse than that, Dad. It's not just about relationships. It's about control—branding. If you're 'out of favour,' like I am now, they make sure you feel expendable. You either toe the line or they break you. If you're valuable, they'll spin it into the golden family narrative. If not... well, you're just left to rot. You didn't help, kicking me out on Christmas Day."

Pete's chest tightened as James's words cut through the air. The weight of what his son was describing—the depths of manipulation, exploitation, and toxic culture at Manic—was almost too much to bear. The mention of kicking James out on Christmas Day added a painful layer of guilt, but Pete couldn't let that derail the conversation. This was bigger than personal failings; it was about the systemic rot that had taken hold of the very industry Pete had dedicated his life to.

Lyra broke the tense silence, her voice calm but firm. "Pete, this isn't just about James. It's about a culture that's been festering for years. Zara's departure was just the tip of the iceberg. What's happening here isn't isolated—it's part of the machine. And it's not just here. You know the 'Baby Bonus' was set up when Toni Green had her baby with Kyler Thompson? Back during the second lockdown and when she was at Bee Manic."

Pete's mind raced, the layers of deceit and exploitation within Manic Radio's culture unfolding before him like a grim tapestry. The "Baby Bonus," James's broken state, Zara's departure—these were symptoms of a deeper sickness, one that had festered unchecked for far too long. The industry Pete had once championed as a place of creativity and connection now seemed like a factory for manipulation and control.

He turned to Lyra, his voice steady but laced with anger. "The 'Baby Bonus'… I remember hearing whispers about it back then, but I thought it was just a rumour. Something for the tabloids to speculate on. Are you saying it was real, and it's still going on?"

Lyra nodded solemnly. "It's real, Pete. I didn't want to believe it at first either, but the evidence is there. HR covers it up well, framing it as part of their 'talent retention strategy.' But it's really about controlling the narrative, keeping the station's image squeaky clean, and ensuring no one questions what happens behind closed doors. Basically, for example, if James got me pregnant, then I'd earn an extra £2,000 a year just for keeping up the 'perfect couple' narrative. And that applies even if I left, as long as the baby was conceived on Manic property. Why do you think they encourage, unofficially, staff to do drink, drugs and have sex all over the place."

"And Kylie is eligible because, you know when she and I were up in Manchester recording the final batch of Headbangers episodes and you were at the Island Awards up there back in November... well, we had sex in the studio, and I didn't use a condom then."

Pete looked at James with a mixture of shock, anger, and sadness, the weight of the revelation settling heavily on his shoulders. The air in the room seemed charged with unspoken pain, and the vulnerability in James's expression only deepened Pete's sense of helplessness.

"You're saying Kylie's pregnancy... it's part of this mess?" Pete's voice was low, almost a whisper, as though speaking louder might make the situation even more unbearable.

James nodded, his gaze fixed on the floor. "She... she knew about the policy, Dad. She used it. When we were in Manchester, she kept pushing for us to do it in the studio. I didn't think anything of it at the time. I was too... too caught up in everything. But now, looking back, it's obvious. She's been using me, Dad. Not just for the shows, not just for the branding... but for this."

Pete ran a hand over his face, the enormity of the situation threatening to overwhelm him. He thought about the industry he had spent decades in, the pride he had once felt in being part of something that connected people through music and shared experiences. Now, that pride was tainted by the realisation of how deep the rot went.

"And... erm... I think I did it again today, got another presenter pregnant... because we had unprotected sex."

Pete froze, unable to process James's last statement fully. The weight of everything—Manic's toxic culture, James's spiralling life, and now the suggestion of another unplanned pregnancy—felt suffocating. He turned slowly, his eyes fixed on James, who was staring at the floor, unable to meet his father's gaze.

"Another presenter?" Pete's voice was barely above a whisper, the words heavy with disbelief and exhaustion. "James... what are you saying? Who?"

James hesitated, the tension in the room thickening. Lyra stepped forward, placing a steadying hand on Pete's arm, as though sensing he was on the verge of breaking.

"Me, Pete," Lyra said softly. "I... I was consoling him, trying to encourage him, and then we... well, made a mistake. I didn't plan it, and I don't think James did either, but we ended up... connecting, in a way that went beyond words."

Pete groaned, as he knew that James had inherited certain genetic flaws from himself, such as having certain equipment be larger than other males. The fact Pete himself had to ensure he used protection with his own wife, Sarah, because the last three times that they had forgotten, she had gotten pregnant, two resulting in James and Chloe, and the third ending in a miscarriage , weighed heavily on Pete's mind as he processed Lyra's words. The implications of this revelation were staggering, and for a moment, Pete felt as though the world had been knocked off its axis. He stared at Lyra, searching her face for any sign that this was some kind of joke or misunderstanding, but her expression was earnest—tinged with regret but also resolve.

"You're telling me," Pete began, his voice low and deliberate, "that you and my son... after everything he's been through, after everything we've been trying to untangle from this toxic mess... you've gone and complicated it even further?"

Lyra met his gaze, her eyes steady but filled with remorse. "Pete, I'm not going to make excuses. It wasn't planned, and it wasn't right. But it happened... nearly four hours ago."

Pete groaned, rubbing his temples as he processed the tangled web of revelations. Lyra's admission was a gut punch, but it was the broader implications—the deep dysfunction at Manic, the calculated manipulation of people like James, and now this—that made the situation unbearable.

He turned to James, who was still slouched in the chair, looking like he wanted to sink into the floor. Pete's voice was steady but edged with frustration. "James, I can't even begin to untangle how we got here. And Lyra—four hours ago? You thought now was the time to complicate things even more?"

Lyra straightened her shoulders, her voice calm but firm. "Pete, I get it. This isn't what you wanted to hear. But I'm not just standing by anymore. This place—Manic—it's eating people alive, and James is one of them. What happened between us wasn't part of some scheme or manipulation. It was two people trying to find a moment of humanity in this hellhole. I caught Cody forcing James to... well, let's just say your son-in-law is a depraved human being and your daughter is just as depraved too."

"You've known, Dad, for 6 months, that Clo's on coke, and yet you let her live with Cody. She... she's not under their thumb... she's got her own schemes... all because of when the two of us were at school," James said, sighing. "Do you remember when I had that friend, Sophia, who'd been in the same year as me at school when I was in Year 12, who'd moved from Cotteridge?"

Pete's brow furrowed as James mentioned Sophia. The name tugged at the edges of his memory, a faint thread leading back to those complicated years when James and Chloe had been teenagers. Cotteridge. Year 12. There had been something about Sophia that Pete couldn't quite place, but the mention of her alongside Chloe's schemes sent a chill down his spine.

"Sophia?" Pete said slowly, searching James's face. "The girl you used to bring round after school sometimes? Always polite, but there was something... reserved about her?"

James nodded, his expression darkening. "Yeah, her. Well, remember Clo used to say I was round other friends to you... I... well, me and Sophia were galivanting round Brum and Wolvo on weekends."

Pete's mind churned as James mentioned Sophia. He remembered those years, though not as clearly as he'd like. He'd been consumed with work at Midlands Manic, as James was 16 at the time, 5 years earlier, and Chloe had just turned 14. Pete recalled the subtle tension in the household during that time—the sibling rivalry that had seemed typical on the surface but now carried an undertone he hadn't recognised back then.

"What does Sophia have to do with Chloe's schemes now?" Pete pressed, his voice firm but carrying a note of cautious curiosity.

"Well, there was a reason I was constantly skint at the time. We'd go on dates, go to restaurants, the cinema, even bowling at the Bowlplex at Star City. We were in love, dad. Chloe found out—about Sophia, about the money, about everything. She threatened to tell you and Mum, claimed she'd make Sophia's life hell at school if I didn't... well, let her in on things... and then we broke up, with Sophia moving back to Cotteridge as her dad got a job at a different bus depot."

Pete leaned back against the studio wall, his hand running through his greying hair as he absorbed James's confession. The pieces of the puzzle began falling into place, and they painted a picture far more complex and painful than he could have imagined. He hadn't realised the extent to which Chloe's manipulations had started so early—or how much they had affected James's life.

"So, Chloe found out you were seeing Sophia, and instead of being supportive, she used it against you?" Pete asked, his voice a mix of anger and disbelief.

James nodded, his eyes fixed on the floor. "She threatened to tell Mum that I'd been sneaking out, spending all my savings, and breaking the rules. But worse than that, she threatened Sophia. Told her she'd spread rumours at school, get her ostracised, make her life unbearable. I couldn't let that happen, Dad. I broke it off with Sophia to protect her."

Pete exhaled sharply, the weight of his children's tangled relationship hitting him like a tonne of bricks. "And this… this dynamic between you and Chloe, it's still happening now?"

James laughed bitterly. "It never stopped. Clo's just found new ways to use it. Now it's Cody, and their whole drug-fuelled circus. They know I'm the weak link, the 'fuck-up.' They've been feeding off that since I started at Manic. Cody's got the newsroom wrapped around his finger, and Clo… well, since she started here in January with her new Ibiza Belters show and has made the feud I had with Stephanie Hirst look like child's play." James rubbed his temples, the exhaustion evident in his voice.

Pete rubbed his own temples, trying to make sense of the revelations that kept coming, each one heavier than the last. Chloe's manipulations, Cody's depravity, and now the toxic work environment at Manic Radio—it all felt like a house of cards, precariously balanced and ready to collapse. His eyes drifted to Lyra, who stood silently, her expression a mixture of guilt and determination.

"Lyra," Pete said, his voice low but steady, "thank you for stepping in when you did. I don't know where James would be without someone looking out for him. But this... this situation is beyond anything I've ever dealt with. Chloe, Cody, Kylie, the parties, this 'Baby Bonus' nonsense—it's all spiralling out of control."

Lyra nodded, her gaze steady. "Pete, I'm here because I care. About James, about you, and about what this industry used to stand for. But you're right. This isn't just a family issue—it's systemic. And unless someone takes a stand, it's only going to get worse. Look, you know I rent Chloe's room at your place, right?"

Pete's expression darkened as Lyra mentioned renting Chloe's room. He nodded slowly, his voice tinged with suspicion. "Yes, I remember you moved in earlier this year, after you split with Si. Why are you bringing this up now?"

Lyra hesitated, glancing briefly at James before meeting Pete's eyes. "Well... I... want to bring James home."

The tension in the studio was palpable as Lyra's words hung in the air. Pete's gaze darted between Lyra and James, trying to process the weight of what she had just said. Bringing James home—a simple suggestion, yet fraught with implications, given the events of the last few months.

Pete let out a long sigh, leaning against the studio wall for support. "Lyra, do you know what you're asking? After everything that's happened—kicking him out on Christmas Day, the state he's in now—it's not as simple as just... bringing him back."

James shifted uncomfortably in his chair, his head hanging low. "Dad, I get it," he muttered, his voice barely above a whisper. "I'm not exactly the poster child for redemption right now. But I'm drowning out there. I thought I could handle it—thought I could fix it on my own—but I can't. Not with Kylie, not with Cody, not with… all of it. If Lyra hadn't stepped in, I... well, Kylie's got her brother, Liam, Cody, Shane and a few others coming over tonight... and guess who's dessert?"

The room fell into an uneasy silence, punctuated only by the faint hum of the studio's equipment. Pete's jaw tightened as James's words sank in. The image of his son—his pride and joy once upon a time—reduced to such a state, caught in a cycle of exploitation and humiliation, was almost too much to bear.

Lyra broke the silence, her voice soft but resolute. "Pete, James needs a way out. Right now. Tonight. Bringing him back to yours isn't just about giving him a place to stay—it's about giving him a lifeline. Somewhere safe, where he can start putting himself back together."

Pete rubbed his face with his hands, his frustration and helplessness plain. "Lyra, do you have any idea how complicated this is? James didn't just end up here overnight. He's been making bad choices for years—choices that have hurt this family, hurt Chloe, and... God knows who else."

"Years? Dad, I've only been at Manic 6 months, been on cocaine length of time. You know what, forget it. I'll just have to go back to being the cum dump and fight to survive another day. Maybe one of these days, Kylie or

Cody or one of the others will finally push it too far, and it won't matter anymore."

****

CHAPTER 3 - Lyra's Worries
Wednesday 16th April 2025

The past fourteen hours had been troubling for Lyra. The tense meeting in her studio with James and Pete had left her shaken, and Pete's steadfast refusal to allow James back into the family home weighed heavily on her mind. Lyra understood Pete's perspective—his frustration, his sense of betrayal, his belief that James needed to take responsibility for his own choices. But she also knew that James was teetering on the edge, caught in a spiral of exploitation and despair.

What was worse was that Kylie had stopped her from leaving with James, with Kylie's best friend, Tina Small and her producer, Lily Jenkins, physically blocking her path as she tried to escort James out of the building. The confrontation had been tense and humiliating, with Kylie smirking from the side-lines, throwing out veiled threats about James's place at Manic Urban and Lyra's own standing within the company. Lyra had managed to keep her composure, but the incident left her fuming. It was a clear reminder of just how toxic and entrenched the culture at Manic Radio had become.

And then there was the realisation that James, like his father Pete, had overly high sperm counts, meaning that, as she and James had had unprotected sex, and she was at the point in her own cycle where she was most fertile, there was a high chance she might now be pregnant. Lyra hadn't been able to stop thinking about it since last night. The possibility filled her with a swirl of emotions—shock, fear, anger, and, unexpectedly, a flicker of hope. It was far too soon to say for sure, but the mere thought of it added another layer of complexity to an already tangled situation.

Getting dressed in a blouse, bomber jacket and trousers, completely the opposite of the other women in the Manic part of the building, who wore halter tops or crop tops, short skirts, and either thigh high socks, fishnet stockings or ripped leggings that tended to dominate the CHR scene, Lyra felt out of place. She was always the outsider in this younger, more carefree world, even though she was in her mid-20s and had worked hard to make a name for herself in the fast-paced world of CHR radio. The vibrant energy of the Manic Vibes team—largely made up of presenters and producers in their early 20s—was both intoxicating and exhausting. They thrived on quick-fire banter, influencer collaborations, and endless social media engagement, all of which Lyra had always found a bit too shallow for her tastes. She liked substance, real connection, and deep conversation—qualities that often felt like rare commodities in the world she inhabited.

Ping

The sound of a notification on her phone, one of the many WhatsApp chats that the Manic presenters were subscribed to, some with schedule and shift updates, some just general chat, and one, which was for presenters under 30 which contained nudes and sex videos of each other.

Lyra glanced at her phone, her stomach twisting as she saw the group chat name flash across the screen: 'Gals and Geezers'. Secretly, Lyra would admit that she sometimes looked in there, especially at photos of James, as she had had a bit of a crush on him since he had joined Manic 6 months earlier. But right now, the thought of seeing

James's life play out in such an unfiltered and exploitative way made her stomach churn. She reluctantly opened the app, hoping it was something harmless for once. Her heart sank as she scrolled through the latest messages.

Photos and videos of last night's "after-work fun" dominated the chat, with Kylie at the centre of most of them. There were selfies of Kylie posing with her clique, bottles of champagne in hand, accompanied by captions like "Another night of chaos! 🍾 💧" and "Who needs rules when you're on top?" Lyra's jaw tightened when she noticed James in the background of one of the photos, tied up, with the breasts of his sister, Chloe, in his mouth, and her husband, Cody, behind him, making James appear utterly powerless and humiliated. The image was a brutal confirmation of everything James had told her the previous evening—about the toxic culture, the manipulation, and the exploitation that thrived unchecked at Manic Radio. Lyra's chest tightened as she struggled to process the sheer depravity on display. This wasn't just workplace banter; this was abuse.

She slammed her phone on the bed of the room she rented from Pete at the Smith family home when another WhatsApp message came through.

"Nott finally got fucked by the cum dump yesterday."

Lyra's heart sank as she stared at the message, her blood running cold. The blunt, vulgar phrasing made her stomach churn. She clenched her fists, breathing heavily as the weight of the situation pressed down on her. It was a direct, cruel jab—meant to humiliate, to belittle, to drag her into the same toxic mire James had been caught in.

"I've seen the CCTV. She's got massive tits, ain't she?"

Lyra looked and saw the message was Ishal, one of the Breakfast presenters, who was dating one of the One Snow Hill property management team, as Manic only leased 3 of the floors, with KMPG being the anchor tenant occupying the remaining floors. Lyra's heart raced, a mix of anger and panic gripping her. The implications of Ishal's comment were clear: the station's toxic culture wasn't limited to the presenters but extended to those managing the building itself. The environment was rotten from the top down, and it was starting to feel like there was no safe place left.

"Double F's for a guess," Cody's response said, and Lyra shuddered, as she knew he was close, having a bust size of 32FF herself. Lyra's face flushed, half from anger and half from the invasive humiliation of seeing her body and personal life turned into fodder for the Manic gossip mill. The fact that Cody—James's brother-in-law, no less—was leading the charge in this vile exchange only deepened her disgust. She clenched her fists tightly, her nails digging into her palms as her thoughts raced.

"Reevesy could bury his cock in her tits and he'd still have them sticking out. After all, he's 10 inches, isn't he?" came another message, the tone crude and callous. "He's probably ruined her pussy for the rest of us."

Lyra felt a wave of nausea rise in her throat as she stared at the screen. The casual vulgarity of the comments hit her like a physical blow. The fact that these people—her colleagues—felt so emboldened to speak about her and James with such crass disregard was both infuriating and deeply unsettling. She wanted to scream, to lash out, to somehow stop this relentless cycle of exploitation and humiliation, but she knew better. The culture at Manic was a hydra; cutting off one head only caused more to grow.

"You know, she'd be the fourth one that Reevesy's got preggers since he started here," a message from Penny Lane, one of the Liverpool drivetime presenters, read. Lyra's grip on her phone tightened as she fought the urge to throw it across the room. The casual cruelty and invasive gossip about James's personal life and her own circumstances were unbearable. She had heard whispers of this toxic behaviour before, but seeing it play out so blatantly in real-time was another matter entirely.

Suddenly a video popped up in the chat, and Lyra saw it was James's face in the thumbnail, and that he was giving a blowjob to a strap on.

Lyra's heart sank further as she reluctantly tapped on the video thumbnail, her breath hitching as the video began to play. The sight of James being degraded, his vulnerability broadcast for amusement, made her stomach churn. The fact that someone had pissed into his mouth midway through the 180 second clip only added to the horror. Hearing James beg for more, as if he was enjoying the experience, sent a shiver down Lyra's spine. It was too much—far beyond anything she had ever imagined witnessing in a workplace environment, let alone one that was supposed to represent the energetic and positive world of CHR radio.

Ping

Ping

Ping

Lyra's phone buzzed relentlessly with more messages flooding the chat. She couldn't bring herself to look anymore. Her heart raced, her chest tightening with every passing second. This wasn't just toxic workplace banter—this was targeted humiliation, a deliberate dismantling of James's dignity and humanity for the amusement of others. The casual depravity sickened her.

Ring

The sound of a call rang out, breaking through Lyra's haze of shock and anger. She glanced at her phone's screen: it was Kylie. Lyra hesitated, her thumb hovering over the green icon as the phone continued to ring. The audacity of Kylie to call her after the barrage of humiliation in the chat was almost laughable if it weren't so infuriating. Lyra took a deep breath, steadying herself, and swiped to answer.

"What do you want, Kylie?" she said, her tone icy.

A mocking laugh echoed through the line. "Relax, Nott. I just wanted to check in. You seemed a bit... stressed yesterday. Look, let's make a deal. You can have Reevesy... but..."

"But what?" Lyra snapped, as she waited for Kylie to finish her sentence, her patience wearing thin. Kylie's pause on the other end of the line stretched unbearably long, her smugness palpable even through the silence.

"You become the hub cum dump. You let everyone have a turn with you—male or female, presenter, or producer, doesn't matter. Full access, no limits," Kylie finished with a smirk in her voice. "And Reevesy gets to profit from it, just like how I currently do with him. Oh, and you stop being so boring, drinking once in a blue moon and not doing drugs. Come on, babe, live a little, snort some coke, get plastered. Hell, Liam can give you some for free."

Lyra clenched her fist, her knuckles whitening as Kylie's words cut through her like shards of glass. The casual cruelty and entitlement in her tone were staggering. The silence that followed was thick with tension, and Lyra could feel her anger bubbling beneath the surface, threatening to spill over.

"Kylie," she said, her voice steady but sharp, "I don't know what sick game you think you're playing, but I'm not part of it. I won't be reduced to your little puppet, and I sure as hell won't let you keep treating James—or anyone else—like this."

Kylie's laugh was icy, a sharp contrast to Lyra's seething anger. "Oh, come on, Lyra. Don't be so dramatic. You're already halfway there—you've already had a taste of Reevesy, haven't you? Everyone knows, as there's blood on the carpet from where he popped your cherry. I can't believe your ex didn't rid you of the pesky virginity... I lost mine when I was 15."

Lyra froze, her grip on the phone tightening as Kylie's venomous words hung in the air. The insinuation, the blatant cruelty—it was almost too much to process. Her heart pounded as the reality of just how far Kylie was willing to go sank in. This wasn't just casual workplace toxicity anymore—this was calculated, systemic degradation designed to break people down.

There was some truth, however, in Kylie's comment. Si, her ex-boyfriend, had been old fashioned in some regards, not wanting to have sex before marriage, his Church of England upbringing and his wrestling career leaving him focused on discipline and tradition. Lyra had respected his boundaries, even if they had clashed with her own desires at times. But now, Kylie's derision twisted that history into something shameful, a weapon to wield against her. Lyra's chest tightened with frustration and humiliation.

"Kylie," Lyra said through gritted teeth, her voice shaking with suppressed anger, "I don't care what you think you know about me or my past. You can spread your lies, you can try to manipulate everyone around you, but you will never have control over me. Not like you have over James."

Kylie chuckled darkly. "Oh, Lyra. Sweet, naive Lyra. You think you're better than this? Better than me? Look around—this is Manic. This is how it works. You either play the game, or you get crushed. If you're not willing to play, you're already losing."

Lyra's anger boiled over. "You're wrong. I won't be a part of this sick culture. And neither will James, not if I have anything to do with it."

Kylie's voice dropped into a mocking sing-song. "Aw, isn't that cute? Lyra thinks she's a hero. Newsflash, darling—you're in over your head. But hey, if you change your mind about my offer, you know where to find me. After all, tonight, Reevesy's going to be split open with 10 different cocks in his arse as some of the Liverpool guys are coming, and even they're not as long as Reevesy, they're thick and twice the girth of his. Even Rory's coming, and he's got a tree trunk in his boxer shorts, guaranteed to ruin any pussy or arse."

Lyra gripped the phone tightly, her entire body trembling with rage as Kylie's words seeped through. The casual cruelty, the outright depravity, and the smug entitlement in her tone left Lyra teetering on the edge of exploding. She took a deep breath, steadying herself as she struggled to maintain control.

"Kylie," Lyra said evenly, her voice sharp as steel, "you can keep your sick fantasies to yourself. If you think for one second I'm going to stand by and let you destroy James—or anyone else—then you've underestimated me."

Kylie snorted, the sound dismissive. "You're adorable when you try to sound tough, Lyra. But let's face it, you're out of your league. You're just one voice in a sea of noise. Nobody at Manic cares about morality or decency—they care about results, numbers, and staying relevant. Even Cal likes to fuck anything that moves, as long as it doesn't mess with the bottom line. So good luck, Lyra. You're fighting a war that was lost before it even started."

Lyra knew from her past 6 years working for Manic, 3 at the original Northern Vibes studios near to the railway station in Stoke and 3 at the Dudley, then Birmingham, hub, and she knew that Kylie wasn't entirely wrong about the culture at Manic Radio. Lyra had seen firsthand how deeply entrenched the exploitation and toxicity ran, from the relentless focus on social media virality to the workplace cliques that thrived on power dynamics. Yet, something about Kylie's words only strengthened Lyra's resolve.

"Oh, and Nott, I've sent you some DMs of James for you to wank to. And if you've got any crotchless panties, James loves them... your granny panties look too old-fashioned for someone in their mid-20s. Spice it up for him, will you?" Kylie's laughter rang out, venomous and mocking, before the call disconnected.

Lyra sat on her bed, her phone still clutched in her trembling hand. The bile rose in her throat as she stared at the blank screen, her anger boiling over. The vile depths of Kylie's manipulation and cruelty felt suffocating, but Lyra knew she couldn't let herself be overwhelmed. She had to think clearly—James's safety and well-being depended on it.

Out of curiosity, she looked at the WhatsApp DM that Kylie had sent to her, and, looking at the photos, didn't realise that her right hand was snaking inside the waistband of her trousers, as the photos of James lying on a studio couch shirtless, his muscular build accentuated under the dim studio lighting, drew her in. Her breath caught as she noticed the vulnerability in his expression—a mixture of exhaustion and quiet despair. The image wasn't overtly sexual, but there was an intimacy to it that stirred something deep within her.

The next thing she knew, she was stroking the most intimate parts of herself, her mind spinning with conflicted emotions—anger at Kylie, compassion for James, and a sudden, unwelcome wave of desire she couldn't fully comprehend.

"Fuck... his cock really... grr..." she muttered, and then realised that she had been drawn into the very web she had sworn to resist. Lyra froze, her hand abruptly still as a surge of shame and anger at herself replaced the fleeting moment of distraction. She pulled her hand away, pressing her palms against her face as if to block out the storm of emotions swirling within her.

"What am I doing?" she muttered under her breath, the reality of her actions hitting her like a slap. The same toxic culture she was determined to fight had found its way into her private thoughts, exploiting her vulnerability in a moment of weakness.

Lyra stood abruptly, shaking her head as if to physically cast off the hold that the situation—and Kylie—had on her. This wasn't who she was. She wasn't going to let Kylie, or anyone else, reduce her to the same games they played. If she wanted to help James, to truly help him, she had to be stronger than this.

"But he could be mine... I could have him pounding my pussy every night... knocking me up as many times as-"

Lyra stopped mid-thought, horrified at the direction her mind had taken. She shook her head violently as if trying to banish the invasive fantasies that Kylie's manipulation and the toxic environment at Manic had planted in her brain. She couldn't let herself spiral, not when so much was at stake—not when James was depending on her, whether he realised it or not.

"But you love him, don't you? Anyway, he loves women with big tits, like you and Kylie... and you've got a strap on in your draw..." Lyra's mind told herself, the intrusive thought a remnant of the toxic environment she had immersed herself in for too long. Lyra clenched her fists, the tension radiating through her as she fought to regain control of her mind. She wasn't going to let Kylie's manipulation twist her into someone she didn't recognise. She wasn't going to play into the same cycles that had consumed others at Manic.

But the irrational side of her started typing a text to Kylie, saying how she wanted James and how his body was screaming out to be dominated by someone who truly cared for him, not just exploited his vulnerability. Lyra froze mid-typing, her thumb hovering over the send button as reality crashed back in. What was she doing? This wasn't the way to help James or herself—it was falling into Kylie's trap, allowing her to manipulate emotions and twist intentions.

Fwoop

The sound of the message being sent shocked Lyra as she realised, too late, what she had done. Her heart pounded, and she stared at the phone screen in horror as the message left her outbox, a digital missile heading straight for Kylie. Panic flooded her veins as she considered the implications. The message had been impulsive, raw, and vulnerable—everything Kylie would use against her.

Seconds later, the familiar ping of an incoming message snapped her out of her daze. She hesitated, dread building as she saw it was the 'Gals and Geezers' chat, and Kylie had screenshotted her reply, adding it into the UK wide Manic Radio group chat, along with the caption:

Kylie Morgan: *Looks like Nott wants to be the next cum dump 😂. Watch out, Reevesy, she's coming for ya! #BigTitsBigDreams*

The chat erupted with laughing emojis and lewd comments. Lyra's chest tightened as her phone buzzed with a flurry of notifications. The humiliation was immediate and suffocating. Her private, impulsive message was now a public joke, weaponised by Kylie in the cruellest way possible.

"You know, Nott, you'll look great when Reevesy's coked up and is breeding you like he bred me," Penny Lane chimed in the chat, her message laced with mockery and derision. Lyra's stomach churned as the notifications kept piling in, a relentless assault of emojis, jeering comments, and explicit jabs that twisted her words and intentions into fodder for the toxic hive mind that thrived within Manic.

****

"I.... I'm not feeling well," Lyra said on the phone, half an hour later, as she contacted the HR team that was based at the hub. "I... ate a bad curry and I'm struggling to keep it down. I think I need to take the day off sick."

She knew that it was 11am, and that someone in the pool of cover presenters would need to step in to cover her afternoon show. But right now, Lyra couldn't bear the thought of stepping into the Manic building or facing the endless humiliation from her colleagues. The toxic comments in the group chats still echoed in her mind, and the thought of encountering Kylie, Cody, or even James in person made her stomach churn.

"Alright, Lyra," came the disinterested voice of the HR assistant on the other end of the line. "We'll mark you as sick for the day. Make sure to log it in the system and let us know if you'll be out tomorrow too. Feel better."

The call ended with a mechanical click, and Lyra dropped her phone onto her bed. She exhaled shakily, her hands trembling as she ran them through her hair. The morning's chaos had left her emotionally drained, and yet she knew this was only the beginning. Kylie wouldn't let this die down anytime soon, and the culture at Manic meant that her humiliation would be fodder for gossip for weeks—if not longer.

A few minutes later, right on cue, the 'Gals and Geezers' chat pinged again, this time Ali Hussain, one half of the Manic Dance Breakfast team based up at the Liverpool hub, chimed in with his signature brand of crass humour:

Ali Hussain: *Hey, guys, it's just come on the cover roster... Stoke & Cheshire. Anyone fancy stepping in for Nott this afternoon? Just make sure you don't catch whatever she's got—unless it's Reevesy! 😂#CumDumpChronicles.*

Kylie responded next with a photo of James with his mouth around a dildo that the opposite end had, attached to it, a printed out photo of Lyra's face, and he was posed in a way that made it appear as though he was worshipping her. The caption read:

Kylie Morgan: *Looks like Reevesy's already practising for you, Nott! #BigTitsBigPlans* 😂

Lyra stared at her phone, a mix of fury and despair washing over her. The group chat erupted in laughter, with emojis, crude jokes, and jeers flooding in. Each notification felt like a hammer blow, pushing her deeper into a corner she hadn't realised she was backed into. The culture of Manic Radio had spiralled so far out of control that even attempting to maintain dignity felt futile.

She tossed her phone onto the bed, fighting the tears that threatened to spill over. The strength she'd shown the night before seemed to evaporate in the face of relentless ridicule and cruelty. For a moment, she questioned why she had ever stayed at Manic, why she had endured the toxicity that had now consumed her life.

But then she thought of James.

Lyra clenched her fists, the image of him humiliated and used driving her anger to a sharp focus. She wouldn't let this culture destroy him—not if she had anything to do with it. James needed someone to fight for him, and if that meant standing up to Kylie and the cliques at Manic, she'd do it, no matter the cost.

****

"You know, big brother," Chloe said, grinning as she and Kylie were sitting on the bed that James was tied to in Chloe and Cody's Central Birmingham apartment, Chloe's thighs around James's head and Kylie kissing her in between her remarks, "you really are the gift that keeps on giving. It's no wonder Kylie and I decided to make you the centrepiece for tonight's entertainment. Now lick your cum out of my pussy, you slut, or I'll make it so you can't wank or sit for a week."

James knew he had to comply, even though incest, to him, was the worst form of degradation, far beyond the humiliation he had endured over the past months at Manic Urban. His mind spun, a chaotic blend of shame, despair, and exhaustion, as Chloe and Kylie pushed him further into submission. The sharp edges of his sister's words cut deeper than any physical act, but James no longer had the will to resist. Every fibre of his being screamed to fight back, to reclaim some semblance of dignity, but he was too worn down, too broken by the toxic environment that had consumed his life.

And then he felt the needle in his arm, another injection of cocaine in his veins, the way Cody preferred to administer the drug to ensure James stayed compliant. The sharp sting was followed by the familiar, overwhelming rush as the drug flooded his system. His heart raced, his thoughts scattering into fragments as the world around him blurred, and then he started licking at his sister's quim as if she were just another part of the endless, degrading nightmare that had become his life.

"Fuck... that's good," he heard Chloe say, her voice a mixture of mockery and satisfaction, as she gripped James's hair tightly, forcing him to continue. James's body obeyed, but his mind detached, retreating to a place where he could try to shield himself from the overwhelming humiliation and pain. He felt utterly powerless, a mere object in the twisted games of those who claimed to love him. "You know Nott has signed up to be your little cum slave, your personal breeding hole. She's probably at Mum and Dad's, fingering herself while imagining you holding her down, breeding her, making her pump out however many babies she can cope with before her body gives out. How many times your cock could make her mew like a kitten in heat." Chloe's words hung in the air, dripping with malice and mockery. James's body moved automatically, his spirit crushed under the weight of her cruel dominance. The rush of the cocaine kept him compliant, but his mind screamed for escape—anything to break free from this unrelenting nightmare.

Kylie laughed, her tone light and mocking as she leaned closer to James's ear. "You know, Reevesy, you might have made 5 women eligible for the Baby Bonus... me, Penny, Zara, your sister and potentially Lyra. You know, I never loved you, really."

James looked at Kylie, shocked, as she said the last sentence. It hit him harder than anything else she had said before. The cold detachment in her voice cut through the haze of drugs, humiliation, and despair, leaving a bitter emptiness in its wake.

"Oh, didn't I tell you?" Kylie said with a grin. "The sex was great, don't get me wrong, and those two years we kept our relationship hidden from the world were fun while we were in Uni, but I was shagging your best mate, Mark, as well, and he paid for my services. A grand a shag he paid me. And then when I joined Manic, those nights I said I had headache and for you to just stay at home and work on your SU sets, I was being ploughed by Cody, Liam and the others. Obviously, when you joined Manic back in October, that spoiled my scheme a bit," Kylie continued, her voice dripping with cruelty as she savoured James's despair. "But then I realised that we could pose as the Golden Couple, the epitome of Manic's 'perfect presenter duo.' You, the golden boy with the looks and charm, and me, the untouchable queen. It was all branding, James—just branding. And you fell for it hook, line, and sinker."

James's breathing quickened, his heart pounding as the words sank in. The layers of betrayal and manipulation Kylie revealed cut through the numbing haze of drugs and humiliation. For months, he had clung to the idea that their relationship, however twisted, had some genuine foundation. Now, that illusion was shattered, leaving nothing but the cold reality of how thoroughly he had been used.

"You're a puppet, James," Kylie continued, her tone matter-of-fact, as though she were explaining a simple truth. "A very handsome, very marketable puppet. You know tonight is our last night together as Nott messaged me earlier."

James's mind raced as Kylie's words sunk in deeper, each sentence hammering away at the fragile understanding he had tried to piece together over the past few months. The words 'puppet', 'marketable', 'branding' all echoed in his head like a broken record. He had been nothing but a pawn in a cruel game, manipulated by the people who should have cared for him the most. His father, Pete, had seen it—the way he had been pulled into a web of lies and exploitation. But even he had pushed him away, leaving him in the hands of people who only saw him as a tool for their gain.

And then James realised something Kylie said, that tonight was his last night—last night to fit into the narrative that she and the others had crafted for him, a narrative he never asked to be a part of, a narrative that had drained him of everything he once held dear. But he was confused what Lyra had to do with it.

"Oh, haven't you heard... she's agreed to be the new Hub Cum Dump in return for taking you on as her personal pimp. She's agreed for you to pimp her out across the office, to let me, Chloe, Cody, whoever wants to use her once you've bred her and made her belly swollen with your sprog, just like my belly is, just like Zara and Penny's are."

James felt his sister's pussy smother his mouth, his mind both in bliss with the cocaine and in confusion with what Kylie was saying, that he was going to be released from his hell. Suddenly Chloe got off him and grinned.

"Oh, big brother, didn't you know... its half past 1, and Kylie's got work, and I've volunteered to cover for your precious Lyra on her drivetime show. We'll be back for 8, when the first of the Liverpool lads come."

James then felt the knots that were keeping his wrists prisoner being loosened, and he knew that either he was being released temporarily or something else was being planned. Chloe leaned in closer, her voice a mix of mockery and false affection as she untied him.

"Enjoy your little break, big brother. You'll need it for later. The Liverpool lads are eager to have their fun, and trust me, they've got plans for you," she whispered, her breath hot against his ear.

James sat up slowly, his body trembling from the mix of drugs and the physical strain of the last few hours. His mind swirled with conflicting emotions—anger, humiliation, and a faint glimmer of hope that Kylie's mention of Lyra could signal a way out of this nightmare.

Chloe and Kylie left the room, laughing and whispering to each other as they gathered their things for their respective shows. James sat on the edge of the bed, his head in his hands, trying to piece together his fractured thoughts. Lyra's name lingered in his mind like a lifeline. Had she really agreed to Kylie's twisted deal, or was it just another cruel manipulation? He didn't know what to believe anymore.

****

CHAPTER 4 - Escape
Wednesday 16th April 2025

James could feel the cocaine of the evening injection in his veins, as Kyler Thompson, one of the Manic Vibes South Coast breakfast crew, had his cock in James's mouth, and Rory Carter, one of the Manic Vibes Chester & Merseyside drivetime crew, had his cock in James's arse, while Penny Lane, Rory's co-host, was bouncing on James's cock like she was riding a mechanical bull, her breathless laughter mixing with the thumping bassline of the CHR playlist echoing faintly from another room. The scene was surreal, a grotesque parody of the energetic chaos Manic Vibes portrayed on-air. James's mind floated between reality and a haze of drug-induced compliance, his body moving on autopilot as the humiliation deepened.

"Fuck, Reevesy, you've had 50 blokes and 20 women in your arse, yet it's still as tight as a choir boy in a Catholic church," Rory said, his Scouse accent carrying a mixture of crude humour and malice. The words barely registered in James's mind, which was a whirl of numbness and fleeting clarity, amplified by the cocktail of drugs pumping through his veins. He felt detached from his body, as though he were watching the scene unfold from outside himself, a spectator to his own degradation.

Penny threw her head back, her laughter grating against James's ears. "Rory, you're too much! Maybe we should get Reevesy a loyalty card for the Hub Cum Dump—ten sessions, and the eleventh's free!" The others in the room erupted in laughter, the sound echoing cruelly through

James's fragmented mind. "You know, Reevesy, I've only got 4 months to go until your sprog comes out my pussy, and I've decided, once I've carried it to term, I'm going to dump it on yours and Nott's doorstep. Oh, yeah, you're homeless and Nott lives in your sister's old room at your dad's house."

James's mind struggled to grasp the barrage of words and mockery, their weight bearing down on him like a suffocating blanket. Penny's cruel taunt about his unborn child hit something deep within him, briefly piercing through the numbing haze of drugs. The thought of an innocent life caught in this twisted cycle of manipulation and degradation filled him with an almost unbearable despair.

Suddenly he felt Kyler's member go deeper into James's throat, making him gag slightly as his body convulsed in protest. The cocaine coursing through his veins dulled the physical discomfort but did nothing to shield him from the emotional and psychological torment. His mind screamed for escape, for any way out of this nightmare, but his body remained trapped, used as nothing more than a toy for the amusement of others.

"That's it, Reevesy," Kyler groaned, his grip tightening on James's head. "You're finally learning your place." The room erupted in laughter again, their mockery cutting through the dim haze like shards of broken glass.

A few minutes later, James felt Rory withdraw, and another cock enter his arse, no lubrication, no condoms, just raw, deliberate cruelty. James winced in pain, his body instinctively recoiling, but he had no strength to resist. The laughter and crude comments from the others filled the room, blending into a cacophony that James tried to block out, retreating further into the corners of his mind. He couldn't let himself break completely—not here, not now. He focused on a single thought: escape.

****

Lyra was curled up on the sofa with Pete and Sarah, Pete having just got home from work whereas Sarah had spent the afternoon in Birmingham, meeting with some of her former Smooth Radio colleagues for lunch.

Ping

Lyra knew that it was the dreaded WhatsApp group chat, probably talking about James and how he was servicing one Manic presenter or another. In a way, she knew that, if she looked, she'd probably be disgusted with what she saw, but in another way, there was some curiosity, especially as her irrational side was curious about if James was-

"Lyra, stop it!" she muttered to herself as her thoughts started to stray. "You need to get James out of Manic, not fall into the same spiral he is. You're going to Hits in a week and half, and you need to get James out of this mess."

Unlocking her phone, she was about to open the group chat when she saw another message from a friend of hers, Emma Toolan, who worked at Bauer at Hits Radio, an email with an attachment for her on-boarding and what to expect at 54 Hagley Road on her first day. Lyra quickly opened it, relief flooding her as she looked over the details of her upcoming new role at Hits Radio. It was the escape she had been craving—something fresh, something far removed from the toxic web of Manic Vibes.

"I'm going to nip down the chippy," Sarah suddenly said, standing up. "Pete, Lyra, do you want anything?"

"Nah, I'm alright," Lyra said, trying not to show how distracted she really was. She'd been caught in the storm of her own thoughts—torn between wanting to focus on her career and a growing sense of responsibility to save James. But it wasn't her job to save him, was it?

She glanced at Pete, who had his eyes fixed on the television, flipping through channels mindlessly. A tiny wave of guilt washed over her. She had been able to escape. She was leaving Manic soon—getting away from the toxic culture and all the chaos that had come to define James's life. But she knew that even if she managed to leave, it wouldn't be enough. Not unless James was willing to do the same.

And not if Pete wouldn't let him move back to the family home, either. She had been thinking about that too—about how Pete seemed to be stubborn on that point, how the argument that had happened on New Years Day, with Pete throwing James into Kylies arms, to how, since then, in the 4 and half months that followed, James had become used and abused by others in the Manic Vibes fold, drowning in the toxic culture of the station. Lyra's thoughts grew darker, her stomach twisting with the weight of her conflicted feelings. She knew that when she had first met James as a member of Manic staff, she had, even though she was dating her ex-boyfriend, gotten a crush on the 5 years younger presenter, him, the 21 year old with the smile and the charm, and her, the 26 year old,

6 year veteran of radio, a bit more jaded but still holding on to the spark that had originally led her to the industry. She had watched him rise so quickly, just as much a part of the machine as everyone else, but somehow more naive, more vulnerable. And now, seeing him descending into this spiralling, drug-fuelled chaos, she couldn't help but wonder where things had gone wrong. Was it his ambition? His naivety? Or had he always been this easily manipulated, even from the beginning?

Her phone buzzed again, pulling her back from her thoughts. It was another message from the WhatsApp group. She stared at it for a moment, her thumb hovering over the screen, unsure whether she was ready to see what had been sent, as it was an image, and although the notification said it was an image, it didn't show what the image was.

And then she noticed it wasn't the Manic group chat, but her old Uni group chat, one that, as a graduate of Staffordshire Uni in Stoke on Trent. Opening it, she saw it was from her best friend, Phillip, who worked as a production assistant at BBC Radio Stoke on one of the few local shows the public service broadcaster produced there, the funding cuts resulting in regional shows instead of hyper-local shows that the local BBC had once been known for. Lyra smiled as she opened the message, the familiar relief of connecting with someone outside the chaotic world of Manic Vibes washing over her.

The photo showed Phillip outside the MediaCityUK studio, grinning widely as he held up a coffee cup with a BBC logo on it. Below the picture, he had written: "First Five Live show about to start!"

Lyra chuckled as she saw her friend's message, as she had heard on the grapevine he was being moved to a national show on one of the BBC's major stations, which was a huge step for him. She quickly tapped out a reply, feeling a renewed sense of hope that maybe there was still some room for integrity and authenticity left in the industry.

"Congrats, Phil! You're killing it. Hope the show goes well. I'm sure you'll smash it, as always. Let's catch up soon!"

She hit send and leaned back into the sofa, trying to shake off the dark thoughts creeping back into her mind. As much as she was excited for her own future at Hits Radio, there was still the gnawing question of what to do about James. She'd tried to distance herself emotionally from his downward spiral, focusing on her new job, her escape from Manic, but there was always a part of her that cared—too much, perhaps.

"Pete, we need to talk," Lyra said, sighing. "I pay rent for my room, as you know, right?"

Lyra watched as Pete grumbled, as if he knew that she was going to try and persuade him to let James return to the family home, something Pete had been adamant against ever since their argument on New Year's Day.

"What about it?" Pete mumbled, not looking up from the television, clearly uninterested in whatever topic she was about to broach. He had been distant recently, locked in his own thoughts, probably still battling his frustration over the state of his son's life.

Lyra took a deep breath, gathering her thoughts. She knew Pete wasn't one to easily change his mind, especially when it came to James. But something in her—perhaps the looming dread of leaving Manic Vibes for good and knowing that James was still caught in its toxic web—compelled her to try once more. She needed to feel like she had done everything she could, even if it meant challenging Pete's stubbornness.

"I think we should let James move back in," she said quietly, her voice a mix of conviction and hesitation.

Pete's head snapped up, his eyes narrowing at her. "What, you serious? After everything that's happened?" His voice had an edge to it, one that Lyra knew well. He was trying to dismiss her suggestion before it could even take root.

"I know it's complicated," Lyra replied, keeping her tone steady. "But it's clear that he's lost. He's stuck in this cycle, and I don't think he's going to pull himself out of it on his own. He needs someone—someone who'll take him in and show him there's a way out. If you don't let him back, then I'm leaving."

The silence that followed was thick, almost suffocating. Lyra's words hung in the air between them, settling heavily like an unspoken ultimatum. Pete's gaze remained fixed on the television, his fingers mindlessly scrolling through the channels, but his mind was elsewhere, wrestling with the truth of what she'd said. He wasn't one to back down easily—especially not when it came to James—but Lyra could see the cracks in his defences, the fatigue in his posture, the weight of the decisions that had piled up on his shoulders.

"I can't just forget what happened on New Year's," Pete muttered, almost to himself. "You don't know what it's been like, Lyra. It's not that simple." He finally looked at her, his eyes darkened with a mixture of anger and sorrow. "We tried to help him. I tried to help him. He's made his choices."

"So, you're happy to see him being used as a toy by his own sister, by his colleagues?" Lyra shouted, her voice getting louder as she became more frustrated, the tears of anger welling up in her eyes. "Do you want him to... you know what, forget it. Tell Sarah that I'm sorry, but I'm not stopping where I'm not wanted."

Lyra stood up and headed towards the stairs, to where the room she was living in, Chloe's room, was, to start packing her clothes. She knew that Sarah was in favour of allowing James back into the house, but she also knew that Pete was stuck in a single mood.

Ping

Lyra noticed that the 'Gals and Geezers' group chat had an image in it, and she knew that it would be something like James being mistreated by one of the others at Manic. Looking at the photo, her heart sank, as it showed James being forced to give oral sex to Liam Price, one of the Manic Vibes East Midlands Drivetime crew, while Rory Carter, one of the Liverpool presenters, stood over him laughing. The caption read:

Liam Price: *Just another Wednesday night at Manic* 🍆 *#CumDumpChronicles*

Lyra's stomach twisted in revulsion. She stared at the image, her heart racing as rage and despair collided within her. James's eyes, glazed and empty, haunted her. He was barely recognisable as the bright, ambitious young man she had first met at Manic six months ago. She had to do something. She couldn't let this continue.

She clenched her fists, her mind racing. There was no way she could leave without at least trying to get James out of this hell. Lyra shoved her phone into her pocket and stormed back downstairs, where Pete was still sitting.

As she stood in front of Pete, she pulled her phone from her pocket and showed him the photo.

"Look, Pete. Look. This is James's fate now, thanks to you kicking him out on New Year's Day. This is what happens when you give up on your son and leave him to fend for himself in a place that preys on weakness. Is this what you wanted? Is this what you're okay with?" Lyra's voice cracked with a mixture of anger and desperation as she thrust the phone towards Pete.

Pete stared at the photo, his face pale and frozen. His eyes darted over the image, and his hand trembled slightly as he reached out to take the phone from her. The image burned into his mind—a stark, undeniable snapshot of just how far James had fallen.

"Lyra… I…" Pete's voice faltered. He set the phone down on the coffee table and buried his face in his hands. "I didn't know it was this bad," he whispered, his voice heavy with guilt.

"He told you yesterday how bad it was, how bad it had become," Lyra snapped, her voice sharp. "He begged for help, Pete! And you turned him away. You left him to this—to them. They've broken him, and every second he stays in that place, he falls deeper into this nightmare. How much worse does it have to get before you do something?"

Pete sat silently, his shoulders slumped, the weight of Lyra's words pressing down on him. He looked at the phone again, the image of James's humiliation staring back at him, unrelenting. His hands tightened into fists, trembling with anger—not at Lyra, not even at James, but at himself. He had failed his son, and now the evidence was staring him in the face.

"I thought… I thought kicking him out would teach him a lesson," Pete said finally, his voice heavy with regret. "I thought he'd wake up, realise he needed to turn things around. But I was wrong. I was so bloody wrong." He looked up at Lyra, his eyes filled with a mixture of guilt and determination. "What do we do? How do we get him out of this?"

"I... I kind of made a deal with Kylie... one my irrational side couldn't resist... one I regret," Lyra muttered, her voice quieter now, the weight of the situation settling in on her. "She phoned me earlier, saying... well, that if she let him go... I'd... I'd become the hub cum dump. Then... then she sent me some photos of James, and the next thing I knew... I was texting her saying that... that I'd agree to it."

Lyra knew that she had made a deal with the devil, and that she had been trying to protect James, especially as he'd fallen deeper into the toxic web, but now she realised the trap she had walked into. The guilt rushed over her like a wave, her hands trembling as she realised just how much she had let herself be manipulated by Kylie's cruel power play. She had let her emotions guide her, and it had almost cost her everything.

Pete's eyes widened in shock at Lyra's confession, his initial guilt now mingling with confusion and concern. He leaned forward, his hands gripping the edge of the coffee table as though steadying himself.

"You what?" he said, his voice low but carrying an edge of disbelief. "Lyra, you're telling me you agreed to... to that? For James?"

Lyra nodded, her cheeks burning with shame. "I didn't know what else to do, Pete. I thought—maybe—if I could get him out, I could deal with the consequences later—especially as in a week and half, I'm heading to Bauer, and so I'd only... only have to endure having nearly everyone's cock or hands on me for a little while. I wasn't thinking straight. I just couldn't stand by and watch him sink any further. Then the bitch sent the private chat into that group chat I just showed you. Look, I... I'd rather suffer knowing I'm leaving Manic anyway instead of James being... being raped."

Pete exhaled sharply, running a hand over his face as he tried to process what Lyra had just said. The air between them was heavy with tension, a storm of emotions threatening to break at any moment. He looked at her, his eyes filled with a mix of anger, disbelief, and a flicker of guilt.

"You shouldn't have done that, Lyra," Pete said quietly, his voice strained. "I know you care about James, but this... this isn't the way. You've let Kylie manipulate you just like she's been manipulating him."

Lyra nodded, biting her lip to stop the tears threatening to spill. "I know. Believe me, I know. But what choice do we have? You saw that picture, Pete. He's not going to survive in that place much longer, not like this. If this is what it takes to get him out, then..." She trailed off, unable to finish the sentence. "I... I'm meant to be meeting Kylie at Chloe's flat on the Priory Queensway in two hours so she can... hand James over. She told me... that I'm supposed to wear... the same clothes as them lot, and that before James gets handed over, I'm to... service him."

Pete sat in stunned silence, the weight of Lyra's words bearing down on him like a storm cloud. He opened his mouth to speak, then closed it again, unsure of what to say. His mind was a torrent of guilt, frustration, and a desperate need to protect his son—no matter the cost.

"You're not going," Pete said firmly, his voice trembling with suppressed rage. "You're not going to let her—let any of them—drag you into that pit. If Kylie thinks she can use James as leverage to pull you into her sick games, she's got another thing coming."

Lyra's eyes flickered with uncertainty. "Pete, I don't think you understand. If I don't go, they'll just keep him there, and they'll make it worse. You've seen what they've done already. How much further are they willing to push? I... I can't let that happen. Anyway, they know James and I slept with each other yesterday, and they... they want to see me get... ruined by James... to be humiliated before they hand him over. Kylie said that... I'd end up being like the rest of them, that I'd have to inhale some cocaine before James... fucks me."

****

Two hours later, the party was in full swing and James had in his mouth Harry Penhurst of the Manic Vibes Cumbria Breakfast team, his arse was being filled by Cody, his own brother-in-law, who was also stroking James's own cock, making him get close to, but not actually, reaching orgasm. The room was a haze of flashing lights, pounding music, and the thick stench of sweat and alcohol. James's body moved mechanically, completely detached from the horrors of his reality, driven solely by the effects of the cocaine and the sheer numbness that had enveloped him. Cody's mocking laughter pierced through the haze, echoing in James's ears as his brother-in-law leaned closer.

"Almost there, Reevesy," Cody sneered, his tone dripping with mockery. "You'll be the star of tonight's entertainment. Don't let the crowd down now."

James felt Cody's sperm fill his hole as Harry also moaned in satisfaction, finishing in James's mouth. The room erupted into applause and laughter, the crowd revelling in James's continued degradation. His mind floated somewhere far away, the cocaine and humiliation blending into a numbing haze. He wasn't sure how much more of this he could take, but he had learned by now that resistance only made things worse.

"You know, big brother," Chloe then said, and James looked to see his sister reaching for his cock while Harry still had his arms pinned. "We've got one final guest coming, and this time, instead of her using you like a mechanical bull, you get to use her." Chloe's grin widened, her voice oozing with malice and twisted glee. "Lyra's coming over. She's finally agreed to join the party. And you're going to break her in, big brother. Make sure she remembers this night forever."

James froze, his drug-addled mind struggling to process what his sister had just said. A wave of nausea churned in his stomach, cutting through the cocaine-induced haze. Lyra? No. She couldn't be here. She shouldn't be dragged into this nightmare. The thought of her—strong, kind Lyra—being brought into this hell twisted something deep inside him.

"Chloe, no," James managed to croak, his voice hoarse and barely audible. "Leave her out of this."

Chloe's laughter was sharp and cruel. "Oh, but she's already agreed, Reevesy. She wants to save you, isn't that sweet? She thinks she can take your place, be the new star of our little show. Isn't she just adorable? You know, I can't wait to suck her nipples, to have her eating me out like a whore, to have her begging Cody to stop."

James's mind reeled at Chloe's words, his heart pounding despite the numbing effects of the cocaine. The thought of Lyra, who had shown him kindness when everyone else had treated him as disposable, being thrown into this twisted nightmare filled him with a new kind of dread. She didn't deserve this. No one did—but especially not her.

"Chloe, please," James begged, his voice breaking as tears streamed down his face. "Don't do this to her. She's not like us. She's... better than this."

Chloe tilted her head mockingly, pretending to consider his plea. "Better than us? Oh, big brother, you're so naive. No one's better than anyone here. She made her choice. She agreed to come, so she's already one of us. And if you're lucky, maybe she'll enjoy it. Just like you have."

James clenched his fists, a flicker of defiance sparking within him. For months, he had let them control him, humiliate him, break him down piece by piece. But the thought of Lyra being dragged into this darkness, of her being used and degraded the way he had been, lit a fire he hadn't felt in a long time.

He couldn't let this happen. Not to her.

"Where is she?" James asked, his voice steadier now, though his body still trembled with the aftershocks of his abuse. "Where's Lyra?"

Chloe smirked, clearly enjoying his desperation. "She'll be here soon. Don't worry, big brother. You'll get plenty of time to... welcome her to the family."

****

CHAPTER 5 - The Next Morning
Thursday 17th April 2025

It had been 12 hours since the previous night, and James woke up to see...

"My Gorillaz posters?" he muttered, taking into his surroundings. The familiar sight of the posters on his bedroom wall brought a strange sense of comfort and confusion. He blinked, rubbing his eyes, trying to shake off the haze of cocaine withdrawal and exhaustion. He wasn't sure how he had ended up back here, in his childhood bedroom at his parents' house. The last thing he remembered was the chaos of the party at Chloe's flat, the humiliation, and then... Lyra.

"Lyra," he whispered, his voice hoarse.

The events of the previous night came flooding back in disjointed flashes. He remembered Chloe's mocking laughter, Kylie's smug taunts, and Lyra walking into the apartment, her face a mix of defiance and fear. She had come for him, despite everything. He didn't know how she had managed to get him out or why she would even try, but she had.

"Give me a minute," a groan from next to him startled James out of his thoughts. He turned his head sharply to see Lyra lying beside him, wrapped in a blanket, her dark hair slightly messy from sleep. The fact she was wearing nothing didn't escape James's notice, or that, unintentionally, she was gripping his erection as if it were the door handle and was holding it that tight, he had come without any realisation or intent. James froze, his mind scrambling to process the scene before him.

"Lyra?" he croaked, his voice barely audible. She stirred slightly, blinking sleepily as she tried to adjust to the morning light streaming through the window. As her eyes focused on James, a flicker of embarrassment crossed her face, and she quickly released her grip, pulling the blanket up to cover herself.

"Sorry," Lyra mumbled, her cheeks flushed. "I—I didn't mean for things to get awkward."

James then chuckled. "Hey, we've already made love once, a couple of days ago, so-"

"Erm, twice, James.... erm, actually, three times. Last night, when I managed to get you free of that bitch of a sister and the others, you were coming down from the drugs, and I… I stayed with you, to make sure you didn't spiral further. We… well, one thing led to another. It wasn't exactly planned," Lyra admitted, her voice soft as she avoided his gaze. "And the other time was... well, Liam injected me with cocaine when I walked in to Chloe's flat, and... well, we fucked in front of everyone... and several of them recorded us."

James stared at Lyra, his mind racing as he processed her words. The mention of Liam injecting her with cocaine and what had followed hit him like a freight train. He struggled to piece together the fractured memories of the night before, his heart sinking as the reality of what they had been pulled into became painfully clear.

"They... recorded us?" James whispered, his voice trembling.

Lyra nodded, her expression a mix of shame and defiance. "Yes. Kylie made sure of it. She wanted to humiliate both of us, to make sure we couldn't just walk away from this. But James..." She reached out, holding his hand. "I've phoned in to work on our way back... your dad drove me to Brum and back her... said that we're both sick... and that I won't be returning for the last week and half of my Manic contract. I... also said that you weren't very well too. As an aside, is it normal for cocaine to still be in one's system 8 hours later when one's had it injected and hasn't ever... used it... before?"

James's heart sank as he realised the full weight of what Lyra had endured to get him out of the nightmare at Chloe's flat. The mention of the recordings made his stomach churn. The humiliation he'd felt over the past few months had been bad enough, but now Lyra had been dragged into it, subjected to the same degrading treatment he'd endured. And she had done it for him.

"I... I don't know," James admitted, his voice barely above a whisper. "Kylie... she made sure I had about 4 or 5 lines a day, or a couple of injections and some lines, so I've never... erm... knew whether it would stay in my system that long." James's voice trailed off, the weight of his confession hanging in the air between them. His eyes moved from Lyra's troubled expression to his own hands, still trembling from the remnants of the drug's grip on him. "I guess I just didn't care, not really. Not about the drugs, or the people... or myself. Why d'you ask, Ly?"

James saw Lyra go red and chuckle. "Erm... I'm horny?" she said, and James chuckled as she said that, a grin on his face that

felt like a momentary break from the heavy tension that had settled between them. The absurdity of the situation — both of them trying to navigate the wreckage of the night — gave James a brief reprieve from the overwhelming feelings of guilt and confusion that had been suffocating him. But the reality was still there, lingering like a shadow.

"You're horny?" James echoed, his chuckle tinged with disbelief. "Lyra, you just... saved me from the most messed-up night of my life, and that's your... response?" His voice faltered, the humour quickly dissipating as the gravity of their situation came crashing down again.

Lyra's grin faded as she bit her lip, clearly realising the absurdity of her attempt at levity. "I know. It's just... you've fucked me in every hole I have, multiple times, and... well, my pussy needs your cock."

James groaned as Lyra said that, but before he could respond, there was a knock on his bedroom door. James knew that, as his bedroom was the only one on the ground floor and so was directly accessible from the kitchen, the knock was likely from his mother or father. He winced, mentally preparing for the awkwardness that would undoubtedly follow.

"James? Are you awake?" Sarah's voice came through the door, her tone soft but laced with concern.

"Uh, yeah, Mum," James replied quickly, his voice cracking slightly as he sat up, pulling the blanket around him as if it would somehow shield him from the chaos of the past 24 hours. Lyra, now fully awake and aware of the tension, shot him a quick, apologetic glance before quickly turning her back to the door. It seemed she was just as keen to avoid this confrontation.

"Can I come in?" Sarah asked.

James hesitated. He didn't want to face his mother in this state, especially with Lyra in his bed. The last thing he needed was another awkward family moment. But at the same time, he knew that pretending nothing had happened wouldn't help either. His life was unravelling, and he couldn't keep hiding from the truth.

"Yeah, come in," James muttered, rubbing his temples as if it might help clear his foggy mind.

Sarah opened the door, grinning. "James, you don't need to hide Lyra. Your Dad told her to stop in your room with you last night to make sure that you weren't alone after everything that happened. He... well, knew you was going to end up coming down from the cocaine, and... well, he knew you and Lyra would probably end up having some private moments to... talk things through."

James froze, his mother's words sinking in. He felt his face flush crimson, mortified that his parents were, in their own way, acknowledging the chaos of the night before. Sarah, however, seemed remarkably unperturbed, as if this kind of situation was just another part of the weirdness of his life.

Lyra, for her part, remained silent, her body tense as she pulled the blanket tighter around herself, clearly trying to avoid any further embarrassment. But then, to James's surprise, she spoke up.

"I just... wanted to make sure James was alright," she said softly, looking at Sarah with a mixture of vulnerability and strength. "He's been through a lot lately... and I didn't want him to be alone."

Sarah nodded, her expression softening. "I get it, love. Don't worry about it. You're both adults, and... to be honest Lyra, I'd rather you date my son than the bitch he was dating before," Sarah said, her voice surprisingly calm. "And as for that daughter of mine, Chloe, she's welcome to that Lane lad... never liked him at all. Pete only went to the wedding because of working at Manic as you know and to do the father of the bride speech. I think Pete would agree with me now that she's better off with him."

James blinked in disbelief at his mother's casual, almost amused tone. The gravity of the situation hadn't quite hit him yet, and here was his mother, discussing his romantic life and the disarray of his past few days like they were chatting about a neighbour's dog.

"Erm... thanks, Mum," James muttered, still processing the fact that Sarah wasn't as horrified as he expected. In fact, she seemed downright nonchalant about everything, even going as far as to imply that Lyra was a better option than Kylie.

"To be fair, James, Sophia, your first girlfriend, was a better choice than the harridan you ended up with. She was a bit naive, but she had a good heart. Anyway, don't worry about it too much. You know your father and I are here for you, whatever you need." Sarah smiled at Lyra reassuringly before turning her attention back to James. "Now, let's talk about what happened last night. I know it's... well, it's a bit of a mess right now, but we need to start figuring out what's going to happen next."

James sighed, rubbing his face in frustration. He was so tired—physically, mentally, emotionally. His mind was still reeling from the events of the previous night, and it felt like everything was slipping through his fingers. But Sarah's pragmatic tone, as always, was oddly comforting. She wasn't pressing him for answers, just gently nudging him towards some form of clarity, even if he wasn't sure he was ready for it.

"Yeah, I know. I just... don't know where to start," he muttered, glancing at Lyra, who gave him a reassuring look.

Sarah raised an eyebrow, sensing the tension. "Well, we'll start by making sure you're alright, James. That's the most important thing right now. Your aunt Helen will be over in an hour."

James groaned, as Helen Carmichael, his aunt, was a GP who worked in Coventry, and she had a habit of popping in unannounced when things were getting particularly chaotic. It wasn't unusual for her to show up with medical advice or a well-meaning but awkward lecture on health and lifestyle. Given the current state of affairs, James could already feel the pressure of her scrutinising eyes.

"Great," James muttered, his tone tinged with sarcasm. "Just what I need."

Sarah, undeterred by his response, placed a hand on his shoulder. "Look, I know this whole thing is a mess, but we need to start taking steps to sort it out. And you're not doing it alone, James. We've all got your back. Anyway, after that, I... well, you know your dad's old boss, Woody Bones."

Woody Bones, the owner of several community radio stations, and previously several local radio stations in the ILR days, had owned Dudley FM, his dad's former station. Woody was a relic of the radio world James had grown up in, long before it had turned into the corporate behemoth that now controlled his life.

"Woody Bones?" James repeated, blinking as he tried to piece together why his mother would be bringing him up now. "What about him?"

"He's asked me to work part-time for one of his new stations," Sarah said, smiling. "Alongside my Reeves Radio Ltd work. South Staffs FM."

James blinked at his mother, trying to process what she had just said. South Staffs FM? The name sounded quaint, almost nostalgic, in stark contrast to the world of corporate radio conglomerates he'd been submerged in. His mother's calm revelation felt like a lifeline, pulling him out of the chaos he had endured for months.

"South Staffs FM?" James repeated, his tone tinged with disbelief. "That's... an actual station? Not just one of Woody's pipe dreams?"

Sarah smiled knowingly. "Oh, it's very real, James. Woody's been working on it for a while now. It'll be covering Perton, Wombourne, Bobbington and parts of South Staffordshire. The beauty of it is that it's local, and it's got that personal touch—something Manic's lost over the years. I've been asked to run it and its sister station, Wolvo Sounds. We've managed to get a lease on a former ILR studio for it... Beacon's old one."

James saw Lyra chuckle at that, as if there was a joke involved in reviving an old ILR studio. Beacon Radio's history, once a proud and vibrant part of the Midlands' local radio scene, was legendary. Its name still evoked memories of a bygone era of radio, when the focus was on community connection rather than corporate homogenisation. James couldn't help but smirk at the irony—his life had spiralled into chaos thanks to the modern radio industry, and now his family was turning to the very roots of local broadcasting for solace.

"Beacon's old studio?" James said, raising an eyebrow. "You're telling me that Woody's bringing back proper local radio? What's next, pirate radio stations making a comeback?"

"James, you dolt," Lyra then said, gently tapping him on the ear, to which James winced as the contact reminded him of how Kylie would playfully tap him before degrading him further. Automatically moving backwards, James didn't realise he was at the edge of the bed and fell flat on the floor with a loud thud.

"Ow," he groaned, rubbing his head as he slowly got to his feet. Seeing Lyra get close to him, James knew on one hand she wasn't Kylie, but the way he had been programmed over the past 4 months, he braced himself instinctively, his body stiffening in anticipation of some kind of ridicule or reprimand.

"James, what's wrong?" Sarah asked, and James could see the concern etched on his mother's face as she looked between him and Lyra. His reaction hadn't gone unnoticed, and it was clear that Sarah was beginning to piece together just how deeply the past few months had affected him.

James hesitated, struggling to find the words to explain. He didn't want to admit how much he had been broken, how even the simplest gestures could trigger memories of humiliation and manipulation. He swallowed hard, his voice shaky as he finally spoke.

"It's... nothing," he muttered, avoiding their gazes. "I just... need to get used to being back here, that's all."

Sarah exchanged a glance with Lyra, who looked equally worried. Lyra reached out, placing a hand gently on James's arm. "James, it's okay," she said softly. "You don't have to pretend. Kylie, your sister and her husband programmed you, didn't they?"

James hesitated, his heart pounding as Lyra's words hit too close to home. He could feel his chest tighten, the weight of the truth pressing down on him. He had spent months trying to survive, trying to detach himself from the humiliations and abuse, but now, faced with the safety of his childhood home and the unwavering concern in Lyra's and his mother's eyes, the facade he had been clinging to was crumbling.

"I…" James started, his voice faltering. He glanced at Lyra, then at Sarah, before finally sitting down on the edge of the bed, burying his face in his hands. "Yes," he admitted quietly. "They… they broke me. Kylie, Chloe, Cody… all of them. They made me feel like I was nothing but a… a toy for their amusement. And I let it happen because I didn't know how to fight back. Or maybe I thought I deserved it. You know how many people I've had in my arse since Dad kicked me out on Christmas Day?"

James took a minute to sigh before continuing. "50 blokes and 8 women, all with their own sick agendas, all treating me like some disposable object. And that doesn't include the countless times they made me do things… things I can't even say without wanting to crawl into a hole and disappear. Even Chloe... made me... fuck her. My own sister making me commit incest, no protection, no condoms, nothing. What's worse is I've got 4... maybe 5... people pregnant. I mean, last night, and the other day, Lyra and I... without protection... and Mum, you know I'm like Dad, an ultra-high sperm count due to some faulty gene that's on Dad's side of the family." James' voice cracked as he admitted this, his face buried in his hands. "Lyra and I might have been... careless. I don't know what to do anymore. I don't know how to fix this."

The room was silent for a moment, the weight of James's confession hanging heavily in the air. Sarah and Lyra exchanged a look, their worry deepening as they realised the full extent of the trauma James had endured. Lyra sat down beside him, gently placing a hand on his shoulder.

"James," Lyra began softly, her voice steady and soothing, "none of this is your fault. What they did to you was abuse, plain and simple. You didn't deserve any of it. And as for what happened between us..." She hesitated, her cheeks flushing slightly. "We'll figure it out together, no matter what happens. You're not alone anymore."

Suddenly the doorbell went, and James braced himself, as he heard the front door open, and his dad greeting his aunt.

"...called me and asked me to give James a checkup. Penelope was also down this end as her job at Wolverhampton Civic Hall had a late finish last night, and she's staying with me this week, so we drove down together. I hope that's okay," Helen said as she followed Pete into the living room. Her voice carried its usual brisk efficiency, the kind that always made James feel like he was back in school being scolded for something trivial.

James tensed as his aunt entered the room, carrying her medical bag. Behind her was Penelope, Helen's daughter, who gave a small wave and a tentative smile as she stepped inside. James hadn't seen Penelope in years—she had been the quiet, bookish cousin who always seemed to blend into the background

Penelope stood by the door, her dark hair tied back into a neat ponytail, looking both curious and concerned. She wore a jacket with the logo of Wolverhampton Civic Hall embroidered on it, clearly not expecting to be roped into a family intervention. Her gaze flicked between James and Lyra, taking in the awkward tension in the room.

"Hey, cousin," Penelope then said, a grin on her face. "And I presume your lady friend is Kylie?"

James's heart sank at Penelope's words. He shook his head emphatically, his voice tinged with frustration as he replied, "No, Penelope. This is Lyra. Kylie and I... we're done. Finished. Over. She's... she's not a part of my life anymore."

"Well how come your Facebook talks about you and Kylie?" Penelope said with a raised eyebrow, pulling out her phone to show James his own Facebook profile. The cover photo was a professionally staged picture of him and Kylie from one of Manic's promotional shoots, both of them grinning and holding microphones with the Manic Vibes logo in the background. The relationship status still read In a Relationship with Kylie Morgan.

James groaned, rubbing his temples as the reality of how much his public image had been shaped and controlled by others sank in. "Penelope, that's not me. It's... it's a facade. Something Kylie and the others put up to keep the 'Golden Couple' narrative alive for Manic. I haven't touched my Facebook in months." His voice cracked slightly as he added, "I don't even know the password anymore. Kylie had control over all that."

Suddenly Penelope coughed something that sounded like James was whipped and then smiled, before chuckling. "Oh, and what does Lyra do then?"

James looked at Penelope, trying to push through the embarrassment and frustration her teasing had caused. He took a deep breath, glancing at Lyra, who was glaring at Penelope.

"I work at Manic Vibes Stoke & Cheshire as their drivetime presenter... but I'm moving to the mid-morning spot on Hits Radio in a few weeks' time," Lyra said.

"Wait, you're replacing Tom Green on Hits Radio?" Penelope interrupted, her eyes lighting up with recognition. "He's leaving? I loved his show! You're the new host?"

Lyra nodded, a small smile tugging at her lips. "Yeah, I guess I am. It's a big step, but... it's time for a change." Her voice was steady, but James could sense the undercurrent of uncertainty. The events of the past few days had clearly shaken her, but she was holding herself together with remarkable resilience.

"Well, good for you," Penelope said, her tone softening slightly. "Although I think he's cute."

James couldn't help but smirk at Penelope's comment, despite the tension in the room. "Tom Green? Cute? He's alright, I guess," he quipped, trying to lighten the mood. "But Lyra here's way cooler. Hits Radio's lucky to have her."

Lyra chuckled softly, nudging James in the arm. "Flattery will get you nowhere, Reeves," she teased, though her smile was genuine. For a brief moment, the heaviness in the room seemed to lift, if only slightly.

"Alright, enough about radio crushes," Helen interrupted, setting her bag on the coffee table. "James, I'm here to check up on you. From what your mum's told me, it sounds like you've had a rough few months. I'm not here to judge—just to help. So, let's start with some basics. How are you feeling physically?"

James hesitated, glancing at Lyra, then at his mother. He felt a surge of embarrassment at the idea of recounting his recent experiences in front of them, but he knew Helen wasn't going to back down. "Tired," he admitted finally. "And... shaky. My body's just... not right. Probably the drugs still in my system."

Helen nodded, her expression neutral but focused. "That's to be expected, given what you've been through. Cocaine leaves the system relatively quickly, but the aftereffects—both physical and psychological—can linger for days, even weeks. How often would you take it?"

James hesitated, glancing nervously at Lyra before answering. "Daily," he admitted, his voice barely above a whisper. "Sometimes four or five times a day. Lines, injections... whatever they gave me. It wasn't... by choice most of the time. They'd push it on me. Said it made me more... cooperative."

The room fell silent. Sarah's face paled, and even Penelope, who had been trying to lighten the mood, looked horrified. Helen took a deep breath, her professional demeanour holding steady despite the clear shock of her nephew's confession.

"That's... a significant amount," Helen said carefully, pulling out a stethoscope and blood pressure monitor from her bag. "We'll check your vitals now, but you'll need a more thorough assessment soon. Withdrawal can be brutal, James, and what you're describing sounds like coercion. You're going to need both medical support and counselling to recover fully. Now, Sarah told me you attended sex parties and were both giving and receiving penetration, right? How many sexual partners do you think you've had over the past few months and when was the last time you had unprotected sex?"

James winced at the directness of Helen's question. He could feel his mother's gaze burning into him, and Penelope's presence didn't help his growing discomfort. His mind scrambled to estimate the answer, though he dreaded voicing it aloud.

"Um…" James began, his voice shaky. "I don't know… maybe 60? 70? Over the last four months, I mean." He hesitated before continuing, his voice dropping even lower. "And the last time was... yesterday, with Lyra."

"Actually, it was 6 hours ago, James," Lyra said, sighing. "About 2am, when you decided that my... backside... was a nice nesting place for your...um... equipment." Lyra's cheeks flushed as she trailed off, clearly embarrassed to be discussing such personal matters in front of his family. James buried his face in his hands, groaning in frustration.

The fact that Lyra then muttered "not that I minded" made James go even redder as Penelope burst into laughter, trying to stifle her amusement behind her hand. Even Sarah smirked slightly, though she quickly composed herself, shooting her nephew a supportive glance.

"Alright, enough embarrassing the poor lad," Helen said firmly, though there was a slight twitch at the corner of her mouth. She adjusted her glasses and set her equipment on the table. "Now, how many of those were male and how many were female?"

James hesitated, his voice barely audible as he replied, "About roughly half and half... including my own sister." He sighed deeply, running a hand through his hair as he struggled to process the enormity of what he was admitting. "Most of them... it wasn't my choice. They pushed me into it, and... I just did what I was told. Kylie... she... some of them would pay her for the use of me, for whatever they wanted. I was... rented out like some sort of object." His voice broke as he spoke, the shame and anger bubbling to the surface. "And yes, with my sister, Chloe... she made me. Said it was all part of the 'family bond'. I didn't even have a say in my own body anymore. I... I think... no, I know, I got 4 people pregnant, and... well, Lyra and I had unprotected sex two days ago and again yesterday and I think I might have got her pregnant and-"

James knew he was rambling as he was spiralling deeper into his thoughts, the weight of his confession pressing down on him like a crushing wave. He stopped mid-sentence, his voice faltering as tears began to stream down his face. The shame, the guilt, and the overwhelming sense of helplessness were too much to contain any longer. He buried his face in his hands, his shoulders shaking as he broke down in front of his family and Lyra.

****

A few hours later, James was sitting in the living room, clutching a mug of tea Sarah had made for him when his phone started vibrating.

Ping

Ping

Ping

Ping

Notification after notification buzzed, flooding James's phone screen. The dreaded WhatsApp group, "Gals and Geezers," was alive with activity. The notifications came in rapid succession, each one twisting the knot in his stomach tighter. He hesitated, his thumb hovering over the screen. He knew it would be bad—he knew it would be the same toxic mess he'd been dragged through for months—but the curiosity and fear gnawed at him.

"Don't," Lyra said firmly, sitting beside him on the couch. Her voice was steady but gentle, a much-needed anchor in the storm of his thoughts. "Whatever they're saying, James, it doesn't matter. You're out of there. They don't own you anymore."

James swallowed hard, nodding slightly but unable to tear his eyes away from the screen. His heart raced as another ping lit up the screen, the group chat preview flashing with a snippet of text:

Rory: *Reevesy's gone MIA! 😂 Guess he's off breeding more 'cum-dumps'. Anyone know where our golden boy's hiding?*

Kylie: *He and Nott are probably off making a porno together. 😂 Hope they're ready for the sequel when he crawls back for more coke!*

James clenched his fists, his entire body tensing as the vile messages scrolled across his screen. Every word felt like a dagger, each comment a cruel reminder of the environment he'd been forced into. He wanted to throw the phone across the room, to smash it, to make it all go away—but he couldn't. It was as if the toxic pull of that world still had its claws in him.

"James." Lyra's voice broke through his haze of anger and humiliation. She reached out and placed a hand gently on his arm, grounding him. "Delete the group. Leave it. Block them all. You don't need this anymore."

Suddenly there was a knock on the door and James looked up sharply, his heart racing at the unexpected sound. He wasn't sure who he expected—perhaps someone from Manic, someone coming to drag him back into the nightmare he was finally trying to escape. Sarah, sensing his unease, stood and moved towards the door.

"I'll get it," she said, her voice calm but firm.

James exchanged a nervous glance with Lyra as they heard the muffled voices from the doorway and then Sarah slamming the door as if it were a final punctuation mark in a conversation she didn't want to continue. A moment later, Sarah walked back into the living room, her expression a mixture of irritation and concern.

"That was Kylie," Sarah announced, her tone clipped. "She's come to 'pick you and Lyra' up for 'work', even though I know Lyra left a voicemail on your HR sickness line to say that you both would be off sick today and that you emailed them a few hours ago, James, to say that you were requesting your 12 month contract at Manic be annulled early and that you're not going to return to work." Sarah sat down with a deep sigh, her gaze fixed on James. "She left when I told her you're not coming with her, but she's not happy. She said she'll be back if you don't call her by tonight."

James's stomach sank. Kylie's grip on his life seemed unrelenting, her refusal to let go of him like a vice. He looked at Lyra, whose jaw was tight with anger, her hands clenched into fists.

"She doesn't own you, James," Lyra said firmly. "You're done with her, with all of them. Let her threaten, let her try whatever games she wants. She can't hurt you anymore."

"But... but... she... she knows something that... well, it could end up blacklisting me from the industry..." James said, stuttering as he knew that there was one thing that he hadn't revealed yet—the secret Kylie held over him, the one that could destroy not only his career but the fragile hope he was beginning to rebuild. He hesitated, his voice faltering as he tried to find the words.

"She knows..." James began, his hands trembling. "She knows that I... she knows that, when I was at uni, and I was a Fresher, that I stole money from the student union bar till," James admitted, his voice barely above a whisper. The words hung heavy in the air, his shame palpable. "I was drunk, stupid, and thought it was funny at the time. Kylie found out—she always finds out everything—and she's been holding it over me ever since. She said if I ever tried to leave her or cross her, she'd leak it to every station in the country. It wasn't a few quid... more like a grand... and I blew it on a... employed woman."

James knew that the euphemism that he had used for a

prostitute would not go unnoticed, and the weight of his confession hung heavily in the room. Sarah's face tightened, her calm composure slipping into something sterner, while Lyra's expression softened, her concern outweighing any potential judgment.

"James," Sarah began, her voice measured but firm, "what you did was wrong. You know that. But you were young, foolish, and clearly influenced by the wrong people. Kylie using this against you now, years later, is manipulation—plain and simple. She has no right to hold your mistakes over your head like this."

Lyra nodded, placing a reassuring hand on James's arm. "And you've changed since then, James. What matters is what you do now, not what you did back then. If Kylie wants to play dirty, we'll deal with it together. But you can't let her keep you under her thumb because of something in your past."

"It gets worse, though, mum. This... lady... was... well, she works now at Manic... and... well, when we had our... paid liaison, I... kind of was heavy handed with her and... well, let's just say, Mum, I may have

injured her in a way that left scars—both physical and emotional." James's voice broke as he admitted this, the words spilling out like poison he had been keeping bottled up for too long. He felt Lyra's hand tighten on his arm, her silent support the only thing keeping him from completely breaking down.

Sarah's expression shifted from stern concern to a mix of disbelief and disappointment. "James... you hurt someone?" she asked softly, her voice laced with pain.

James nodded, his eyes fixed on the floor. "It was an accident," he whispered. "I didn't mean to hurt her, but I was drunk and stupid, and I... I didn't realise how rough I was being. I... I apologised, and she accepted it... after I... paid her off."

The silence in the room was deafening, broken only by the muffled ticking of the living room clock. James felt as though the weight of his confession was pressing him into the sofa, suffocating him. He couldn't bear to meet his mother's gaze, nor Lyra's, as his darkest secret spilled into the open.

Sarah inhaled deeply, her hands gripping her knees as she composed herself. "James," she said finally, her voice low and trembling with a mix of emotion, "what you've just told me… it's serious. You know that, don't you?"

He nodded, barely able to find the courage to respond. "I know," he croaked, his voice hoarse. "But it gets worse... Lorna... you know her, Ly, one of Cody's colleagues in the newsroom... she's the one who it was... she was one of those who forced me over the past couple of months to do things to her... made me drink her piss and then clean her out with my tongue. She kept saying it was payback for what I did back then." James's voice cracked as he relayed the full extent of the humiliation and manipulation he had endured. "She used it against me, just like Kylie. Every time I tried to say no, she'd bring it up, and I'd just… shut down."

Lyra's jaw tightened, her hands balling into fists as she listened. "That's not payback, James," she said firmly. "That's abuse. They used your past against you to control and hurt you. None of this is on you anymore. It's on them." Her voice trembled slightly with anger, her protective instincts flaring as she looked at James. "We'll figure this out. But first, you need to focus on healing. We'll deal with Kylie, Lorna, and the rest of them later."

Sarah stood abruptly, her hands on her hips as she processed everything James had just revealed. "James," she said softly but with steel in her tone, "you've made mistakes—serious ones—but no one has the right to do what they've done to you. We'll help you, but you need to let us. No more keeping this to yourself."

James nodded, his voice barely audible as he replied, "Okay."

"Good." Sarah turned to Lyra, her expression softening slightly. "Lyra, thank you for standing by him. I can see how much you care for James, and I'm grateful he has someone like you in his corner."

Lyra gave a small nod, her cheeks flushing slightly. "He's worth it," she said quietly. "Even if he doesn't always believe it."

Sarah smiled faintly before glancing back at James. "Right, first thing's first. We're going to get you some proper help, James—medical, psychological, whatever you need. And as for Kylie…" Her eyes narrowed. "I'll deal with her if she comes back here. She won't get away with this."

James blinked in surprise at the determination in his mother's voice. For the first time in what felt like forever, he felt a glimmer of hope—a tiny spark that maybe, just maybe, he could start to piece his life back together with the help of the people who truly cared about him.

As the room fell into a contemplative silence, the weight of James's revelations still lingered. But amidst the heaviness, there was also a sense of resolve—a shared understanding that this was the beginning of the end of Kylie's reign over his life. And though the road ahead was uncertain, for the first time in months, James felt like he wasn't walking it alone.

****

CHAPTER 6 - The Phone Calls Intensify
Friday 18th April 2025

James stared at his phone as it buzzed relentlessly on the coffee table. The notifications from WhatsApp had mercifully stopped after he muted the Gals and Geezers group, but Kylie had now resorted to direct phone calls. Every minute or so, her name flashed across the screen, her persistence a suffocating reminder of the hold she still thought she had over him.

The house was quiet save for the distant hum of the washing machine. Sarah had gone out to run errands, and Pete was upstairs sorting through old files, giving James a rare moment of solitude. Or it would have been, if Kylie wasn't so determined to intrude on it.

Ring

Again.

This time, however, it was a 0151 number that James didn't recognise, but he had an inkling it might be related to Kylie or someone else from Manic. His stomach churned at the thought.

He hesitated before reaching for the phone, his thumb hovering over the green answer button. Against his better judgement, he picked up, his voice cautious.

"Hello?"

There was a pause, followed by a voice that James knew was one of the staff from the Speke hub of Manic.

"Good afternoon, its Louise from Manic Vibes. We're just going to wait for a moment and then put you through to the studio."

James's heart sank. He had no idea why they'd be calling him or what they could possibly want, but the mention of the studio made his pulse quicken. His mind raced through worst-case scenarios—had Kylie escalated her manipulation? Was this some stunt to publicly humiliate him?

Looking at the clock, he noticed it was only 9am, so it would be the breakfast shows across the different regions, and suddenly the sound of the Manic Vibes West Midlands breakfast show intro jingles filled the line, accompanied by the unmistakably high-energy voices of Hayley Pearson and Lorcan Anderson, two people who had paid Kylie for the privilege of using James as their pawn in the toxic games Manic had normalised. James's grip on the phone tightened, his knuckles white as he braced himself for whatever was coming next.

"...and we've got a very special caller on the line, one who's made the news this morning after some very saucy pictures appeared in the Daily Mail of him and Lyra Nott at a very... high powered... party, its none other than Manic Urban's very own Jimmy Reeves."

James's heart plummeted as the words hit him like a freight train. His mind scrambled for an explanation, a way out, but the damage was already done. The Daily Mail? Saucy pictures? What on earth had Kylie or someone else leaked this time?

"Er... hi," James croaked, his voice trembling with a mixture of fear and anger.

Hayley's chirpy tone didn't falter, the grin practically audible through the phone. "Jimmy, my man, how are ya? We've all seen the pics, the front page of you and Lyra Nott, both high on cocaine, her in a position that would make a yoga instructor blush, and you... well, let's just say it looks like you were the life of the party! Care to comment on the, er, festivities?"

James's stomach churned, a cold sweat breaking out across his forehead. He struggled to find his voice, his mind racing with a mixture of anger and humiliation. Kylie's reach had clearly gone further than he anticipated, and now his private life was being turned into entertainment fodder.

"I... I have no comment," James stammered, his voice shaking as he fought to maintain his composure. "And, honestly, I don't appreciate being dragged into this on-air without warning."

Lorcan's laugh was sharp, almost cruel. "Aw, come on, Jimmy! You're a public figure now, mate. People are curious. And besides, you and Lyra looked like you were having a great time. Now, a witness says that you were, quote, so high that you couldn't tell which way was up, and Lyra was leading you around like a puppy. Care to clarify for the listeners, Jimmy? Were you the party animal of the night, or was this just a misunderstanding?"

James's grip tightened on the phone as he forced himself to remain calm, though his insides were churning. He knew any response could be twisted and used against him. This wasn't an interview; it was a trap.

"I've already said I have no comment," James replied, his voice firm despite the tremor beneath it. "And furthermore, Lyra doesn't deserve to be dragged into this - she's innocent in all of-"

"Be that as it may, Jimmy," Hayley interrupted, and James knew that she was about to steer the conversation into even murkier waters. Her voice, still chipper and faux-friendly, carried a sharp edge. "But you have to admit, these photos are something else. I mean, the chemistry between you two—it's electric! Our listeners are dying to know: is Lyra the new leading lady in your life? Or is this just another one of those Manic Vibes party stories we keep hearing about? Several Manic Vibes presenters have come out saying you are the father of their soon-to-be-born children, including Manic Vibes Chester and Merseyside drivetime host Penny Lane, our own Kylie Morgan, myself, Ibiza Belters host Clo Reeves, Manic Vibes Tayside host Tamina West, as well as former Manic personalities Toni Green and Zara Love. What do you have to say to these allegations?"

James's blood ran cold as the words hit him. His jaw tightened, and he had to fight back the urge to hang up the phone. The audacity of the situation was almost laughable, if it weren't for the fact that it was playing out in front of countless listeners. Kylie and her allies had clearly orchestrated this stunt, using it to humiliate him further and drag his name—and Lyra's—through the mud.

"I'm not going to dignify that with a response," James said firmly, his voice finally finding a steadiness he didn't feel. "This is my private life, and I won't let it be turned into entertainment for your show. If you want to talk about radio, music, or anything related to my work, fine. But this? This is harassment."

"Oh, but its public record, Jimmy," Lorcan then jumped in, his tone dripping with mock sincerity. "When you're in the spotlight, your private life becomes fair game. And our listeners love a bit of gossip with their morning coffee. Besides, if there's nothing to hide, why not set the record straight?"

James clenched his jaw, the anger bubbling just beneath the surface. He was done playing their game, done letting them dictate the narrative. He took a deep breath, steadying himself before speaking.

"Because it's none of your business," James shot back, his voice sharp and unwavering. "What's being aired here isn't journalism or entertainment—it's exploitation. I've been through hell these past few months, and you're only making it worse. If you want to drag me through the mud, fine, but leave Lyra out of it. She's done nothing to deserve this."

"Funny you should say that, we've got her on the line right now," Hayley said and James shuddered, as he knew Lyra was in the shower, and so wouldn't know what he was saying. Suddenly the sound of running water stopped, and the line crackled before Hayley's voice came through again, too cheerful for James's liking. "Good morning, Lyra. Now, for listeners who don't know, our dear colleague from Manic Vibes Stoke & Cheshire is leaving

Manic soon for Hits Radio, and this little photo scandal couldn't have come at a more dramatic time, could it? In fact, a statement by the other side says that they are reviewing your upcoming contract and there are rumours from a source within Bauer that your new show might not be approved due to these allegations. How do you feel about that, Lyra?"

James's stomach churned as he heard Hayley's words. This was no longer just about humiliation; they were actively sabotaging Lyra's career. He tightened his grip on the phone, his knuckles turning white. Before Lyra could respond, he interrupted.

"Hayley, that's enough," James snapped, his voice firm and commanding. "This has gone beyond gossip or fun morning banter. You're playing with people's lives. Do you realise that? Anyway, if we really want to talk, what about the time I covered for Lorcan a few months ago on this show and while we were on air, you were snorting cocaine as if it had gone out of fashion yourself? Or when Lorcan walked in on me in the Manic Urban studio and demanded I service him because he had paid Kylie £50 for the privilege? How he made me beg for the right to have him... have him rape me. Are we going to air those stories next, or is it only my humiliation on the menu for today?"

The line fell silent for a moment. James could almost hear Hayley and Lorcan exchanging panicked glances, their on-air composure faltering. This wasn't part of the script they'd prepared, and they clearly hadn't expected James to fight back.

Hayley recovered first, though her voice was noticeably less perky. "Well, Jimmy, it sounds like you've got quite a lot on your chest this morning. We're always here for a chat, but maybe we'll leave this one for the HR department to handle, yeah? Anyway folks, we'll have more from Lyra and Jimmy after this hit from Calvin Harris and Ellie Goulding – 'Miracle.' Don't go anywhere!"

The upbeat music kicked in, but James was already fumbling with the phone, ending the call. The anger coursing through him was almost palpable. His breathing was ragged, his hands trembling as he slammed the phone down on the coffee table.

Ring

Another 0151 number, a Liverpool number, and James froze as he stared at the screen. The relentless calls, the toxic manipulation—they weren't stopping. His hands shook as he debated whether to answer, but this time, he let it ring out, unwilling to subject himself to any more of Manic's games.

Ring

This time a different 0151 number, one which was in James's contact list as Manic's HR department. James groaned, reluctantly answering the call, knowing he couldn't avoid it forever.

"Hello, this is James," he said cautiously, his voice still shaky from the previous call.

"James, it's Charlotte from HR," came the polished, clipped tone on the other end of the line. "We've received multiple complaints this morning about the nature of your comments on the West Midlands breakfast show. We are calling you to inform you that you are being suspended without pay pending an internal investigation. Furthermore, we are reviewing your contract due to the reputational damage this has caused to Manic Vibes and the wider Manic Radio network."

James's stomach dropped, the words hitting him like a punch to the gut. He gripped the phone tightly, his knuckles white as he fought to keep his composure. His mind raced, replaying the morning's events and the escalating chaos that seemed intent on destroying what little stability he had left.

"Charlotte," James began, his voice strained but steady, "I was ambushed live on air with deeply personal and defamatory accusations. I only defended myself. Are you seriously penalising me for that?"

"In accordance with section 12, subsection G, paragraph 8 of your contract," Charlotte continued, her tone devoid of sympathy, "any behaviour, on or off air, which could reasonably bring the Manic Radio brand into disrepute is grounds for suspension and review. Your comments regarding illegal substances and allegations of inappropriate conduct among your colleagues fall under this clause. While we understand the situation may have been emotionally charged, the nature of your statements cannot be ignored. You'll receive further details by email shortly."

James took a deep breath, his anger simmering just beneath the surface. He knew the clause Charlotte was referring to, but the irony of it being used against him—after everything he'd endured at Manic—was almost laughable.

Then he remembered that yesterday, he had emailed HR with a letter of resignation, requesting immediate termination of his contract and citing the hostile work environment as the reason. Taking a deep breath to steady himself, he decided it was time to remind Charlotte of the facts.

"Charlotte," James said, his voice firm and controlled, "I sent you an email yesterday, officially resigning from my contract. I requested that my resignation take immediate effect due to the toxic and abusive environment I've endured at Manic. Have you reviewed it?"

There was a pause on the line, the sound of clicking keys faintly audible in the background as Charlotte presumably searched for the email. James felt his heart pounding in his chest as he waited for her response.

"Ah, yes, Mr Smith, however we have decided not to accept your resignation at this time," Charlotte's voice came back, colder than before. "This is due to there being 6 months left on your contract, and therefore you are required to complete the remaining 6 months, as it states that you have to provide a 6 month notice period. Your request to resign without serving this six-month notice period is being reviewed by legal, and we will contact you once a decision has been made. Please note, this may take some time due to the complexity of your case."

James's heart sank. He had expected some resistance, but he hadn't anticipated being forced to stay in a job that had become nothing short of a prison. The thought of remaining at Manic for another six months, trapped in the toxic culture and manipulative environment, made him feel physically ill.

"Charlotte," James's voice was low, strained, "You can't be serious. After everything that's happened, you're going to force me to stay at Manic? To finish out my contract in a place where I've been abused and humiliated by my colleagues, my superiors, and the very people who should have been protecting me? How does that make any sense?"

"I understand this is difficult, James, but it's company policy," Charlotte replied, her tone still detached. "We are reviewing the situation, and until further notice, you are suspended without pay. Furthermore, you are reminded that the exclusivity clauses still apply, and you will not be permitted to entertain offers from other media organisations during this time. We will be in touch shortly with further details."

The line went dead before James could respond. His mind was spinning as he dropped the phone onto the coffee table. The weight of the call, the suspension, the ongoing power struggle with Manic, all of it was crushing him.

He sat there for a long time, staring at the phone, feeling his anger slowly dissolve into a cold sense of helplessness. His hands trembled as he thought about the coming months—six months of being shackled to the very company that had exploited him, humiliated him, and now, thanks to Kylie's manipulations, continued to pull his strings.

Ping

James's phone buzzed again, pulling him from his spiralling thoughts. He hesitated before glancing at the screen, his heart skipping a beat when he saw the subject line: "HR Update - Immediate Action Required."

With a deep sigh, he opened the email. It was from Manic's HR department, and the contents were stark and impersonal.

From: *charlotte.mcdonald@manicradio.group*

To: *jamie3443snetta@yahoo.co.uk*

Subject: *Immediate Action Required: Status of Your Employment*

Dear Mr Smith,

Further to our telephone conversation, we regret to inform you that due to the ongoing situation, your request for resignation has been temporarily halted. As per your contract, you are obligated to serve the six-month notice period before your employment can be terminated, regardless of any circumstances.

During this period, you are expected to comply with all company policies, including attendance and participation in all mandatory meetings, as outlined in your contractual obligations.

Please be aware that the allegations made against you, including those aired on the West Midlands breakfast show, are being reviewed as part of the internal investigation. We take these matters seriously and ask for your cooperation as we work to resolve them.

If you have any further queries, please contact the HR department.

Regards, Charlotte McDonald HR Manager, Manic Radio Group

James stared at the screen, the words blurring in his vision as he read and re-read them. He felt his heart sink into his stomach. Not only was he still trapped, but the fight was being taken out of his hands. Six more months? He couldn't bear it.

The overwhelming frustration built inside him, a pressure cooker of emotions that seemed to have nowhere to go. He could hear the faint sounds of his family upstairs, the hum of life going on around him, but it felt as though he were in a bubble—trapped in his own personal hell, with no escape. Every attempt to fight back, every plea for freedom, was shot down, leaving him with nothing but more chains.

Suddenly he heard squealing from upstairs, and chuckled, as he knew that Lyra was in the room that she rented, and that the squealing was not of a painful or embarrassing nature, but a sound of relief, one James recognised from the few times they had made love, the sound of Lyra coming close to orgasm. The realisation brought a brief, almost surreal moment of levity amidst the chaos in James's mind. He chuckled softly to himself, shaking his head at how even in the direst circumstances, life found ways to remind him of its absurdity.

Heading upstairs, James knew that Lyra would possibly object to him walking in on what was now her domain, but the need for the toilet was important as he hadn't been all morning, and that the bathroom was right next to her room. He hesitated for a moment outside the door, the muffled sound of Lyra's voice—soft, breathless, and clearly lost in her own moment—making him blush slightly. The last thing he wanted was to intrude or embarrass her, especially after everything they'd been through in the past 24 hours.

"Fuck... James... Grrr..." he heard as he passed, seeing through the door crack that she was laying on a towel, a strap-on being used as a dildo as she pleasured herself. Carrying on to the bathroom, James looked in the mirror and noticed that, despite being 22, he was starting to get grey hair around his temples, a stark reminder of the stress that had aged him far beyond his years. He sighed, gripping the edge of the sink as he stared at his reflection. The events of the last few months had left their mark— not just physically but emotionally and mentally. He was barely holding it together, but the knowledge that Lyra cared enough to stick by him was a sliver of hope he desperately clung to.

After finishing in the bathroom, James washed his hands and splashed cold water on his face, trying to shake off the heaviness that lingered in his chest, when he felt a pair of arms around him, and a kiss on the side of his neck.

"Those idiots rang me while I was in the shower to put me on air at the same time as you. I heard what you said,

James. You did well. You didn't let them get away with it. But this fight... we need to plan it carefully," Lyra whispered into his ear, her voice soft but firm, a hint of determination beneath her usual calm.

James stood there for a moment, his back pressed against her chest as she held him. He could feel the warmth of her body, the steadiness of her embrace, and for the first time in days, he felt a flicker of hope that he might not have to go through this alone. The whole situation—Manic, Kylie, the manipulation—had seemed so insurmountable, but Lyra's unwavering support was something he could latch onto.

"Thanks, Lyra," James muttered, finally finding his voice, though it cracked slightly. "For sticking with me. I don't know where I'd be without you right now. You know HR have emailed me to say they're making me stick to the 6 months' notice. Hang on... when was your contract up, Ly?"

"My contract would have been up next Friday anyway, which is why I didn't opt for the annual renewal and opted to leave quietly," Lyra continued, her arms still wrapped around James as they stood in the small bathroom. "But seeing how they're treating you, I'm glad I didn't renew. James, they're doing this to you because they think they can control you, just like they've always done. But if we stick together, we can fight this. You don't have to stay there for another six months. Anyway, mister, I need you in my room... this dildo isn't satisfying me as much as I want your cock pounding me. You've always been better at giving me what I need than any toy ever could," Lyra finished, her breath warm against James's neck as she planted another soft kiss just below his ear.

James chuckled nervously, feeling a mix of embarrassment and flattery at her boldness. "Lyra, you know I appreciate your... enthusiasm, but after everything that's happened, I'm not sure I'm in the best headspace for, uh, 'activities.'"

"I'm trying to take your mind off the morons at Manic," Lyra whispered, her voice softening as she tightened her embrace. "A bit of stress relief wouldn't hurt, would it? But only if you're okay with it, James. No pressure. Just know I'm here for you—in every way you need."

James sighed, turning around to face her, his hands resting gently on her shoulders. He could see the genuine care in her eyes, a mix of concern and affection that made his chest tighten. Lyra had been his anchor through the chaos, and the thought of letting her down weighed on him. But he also knew she was right—he needed to take a step back from the storm that had consumed his life, even if only for a moment.

"Lyra," he began softly, brushing a strand of hair from her face, "you've already done so much for me. More than I could ever ask for. I just... I don't want to drag you down with all of this."

"You're not dragging me down," Lyra interrupted, her voice steady. "We're in this together, James. Whatever happens, we'll face it as a team. But you need to stop carrying the weight of the world on your shoulders alone. Let me help you."

James nodded, a small, grateful smile tugging at the corners of his lips. "Alright, Lyra. Let's go back to your room. But, um… let's keep things light for now.... no... you know, toys or anything like that."

"Strictly vanilla is what I was thinking," Lyra said with a soft chuckle, taking James's hand and leading him gently back to her room. The dim light filtering through the curtains cast a calming glow over the space, the faint scent of lavender from a diffuser adding to the tranquil atmosphere. It was a stark contrast to the chaos James had been navigating for months—a brief, much-needed sanctuary. "You know, like what we did on Monday, just pure tender love."

****

"We need to sort your dear brother out," Kylie said, sitting cross-legged on the bed in Cody and Chloe's Birmingham apartment. Since the party, she had moved into the spare room, turning it into her personal command centre of chaos. The room was cluttered with printouts of screenshots, messages, and photos—all part of her twisted effort to keep control over James and his public image. Chloe, sitting on the sofa with a glass of wine in hand, smirked at Kylie's determination.

"You mean, break him further," Chloe corrected, her tone dripping with malice. "He's already a wreck, thanks to you. What more do you want from him? I thought you were done using him after the party."

"Oh, sweetie," Kylie said with a saccharine smile, leaning back against a pile of cushions. "I'm never done. James isn't just some fling or a pawn—he's a project. A failed one right now, but we can fix that. The problem is that Lyra has gotten to him, and now he thinks he can wriggle free from us."

Chloe raised an eyebrow, swirling her wine lazily. "Lyra's not stupid, you know. She's not like James—she won't play along. If anything, she's going to be the one who breaks him out of this mess. You're wasting your time."

Kylie's eyes narrowed, her smile fading. "That's where you're wrong. Lyra's just as vulnerable as James. She just hides it better. But everyone has a breaking point, and I'll find hers. If she wants to protect him, she'll have to make sacrifices. And if she doesn't…" Kylie let the threat hang in the air, her smirk returning. "Well, let's just say Bauer's shiny new host won't be so shiny after I'm done with her. You see, my second cousin works at The Lantern, as one of the HR people within Bauer, and he can make sure that Lyra's new job can go up in smoke before she even starts. All I have to do is make the right call, share the right photos, and Lyra's bright future at Hits Radio will be nothing more than a footnote in her CV. Then she'll have no choice but to come crawling back to Manic. Anyway, where's that useless husband of yours? I need his cock to fill me."

Chloe chuckled. "Pregnancy does make you horny, doesn't it?" she said, rubbing her own 4 month bump. "You know, it's a good idea, making James think my baby is his, even though its Liam's. Pity Cody's firing blanks otherwise we could have just pinned it on him. But Liam's clueless enough not to realise we've spun this web around him, too. Good job Manic makes us do a DNA test when we get to Week 8 of our pregnancies and has the blokes keep their DNA on file, so we know which of the men at Manic is the father of which child. But with James... well, he doesn't need to know that, does he? He's already shattered enough to believe anything we tell him." Chloe sipped her wine, her smirk widening. "And let's be honest, James is the perfect scapegoat. If he tries to fight back, we've got more than enough dirt to bury him."

Kylie leaned forward, her eyes gleaming with twisted delight. "Exactly. Which is why we know Zara, Penny and I are all carrying James's baby, and we're making it out that Toni and Hayley are also pregnant with his children, too. James doesn't need to know the truth, and with the chaos we've engineered, he'll believe every word we say. He's too broken to question it. Besides," Kylie added with a sly smile, "the more tangled his web becomes, the harder it'll be for him to ever leave Manic. If he even thinks about walking away, we'll make sure the whole world knows about his 'children'—real or not. Let's see how he handles being the face of the next tabloid scandal."

Chloe set her wine glass down, leaning back on the sofa. "You're playing a dangerous game, Kylie. If this blows up, it won't just take James down—it could drag the rest of us with him."

Kylie shrugged, her expression one of mock innocence. "Oh, darling, that's the beauty of it. If it all goes wrong, James will take the fall. Not me, not you, not any of us. He's the perfect scapegoat. And as long as Lyra stays in the picture, we've got leverage. Bauer might be all prim and proper, but even they won't touch someone with the kind of dirt we can throw at her."

Chloe's eyes narrowed. "And what if James finally grows a spine? What if Lyra manages to pull him out of this mess and they expose us?"

Kylie laughed, a cold, sharp sound that echoed through the room. "Expose us? Please. No one will believe a word they say. Manic owns the narrative, and we've made sure James's reputation is already in tatters. As for Lyra…" She trailed off, her smile turning into a smirk. "Let's just say I've got a few tricks up my sleeve to ensure she won't be a problem for much longer. She wants to play the hero? Fine. But heroes always fall, and I'll make sure her fall is spectacular."

Cody entered the room then, a grin on his face. "Did I hear more plotting and brewing. Oh, by the way, I think we should thank Suzie for leaking those photos that her own useless husband had taken at the party. Do you think she knows her fiancé is the father of our little one, Clo? After all, he's like the rest of us at Manic, has a wondering dick and shags anything with a pulse."

"Oh, yeah, she knows that he's a cheating bastard, but she's too wrapped up in the Manic bubble to care," Chloe replied, her tone dripping with amusement. "Suzie's loyalty to Manic—and her desperation to stay relevant—makes her the perfect pawn. She'll do anything to keep her place at the table, even if it means throwing her fiancé under the bus."

Kylie smirked, leaning back against the headboard. "Typical Manic behaviour. Everyone's so busy stabbing each other in the back, they don't notice when they're next on the chopping block. It's what makes this place so… efficient."

Cody chuckled darkly, taking a seat on the edge of the bed. "You know, for all your scheming, Kylie, you'd make a damn good regional manager. Maybe you should pitch that to Cal. After all, if anyone knows how to keep this circus running, it's you."

Kylie tilted her head, considering the suggestion. "Oh, Cody, babe," she said, reaching into Cody's jeans. "I'm already planning to dethrone him. After all, I've found out about his daughter who was put up for adoption when she was born."

Kylie's words hung in the air like a chilling prelude to her next scheme. Cody raised an eyebrow, curious but slightly wary.

"Cal's daughter? Now that's a twist I wasn't expecting," he said, his voice dripping with intrigue. "What's your plan for that little gem?"

Kylie's smirk widened as she toyed with Cody's belt, her movements deliberate. "Let's just say I have my ways of finding leverage on anyone who might stand in my way. Cal thinks he's untouchable, running the show like he's some sort of corporate king. But even kings have skeletons, and his just happen to be very well hidden. You see, he and a certain Cassie Longton dated when she was 14 and he was 16, and lived in Altrincham, and he got her preggers. It so happens that she is, now, on her third child, the second one she's had with him, and Cassie's name is... Toni Green... and that his degree in Business Management wasn't earned... he told me a few weeks ago while we were fucking that he brought his degree online to meet the job qualifications when he applied for Manic Radio's managerial training scheme. Cal has more skeletons in his closet than a haunted house on Halloween, and I intend to rattle every single one of them when the time comes."

Kylie leaned back smugly, her fingers deftly pulling Cody's belt free. "I'm just biding my time. Once I've got James and Lyra out of the way, and Chloe's little drama with Liam playing out perfectly, I'll make my move. The beauty of it all is that no one sees me coming. They're too busy watching the chaos I'm causing elsewhere."

Cody chuckled darkly, his grin widening as he leaned closer. "You're dangerous, Kylie. That's what I like about you. But if you're really planning on taking down Cal, you'd better have all your ducks in a row. He's not going to go down without a fight."

"Oh, he'll fight," Kylie purred, her voice dripping with confidence. "But by the time I'm done, he'll be too busy trying to cover up his scandals to realise I've already taken his throne. He's nothing more than a stepping stone, Cody. Just like James. Just like everyone else."

Chloe, who had been lounging on the sofa with an air of detached amusement, raised her glass in a mock toast. "Here's to Kylie Morgan, the queen of chaos and manipulation. May your reign be as scandalous as your schemes."

****

CHAPTER 7 - A Last Minute Cancellation
Friday 25th April 2025

From: *lionel.morgan@bauermedia.co.uk*

To: *nottyly45@hotmail.co.uk*

Subject: *Withdrawal of Job Offer*

Dear Miss Nott,

We regret to inform you that, due to recent developments concerning allegations involving your conduct while employed at Manic Radio Group, Bauer Media has decided to withdraw the previously offered position of mid-morning presenter at Hits Radio.

While we understand this news may come as a disappointment, we must uphold the integrity and reputation of Bauer Media and its associated brands.

We thank you for your interest in the role and wish you the best in your future endeavours.

Kind regards,

Lionel Morgan

Talent Acquisition Assistant

Bauer Media Group

Lyra couldn't believe it. It was only 3 days until she had been due to start at Hits Radio, a position she had been working towards for years. The email felt like a punch to the stomach, and she stared at it in disbelief, her mind racing to piece together what could have gone so wrong, so quickly.

She sat on the edge of her bed, clutching her phone as if the device itself were responsible for the betrayal. The words blurred in front of her, but the meaning was crystal clear: everything she had fought for, every step she had taken to escape Manic Vibes, had just crumbled. And she knew exactly who was behind it.

"Kylie," Lyra muttered under her breath, her grip tightening on the phone. It had her fingerprints all over it—the photos, the rumours, the endless attempts to drag Lyra into the mud. Kylie had succeeded in ruining her shot at Hits Radio, and Lyra could feel the rage bubbling beneath the surface.

Attached to the email was several media clippings, including photos of her taking cocaine, having sex with James at Chloe's flat, and even the infamous images from the Daily Mail scandal. Lyra scrolled through the attachments, her stomach turning with each click. The captions were brutal—twisted, exaggerated versions of events, designed to destroy her reputation. Each image, each headline, felt like a knife in her back. She knew this wasn't just about her—it was about James too, and the way Kylie had orchestrated everything to pull them both down.

Ping

Lyra looked at the notification and saw that it was a WhatsApp message from Kylie, with a link to Pornhub, an infamous platform for explicit content. Her blood ran cold as she hesitated, knowing full well what she might find. Taking a deep breath, she tapped the link, her hands trembling.

The page loaded, and there it was—a video titled "Manic Radio's Naughty Nights: Lyra Nott and Jimmy Reeves Caught on Camera!" The thumbnail alone was enough to make her stomach churn. It showed a blurred image of her and James from that disastrous night at Chloe's flat, clearly recorded without their consent.

Pressing play on it, she noticed it was unedited, uncut and raw footage from the very night she had tried so hard to forget. Lyra's face burned with humiliation as she watched the first few seconds of the video, her and James clearly identifiable, despite the poorly pixelated attempt at anonymity. The sounds, the angles—everything about it screamed exploitation.

She stopped the video, unable to watch any more, and dropped her phone onto the bed as if it were radioactive. Her chest tightened, and her breaths came shallow and quick. Tears pricked her eyes, but she fought them back, knowing that breaking down wasn't going to fix anything.

Her mind raced. Kylie had gone too far this time—beyond malicious gossip, beyond sabotage. This was an outright violation of her privacy, her dignity, and her humanity. And worse, it wasn't just her reputation at stake; James's career, his mental health, and whatever shred of self-respect he had left were all hanging by a thread.

Lyra stood up abruptly, pacing the room. She had to do something. This couldn't stand. But what? Going to the police seemed like the obvious answer, but would they take her seriously? Would they even be able to do anything before the damage was irreversible?

She grabbed her phone again and called James, who had gone to Wolverhampton to see if he could reenrol at the University of Wolverhampton, having back in January left the establishment, his final year only one semester completed of the trio. The irony that he had mostly written his dissertation in that first semester during the two months prior to signing with Manic meant that he was technically ahead of schedule on his academic work. However, the chaos of the past few months had derailed him completely. Re-enrolling felt like his first step toward reclaiming some semblance of a future—a path away from the toxic grip of Manic and the trauma Kylie had inflicted.

James answered after a couple of rings, his voice tentative but calm. "Lyra? What's up?"

"James," Lyra said, her voice tight with controlled fury. "I just got an email from Bauer. They've withdrawn the job offer. And it's not just that—Kylie's leaked a video of us from that night. It's all over Pornhub."

There was a long pause on the other end of the line. James didn't respond immediately, and Lyra could almost hear the gears turning in his head as he tried to process what she'd just told him.

"She… what?" James finally said, his voice low and shaky. "Lyra, I'm so sorry. This is all my fault. If I hadn't—"

"Don't," Lyra interrupted, her tone sharp. "This is not your fault, James. This is Kylie's doing. She's the one who's orchestrated all of this. And we can't let her get away with it."

Ping

The sound on her tablet of another notification, this time another email. Lyra picked up her tablet, her heart sinking further as she opened the email.

From*: charlotte.mcdonald@manicradio.group*

To*: nottyly45@hotmail.co.uk*

Subject*: Offer of Job - Manic Vibes West Midlands Drive*

Dear Miss Nott,

We hereby offer you the position of Drivetime Presenter for Manic Vibes West Midlands, effective immediately. This offer is being made following your previous contributions to the network and recognition of your ability to engage listeners across key demographics.

The position will require you to begin as early as Monday 29th April 2025, based at our One Snow Hill studios. Please note that acceptance of this role will include compliance with our updated Talent Agreement, which includes exclusivity clauses and a requirement for participation in all promotional activities associated with the station.

The salary for this role will be £40,000 per annum, plus stock holdings in Manic Radio Group.

We look forward to your confirmation and hope this opportunity marks the next exciting chapter in your career.

Kind regards,

Charlotte McDonald

HR Manager, Manic Radio Group

Lyra forgot she was on the phone with James as she read the email and laughed, as if Manic were mocking her outright. The audacity of the situation was too much to process. Manic, the very organisation she was desperate to escape, was now offering her a position as if it were some grand opportunity—as if they hadn't been complicit in dragging her name through the mud.

"James," she said, regaining her composure, "you're not going to believe this. Manic just offered me drivetime on their West Midlands station. Effective Monday... with... a pay rise too."

James's voice crackled with disbelief when he replied, "Wait, what? After everything that's gone down, they're offering you a job back at Manic? That's... that's insane."

Lyra couldn't help but let out a bitter laugh. The absurdity of it all felt like a slap in the face. She could feel the heat rising in her chest, the anger welling up, but there was something else too—an eerie, dark sense of resignation. She had spent months fighting to get away from the toxic environment at Manic, and now they were dangling this job in front of her as if it were a lifeline. They knew exactly how vulnerable she was right now.

"They're playing me, James," she said, her voice low and venomous. "They think I'll come crawling back because I've been blacklisted from everywhere else. They know I'm desperate. But I'm not falling for it."

James let out a heavy sigh on the other end. "I don't even know what to say. This whole thing's turned into some weird nightmare, and no matter what we do, we're just stuck in it. I've just spoke to the Vice-Chancellor and... well, it seems Manic have interfered here too."

Lyra's stomach churned again as she processed James's words. "What do you mean, they've interfered?" she asked, her voice tight with a mix of frustration and disbelief.

"I mean," James said, taking a deep breath, "the university has started to put pressure on me to stay quiet about the whole situation. The Vice-Chancellor said there were 'rumours' from some 'anonymous sources' about why I left the university last semester, and how my 'personal life' was... affecting my professional reputation. It's like they've been doing everything they can to screw with us, Lyra. They're pushing me into a corner, too."

Lyra sank back onto the edge of her bed, the weight of everything bearing down on her. The realisation hit her hard—Manic, Bauer, and now even the university, were all part of a system working to crush their careers, playing their part in the web of lies and manipulation that Kylie had spun. She couldn't shake the feeling that they were all circling, waiting for her to make a wrong move.

"I'm so sorry," James said, his voice barely above a whisper. "None of this should have happened. None of it. Manic... they've won, haven't they?"

Lyra could hear the defeat in James's voice, and it lit a fire in her that she didn't know she still had. She stood abruptly, pacing the room as her mind raced. She refused to let Kylie, Manic, or anyone else dictate the course of their lives any longer. They had taken so much from her already—her dignity, her career prospects, her sense of control—but they weren't going to take her resolve.

"No, James," Lyra said firmly, her voice cutting through the silence. "They haven't won. Not yet. They think they've backed us into a corner, but what they don't realise is that we still have a choice. We can fight back. And we will."

James let out a hollow laugh on the other end of the line. "Fight back? Lyra, how? They've got everything—the media, the industry, even the university wrapped around their little finger. If I hadn't joined Manic, I wouldn't have got on cocaine, wouldn't have been in the situation, you'd be heading to Bauer without all this shit, and I'd probably still be finishing my degree, lining up job prospects like a normal twenty-two-year-old. It's all my fucking fault."

Lyra could hear, in the background, the sound of a pub, and knew that James was probably at The Hogshead on Stafford Street, his usual haunt when things got too heavy. The clink of glasses and low murmur of conversations painted a picture of James sitting in a corner nursing a pint, drowning in his guilt. Lyra tightened her grip on the phone, her heart aching for him.

"James, stop," she said sharply, interrupting his spiral. "This isn't your fault. It's theirs—Kylie, Chloe, Cody, everyone at Manic who's played a part in this mess. They've exploited you, manipulated you, and tried to destroy everything you've worked for. But you are not the villain here. You're a victim, just like me."

There was silence on the line for a moment before James sighed heavily. "It doesn't feel that way, Lyra. Every step I've taken since joining Manic has been a mistake. I mean, before I became the hub cum dump, I was joining in with the others when Zara was being treated the same way. I didn't stop it, Lyra. I laughed along with the jokes, I joined the crowd. And now it's me in the firing line, and I don't know how to fix it."

Lyra exhaled slowly, trying to keep her composure. She knew James was carrying a mountain of guilt, not just for what had been done to him, but for his complicity in the toxic culture that Manic had bred. But guilt wasn't going to fix anything. They needed a plan.

"James," she said softly but firmly, "what happened with Zara and the others... it's a symptom of the system we're up against. Manic thrives on creating this environment where people turn on each other. It's how they keep control. But we can't let them win. You can still make this right—by standing up to them. By standing with me."

James let out a bitter laugh. "Stand up to them? Lyra, they've got everything. The media, the industry, even bloody HR. What am I supposed to do? Post a heartfelt tweet and hope someone listens? This isn't a rom-com where the underdogs win in the end. This is real life, and they've already crushed us."

****

"Stand up to them? Lyra, they've got everything. The media, the industry, even bloody HR. What am I supposed to do? Post a heartfelt tweet and hope someone listens? This isn't a rom-com where the underdogs win in the end. This is real life, and they've already crushed us." James said, sighing. He was sat in the Hogshead, and opposite him was Chloe, a grin on her face as she nursed a gin and tonic. She had spotted him as she walked in, clearly having anticipated his presence. James knew he should have left the moment she sat down, but his exhaustion and anger kept him rooted to the spot.

"You know, James," Chloe said, after James finished the call to Lyra. "Cal was saying last night when I was at work that he'd happily have you back at Manic, joining me on my show, if you apologise to everyone. Just think, the father of my child and big brother joining me on the Ibiza Belters show would be the ultimate PR win for Manic. They'd love to spin it as a 'family reunion' narrative. You could rebuild your reputation, maybe even climb back to the top. All you have to do is stop fighting and fall back in line."

James stared at her, his blood boiling at the smugness in her tone. Chloe was revelling in her position, her drink in hand as if she'd already won. He clenched his fists under the table, his knuckles white as he resisted the urge to throw his pint in her face.

"You really think I'm going to just roll over and let you and Kylie destroy what's left of my life?" James said, his voice low but shaking with barely contained fury. "You've already humiliated me, blacklisted me from the industry, and dragged Lyra into this nightmare. And now you want me to apologise? To you? To the people who raped me? Are you even listening to yourself?"

Chloe's smirk faltered slightly, but she quickly recovered, leaning back in her chair with an air of nonchalance. "Oh, come on, James. Don't be so dramatic. You're overreacting. It's just the way things work at Manic. Everyone plays the game, and you're not special. Besides, you had your fun too. Don't act like you're some innocent victim in all of this. Anyway, with Dad being a freelancer at Manic with his Goldies WM Drivetime show, his job is in jeopardy too if you continue pushing this narrative about what happened to you. Anyway, I noticed you didn't tell your girlfriend that I was here... did you?"

James felt his stomach churn as Chloe's words sank in. She was playing the same manipulative game Kylie had mastered, twisting reality to suit her narrative and dangling the threat over his head like a noose. The mention of their father, Pete, only fuelled his anger. He slammed his pint down on the table, causing a few nearby patrons to glance over.

"Chloe," he hissed through gritted teeth, "you don't get to rewrite what happened. You and the rest of them treated me like dirt, used me, humiliated me—and now you want me to grovel and play happy families on air? For what? To make you and Kylie look good? To save your pathetic careers while I'm left picking up the pieces of my life?"

Chloe smirked, swirling the ice in her glass as if his anger were nothing more than a mild inconvenience. "James, you need to stop thinking about yourself for once. This isn't just about you. It's about Dad, me, and even Lyra.

You think Bauer's going to stick with her now? You think anyone's going to touch you after this? Manic is your only option, whether you like it or not. Anyway..."

James noticed Chloe place the glass on the table and open her purse, revealing a syringe with a solution in it. moving so she was sitting close to James, close enough to be unable to move a slip of paper between the siblings. The next thing he knew, she was stroking his arm, the Gorillaz t-shirt he was wearing crumpling slightly under her touch as she felt for a vein.

Trying to move his arm away, he noticed that she placed the needle of the syringe against his skin, her grip firm and unrelenting. Panic surged through James as Chloe leaned in closer, her voice low and dripping with menace.

"Relax, James," she whispered, her breath warm against his ear. "This is just a little reminder of who's really in control. You think you can walk away from all of this? From us? Think again."

And then it pierced his skin, the needle sliding in with practised precision. James's mind raced as a cold rush of liquid entered his vein. His vision blurred momentarily, and a wave of nausea rolled over him as he pushed Chloe away with as much strength as he could muster. She stumbled back slightly, her smirk replaced by a flash of annoyance.

"What the hell did you just do to me?" James spat, his voice rising as he rubbed his arm, the faint sting of the injection still fresh. The surrounding patrons in the pub turned their heads, murmurs rippling through the room.

Chloe composed herself quickly, smoothing her dress and flashing a saccharine smile at the onlookers. "Calm down, big brother," she said sweetly, her voice dripping with false innocence. "It's just a little pick-me-up. You've been so down lately—I thought you could use a boost. It's not any old cocaine, y'know. It's got an additional kick as it's got something you haven't had before, a nice bit of pharmaceutical grade 'booster' in it. Helps with focus. Keeps you sharp for decisions. You wouldn't want to miss out on the next big move, would you, James?"

James recoiled, his mind spinning in panic as the warmth from the injection spread through his veins. He could feel the dizziness creeping in, the confusion beginning to cloud his thoughts. This wasn't just another dose of something to numb him—it was something else, something more sinister. He could taste the bitter aftertaste of manipulation in the back of his throat. The cold grip of fear tightened around his chest.

"You've got to be joking," he muttered, his voice trembling with a mixture of rage and disbelief. "What the hell is wrong with you, Chloe?"

Chloe gave a mockingly sweet laugh, her eyes gleaming with malice. "Oh, big bro, don't you know? You were always the golden boy, always the one who Dad took to work... the one who used me as cover at school when you were dating Sophia."

Sophia, James remembered, was his Sixth Form girlfriend who he had been besotted with, until she had left him for his best friend, Alan Harper, a fellow Sixth Form student. The mention of Sophia's name stung James, not because of the relationship itself, but because it reminded him of a simpler time—before Manic, before Kylie, before Chloe had become a twisted caricature of the sister he used to know. He shook his head, trying to clear the fog creeping into his mind from whatever Chloe had injected into him.

"You're insane," James spat, his voice shaking as he tried to steady himself. "I don't know what you're trying to prove, but I'm done playing your games. I'll never go back to Manic. Not for you, not for Dad, not for anyone."

Chloe leaned in closer, her smirk widening. "Oh, James, you'll come back. You always do. You think you're better than us, but you're not. You're just as much a part of this as anyone else. You can run, but you can't escape who you are. And as for Lyra..." Chloe paused, her voice taking on a more sinister edge. "Well, let's just say she might not be there to save you next time."

Suddenly Chloe brought James's hand down onto her thigh, moving it up towards the hem of her dress, before slapping him and screaming.

The sharp crack of Chloe's slap echoed through the pub, cutting through the low murmur of conversation like a knife. Heads turned, and all eyes fell on James and Chloe. Chloe's dramatic gasp and wide, tear-filled eyes painted a picture that was entirely different from the truth.

"James, how could you?" Chloe cried, her voice loud and trembling with faux outrage. "Don't you dare touch me like that!" She clutched at her thigh, pulling the hem of her dress down as though she had just narrowly escaped something unspeakable.

James reeled back, stunned by the audacity of her performance. His head spun, a toxic cocktail of rage, confusion, and whatever Chloe had injected into him making it hard to focus. He stammered, trying to form words, trying to explain, but Chloe's crocodile tears had already done their damage.

A burly man at the bar stood up, glaring at James. "Oi, mate," he said, his voice low and dangerous. "What's going on here? You think you can just assault a woman in broad daylight?"

"No, that's not—" James began, but his words were drowned out by Chloe's loud, exaggerated sobbing.

"He's been harassing me for weeks," Chloe wailed, clutching at her gin and tonic for added effect. "Ever since… ever since I tried to help him. He's spiralling, drinking all the time, using drugs. I didn't want to say anything because he's my brother, but… but he's dangerous!"

****

Pete was sat in Studio A1, the Manic Goldies West Midlands studio, ready to present his afternoon drivetime show when his producer, Rachel Powell, walked in, a frown on her face.

"Pete, just passed the news room and they're going to be leading the evening news on an article about an arrest in Wolverhampton of someone on suspicion of attempted rape," Rachel said, sighing.

Pete's heart sank at Rachel's words. His first instinct was to dismiss it as another grim headline, but a gnawing sense of dread began to creep in. Wolverhampton, attempted rape... it was too close to home. And given the chaos surrounding James, Pete couldn't shake the feeling that his son might somehow be involved.

"Did they say who it was?" Pete asked, trying to keep his voice steady, though the tension in his chest betrayed him.

Rachel hesitated, her expression a mix of discomfort and concern. "Not officially, no," she said, shifting awkwardly. "But there are whispers... some people are saying it might be James. Apparently, he tried to rape your daughter, Chloe."

Pete scoffed. "She's no daughter of mine. Knowing that bitch, she's probably claiming James did something to deflect from her own mess," Pete said, his voice sharp with a bitterness he rarely allowed to surface. His grip on the desk tightened as he struggled to maintain his composure, but the thought of Chloe using such a serious accusation as a weapon against James made his blood boil.

Rachel raised an eyebrow at Pete's response but wisely chose not to press the matter. Instead, she placed a stack of papers on the desk, containing the afternoon show's running order. "Well, let's focus on the show for now. If you need to step out or address anything, just let me know. We've got your back, Pete."

Pete nodded, grateful for Rachel's professionalism. "Thanks, Rach," he muttered, flipping through the papers absentmindedly. But his mind was elsewhere, racing through the possibilities of what could have led to such an explosive situation.

****

CHAPTER 8 - Release
Saturday 26th April 2025

"Do you understand that we are releasing you on police bail and that you are not to contact the complainant or any witnesses, directly or indirectly, as part of these conditions?"

James nodded, his expression weary and hollow. The events of the past 24 hours had left him emotionally drained, his mind a whirlwind of confusion, anger, and despair. He sat in the cramped interview room at the Wolverhampton police station, his hands trembling slightly as he processed the officer's words. The fluorescent lighting buzzed faintly overhead, casting a harsh glare on the stark white walls.

"Yes, I understand," James replied, his voice hoarse from the hours of questioning.

The officer handed him a sheet of paper outlining the bail conditions. "You'll also need to return on the date listed for further questioning. Until then, stay away from your sister, Chloe Lane, and anyone involved in the case. Any breach of these conditions will result in your immediate arrest. Do you have any questions?"

James shook his head silently, his gaze fixed on the paper in his hands. His fingerprints were still faintly visible on his fingertips, a lingering reminder of how deeply entangled he'd become in this nightmare. He wanted to argue, to scream that Chloe had set him up, but he knew it would fall on deaf ears. The system was stacked against him, and Chloe's performance in the pub had been convincing enough to warrant his arrest.

As the officer opened the door, James saw Lyra waiting for him, her face entangled with worry, her eyes scanning him with a mix of relief and concern. Before James could say anything, the man standing next to Lyra spoke up.

"Right, officer. Firstly, I am not happy that you have held my client for as long as you have without sufficient evidence or charges. I would appreciate it if we could get a full explanation of the reasoning behind the arrest and why it took so long for him to be released," the man said, his tone sharp but measured.

James was confused, as he had never met the man before, and was wondering why he was saying that James was his client. Looking at the man, he then recognised that he had the same facial features as Lyra, and that their eyes were the same. Lyra then discreetly mouthed to James two words. "Trust me."

James gave a slight nod to Lyra, his confusion mingling with curiosity as he studied the man. The resemblance between him and Lyra was undeniable—the same sharp cheekbones, the same intense, piercing gaze. The man exuded a calm but commanding presence, his tailored suit adding to his air of authority.

The officer hesitated, clearly caught off guard by the newcomer's assertiveness. "Sir, I can assure you that everything was conducted within protocol. Mr Smith was detained based on the allegations made and the evidence presented at the time."

"Allegations which are clearly fabricated," the man cut in smoothly, his tone dripping with controlled disdain. "And yet you held him for hours without any substantial proof beyond the word of a so-called witness who conveniently shares a history of conflict with my client. If this is how Wolverhampton Police handles justice, it's no wonder public trust is at an all-time low."

The officer bristled but didn't argue further. "I'll pass your concerns on to the appropriate department. If you have further issues, you can lodge a formal complaint."

The man gave a curt nod, clearly dismissing the officer as he turned to James. "Come on, James. Let's get you out of here."

James followed him out of the station, his mind still racing with questions. Lyra fell into step beside him, her hand brushing against his in a silent gesture of reassurance. As they reached the car park, the man turned to face James, his expression softening slightly.

"James, I'm Theodore Nott," he said, extending a hand. "Lyra's older brother and, more importantly, a solicitor specialising in criminal defence. Lyra called me last night and told me everything. I did try and get to see you but the idiot on the front desk claimed I wasn't even a registered solicitor, so I had to make my own arrangements. I'll be representing you from now on. No more cops dragging you around without a solid reason."

James stared at Theodore, still struggling to process the whirlwind of events that had just unfolded. He shook Theodore's hand, but it felt surreal. Lyra's brother was a solicitor? That was something James hadn't known. The weight of the past few days—the arrest, the humiliation, the uncertainty—seemed to lift, if only slightly, as he realised that someone with actual power was now on his side.

"Thanks," James muttered, his voice still thick with exhaustion.

Lyra's expression softened as she smiled up at him, her worry fading a little as she gave his hand a reassuring squeeze. "I told you, we've got your back. No one is going to let them get away with this."

"Right, James, the first thing I'm going to do is file a complaint with the Independent Office for Police Conduct (IOPC) regarding the way you were treated," Theodore continued, his tone calm but firm. "From what Lyra has told me, it seems like there's been a gross mishandling of this case from the start. Chloe's accusations don't hold water, and the way the police detained you without sufficient evidence is unacceptable. We're going to challenge this every step of the way."

James nodded numbly, the weight of his release still pressing heavily on him. "I appreciate it," he said quietly, his voice hoarse. "But I'm just… I'm so tired. I don't even know where to start with all of this."

Theodore placed a hand on James's shoulder, his grip firm but reassuring. "We start by building your defence. Every single detail matters—what happened that night, Chloe's behaviour, your relationship with her and others at Manic. We'll tear her story apart piece by piece. But for now, you need to focus on getting some rest. You've been through hell, and it's not over yet, but you don't have to face this alone."

Lyra stepped closer, her presence steady and comforting. "Theo's right, James. We're in this together. Let's just get you home for now, okay?"

****

Pete was sat in the living room of the Smith family home in Pensnett when he heard Lyra's car pull up outside. He had been pacing the room, the news of James's arrest cycling through his mind like a broken record. His heart was heavy with worry and frustration, compounded by the guilt of knowing how deeply his decisions had affected his son's life. The door opened, and he turned to see Lyra leading James inside, followed by a man Pete didn't recognize but who shared Lyra's striking features.

"James," Pete said, his voice breaking as he moved forward to envelop his son in a tight, desperate hug. "I'm so sorry, son. I should've done more, been there more."

James, still reeling from everything, returned the embrace, his body tense but slowly relaxing into his father's arms. "It's not your fault, Dad," he whispered, though the words felt hollow even to him.

Lyra introduced the newcomer, "Pete, this is my brother, Theodore. He's here to help. He's a solicitor."

Theodore extended a hand to Pete, his grip firm. "Pleasure to meet you, Mr. Smith, under better circumstances, I hope. I've already started on James's case. We're going to challenge this arrest on every front."

Pete nodded, his gratitude mixed with a rush of hope. "Thank you, Theodore. We need all the help we can get." He turned his attention back to James, his eyes scanning his son for any signs of harm. "Are you okay, physically? Did they treat you well?"

James gave a slight, tired nod. "I'm fine, Dad. Just... tired. Chloe... she... she drugged me in the pub... cocaine... injected me."

Pete's face darkened with a mix of fury and disbelief as James's words sank in. "She what?" he demanded, his voice rising with anger. "Your own sister injected you with cocaine? In public? What kind of madness is this?"

James sank onto the sofa, running a hand through his hair as he avoided his father's intense gaze. "She claimed it was to help me 'focus,'" he said bitterly. "But we both know it's just another way for her to mess with me. And then… she staged it. She grabbed my hand and screamed, making it look like I'd assaulted her. That's why I got arrested. The police drew blood but assumed that I had injected myself with cocaine and tried to sexually assault her. I... I didn't even go to her, she came to me in the pub."

Pete clenched his fists, pacing the room as he struggled to contain his rage. "This has gone too far. She's not just trying to ruin your career; she's trying to destroy your life. I can't believe my own daughter would do something like this. Chloe… she's crossed every line imaginable."

Theodore stepped in, his voice calm but firm. "Mr Smith, I understand your frustration, but right now, we need to focus on the facts and building James's defence. Emotional reactions won't help us, but evidence will. I'll file for a full disclosure of the evidence the police are using, including Chloe's statement and any CCTV footage from the pub. There is one thing we need to discuss... money. Now-"

"Come on, Theo," Lyra said, frowning. "James and I are-"

"Ly, sis, I'm not going to charge you for my services, if you'd let me finish. All I'm going to have to charge you for is the experts I have to engage, such as toxicologists or forensic analysts, and any court fees that come up. I'll handle the legal side pro bono. This is about justice, not profit." Theodore's tone was reassuring, and his sharp gaze softened as he looked at his sister and James. "I just need you to trust me and be honest about everything."

James nodded slowly, his exhaustion evident. "Thank you, Theodore. I don't know how I'm going to repay you, but… thank you."

Theodore gave a slight smile. "We'll worry about repayment later. Now, Lyra, you mentioned to me earlier you've got a copy of the records that James's aunt made of her medical examination a couple of weeks ago, yes?"

"Yep, let me nip upstairs and I'll get the copy of what Helen compiled, including the number of times he had been sexually assaulted," Lyra said, already heading upstairs to fetch the file.

James watched her go, the sound of her footsteps fading as she ascended the stairs. He slumped back into the sofa, his body heavy with the accumulated weight of the last few days. Theodore settled into the armchair across from him, opening a sleek leather briefcase and pulling out a notebook and pen.

"B... before we start... do you think if I knew where there were... were a cache of drugs were, it'd help?" James said, looking at Theodore.

Theodore's pen paused mid-note, and he looked up sharply, his eyes narrowing as he processed James's words. "A cache of drugs?" he repeated, his voice steady but laced with curiosity. "What do you mean, James? Are you saying you know where drugs are being stored or distributed?"

James hesitated, his hands fidgeting nervously in his lap. "They... they had... a broom closet at One Snow Hill... where Manic in Birmingham is based... lots of cocaine... the third floor, next to Studio C7."

Theodore's pen froze, and his brow furrowed as he leaned forward, resting his elbows on his knees. "James, this is serious. Are you saying there's an active drug cache inside Manic Radio's Birmingham hub?"

James nodded hesitantly, his voice barely above a whisper. "I've seen it. They... they moved the cocaine in on the 12th of April, when the hub at The Waterfront was being closed and things were moving to the One Snow Hill studios. There was also, as of a couple of weeks ago, drugs at my ex-girlfriend's flat in Great Bridge, and at Chloe's apartment in Birmingham. Kylie... she... I think she's moved in with Chloe and Cody, her husband, though."

Theodore's eyes sharpened, and he quickly began scribbling notes in his notebook, the calm efficiency of his demeanour belying the gravity of the situation. "James, this is critical information. If what you're saying is accurate, this could be a turning point—not just for your case, but for exposing the wider corruption within Manic Radio. However, we need to tread carefully. Allegations like this, especially against a high-profile organisation, require evidence. Pete, you're going to be at work there Monday, right?"

"I'm actually going in in an hour to do my Saturday Goldies phone-in show," Pete said.

Theodore nodded thoughtfully. "Pete, if you're comfortable, I'd suggest keeping an eye out for anything that might corroborate James's account. I'm not asking you to put yourself in danger or compromise your position, but any observations—anything at all—could be invaluable."

Pete chuckled. "Well, to be fair, I'm booked in Studio C3, as after my show I'm doing some pre-records for a Manic Rock overnight show, so I'll be near the closet. On a Saturday, as my show is usually the only live show coming from Brum, it's the old guard who are duty management, not the coke heads of James's generation, and they'll be on the fifth floor in the canteen or their offices, listening to the shows on the air, not lurking around the studios. I'll take a discreet look and see if I can find anything, but I'll tread carefully. The last thing we need is for them to realise someone's onto them."

Theodore gave a small nod of approval. "Good. Stay safe, Pete. If you do find anything, don't touch it—just observe and make a note of what you see. If there's an opportunity to take pictures discreetly, that could be helpful, but don't risk exposing yourself."

James shifted uncomfortably on the sofa, guilt flickering across his face. "Dad... I don't want you to get in trouble because of me."

Pete placed a reassuring hand on James's shoulder. "Don't worry about me, son. This isn't just about you—it's about standing up to what's wrong. They've hurt you, and they've hurt so many others. If I can do something to help, I will."

Lyra returned to the room, a thick folder in her hands. She placed it on the coffee table in front of Theodore, who immediately opened it and began scanning the contents. Inside were detailed medical records and notes compiled by Helen, outlining the extent of James's injuries and the repeated instances of abuse he had suffered at Manic.

"This is damning," Theodore murmured as he read through the pages, his expression darkening. "It paints a clear picture of a systemic pattern of abuse within Manic Radio. There's forced anal penetration, broken ribs, even... shit, gonorrhoea. Ly, did you know James has gonorrhoea?"

"Yes, and no. I... I mean, Theo, I know he has, but... well, only after we had unprotected sex a couple of weeks ago. And... well, Theo, I may have joined the list of James's growing list of infected partners. But before you jump to conclusions, I've already got anti-biotics, so don't worry. It's just the Pill I forgot to obtain."

"Wait, sis, you forgot the Pill?" Theodore's words trailed off as he raised an eyebrow, his solicitor façade briefly replaced by the older brother in him. "Lyra, are you trying to tell me...?"

Lyra shifted uncomfortably, her cheeks flushed. "Look, Theo, this isn't exactly the time to get into my contraceptive choices, alright? I'm dealing with it. Anyway, Mum's always pressuring me for a grandchild, especially as you've given her 5, and I'm 27, so I'm not exactly a spring chicken anymore, am I?" Lyra tried to deflect with a weak laugh, trying to downplay the situation. James, on the other hand, looked mortified, his face a mix of guilt and awkwardness.

"Great, so that's 5 potential mothers on my list now— Lyra, Chloe, Kylie, Zara, and Penny, all dragged into this mess," James muttered, running a hand through his hair in frustration. "And I'm the one stuck in the middle of it all, with no clue who's telling the truth anymore." He looked at Lyra, his voice softening. "But if you... you know... are pregnant, I'd... I'd be there for you. No matter what."

Lyra gave him a small, reassuring smile, placing a hand on his knee. "James, let's not get ahead of ourselves. Right now, the focus is getting you out of this nightmare. Anything else can wait."

Theodore chuckled. "Well, Lyra did mention to me that Manic take DNA from all their male presenters when they sign their contracts, is that right, James?"

James nodded slowly, his expression clouded with a mixture of shame and anger. "Yeah, they did," he said quietly. "It was part of some so-called 'health and safety' initiative when I joined. They claimed it was for emergency identification purposes or some nonsense, but now... now it feels like just another way for them to control us."

"That's funny," Pete said, and James looked at him, confused. "I never had mine took when Manic brought out Breeze Media back in 2019, when Midlands Manic became part of the Manic Radio Group back then. There again, as I'm 52, they probably see me as an old fart and not worth the trouble," Pete finished with a wry smile, trying to inject a touch of levity into the tense atmosphere.

"Unless it's to do with the baby bonus," Lyra interjected, and James noticed Theodore perk up at the mention. He adjusted his glasses and leaned forward, his expression turning serious.

"Baby bonus?" Theodore asked, his voice sharp with curiosity. "What's that about?"

Lyra glanced at James, who looked down, clearly uncomfortable. Taking a deep breath, she explained, "Manic has this... policy. They call it the 'baby bonus.' It's part of their branding strategy. If a presenter has a child while employed with them, they incentivise it with bonuses and promotions. They say it's to create 'family-friendly branding,' but it's really just another layer of manipulation. They even require DNA tests for all babies born to female staff or partners of male staff, supposedly to 'confirm' paternity."

Theodore's face darkened as he absorbed the information. "So, they're essentially encouraging employees to have children while weaponizing it for their own PR purposes?

And using DNA tests as another form of control? That's insidious."

James nodded, his voice subdued. "They told me Chloe's baby is mine, but I don't even know if that's true. I'm not sure about Kylie's baby either. And now... now Lyra might be... and I don't even know if I can protect anyone, let alone myself."

Theodore placed a hand on James's shoulder, his tone firm but reassuring. "We'll deal with all of it, James. One step at a time. The DNA records they've taken? That might actually work in our favour. If we can get access to those records, we can prove whether or not you're actually the father of these children. And if they're fabricating claims about paternity, we can expose that too. It's just more evidence of their unethical practices. Now, James, have you ever heard of GDPR?"

James nodded hesitantly. "Yeah, I've heard of it. Data protection and all that. Why?"

Theodore leaned forward, his sharp gaze fixed on James. "The General Data Protection Regulation protects individuals' personal data. What Manic is doing—collecting and using your DNA, potentially without proper consent or for purposes beyond what you agreed to—could be a massive breach of GDPR. If they've mishandled your data, we can file a complaint with the Information Commissioner's Office (ICO). It could open a legal avenue to challenge them."

James blinked, the weight of Theodore's words slowly sinking in. "So, if they've violated GDPR... we could actually take them down?"

Theodore nodded, a faint smile tugging at the corners of his mouth. "It's not just about taking them down, James. It's about holding them accountable. Legally, you're entitled to copies of what data they hold on you too, be it your HR file, DNA records, or anything else they've gathered. We can submit a subject access request to Manic Radio Group, compelling them to provide all the data they have on you. If they refuse or provide incomplete information, that's another breach of GDPR."

Pete looked at Theodore, his brow furrowed. "But would that be enough to get them to back off? They've got lawyers of their own, probably the best money can buy."

Theodore adjusted his tie, a steely determination in his eyes. "They might have money, Mr Smith, but the law isn't entirely on their side. If we can show a pattern of abuse, data mishandling, and unethical practices, they won't just be dealing with me—they'll have regulators, watchdogs, and potentially the courts breathing down their necks. Organisations like Manic thrive on intimidation and secrecy. If we shine a light on their actions, they'll lose the one thing they rely on most: control."

James rubbed his temples, the enormity of what Theodore was saying washing over him. "Okay, so... what's the plan? How do we even start fighting something this big?"

Theodore leaned back, tapping his pen against his notebook. "First, we gather evidence. The medical records Helen compiled are a strong start. Pete, anything you notice at work that corroborates James's account of the drug storage would be invaluable. Lyra, you mentioned to me that Bauer withdrew a job offer due to allegations related to your time at Manic. One of the partners at the firm specialises in employment law, so she might be able to help you challenge that withdrawal if it was based on false information or defamatory claims. We'll also file a GDPR subject access request to Manic Radio Group to obtain everything they have on both of you—James and Lyra."

Pete leaned forward, his elbows on his knees, his expression pensive. "What about the drugs James mentioned? If they're really storing cocaine at the studios, wouldn't reporting that to the police escalate things?"

Theodore nodded, his face serious. "Potentially, yes. But we need to be strategic. If we report it without solid evidence, Manic could turn it around, claim James is trying to smear them out of spite. We can't give them any ammunition. Pete, if you can discreetly document anything you see—dates, times, even photos if possible—we can use that information to build a case. Once we have enough evidence, we'll involve the authorities."

Lyra placed a hand on James's arm, her touch grounding him. "We've got this, James. You're not alone anymore. They can't keep getting away with this."

James exhaled shakily, the smallest glimmer of hope breaking through the fog of despair. "Alright," he said quietly. "Let's do it. Whatever it takes."

Theodore smiled faintly, his determination evident. "Good. We'll take it one step at a time. They've underestimated you, James. They think they've already won. But they haven't seen what we're capable of yet."

Pete stood, his expression resolute. "I'll do whatever it takes to help. They've messed with my family for too long. It's time to put an end to it."

The room fell silent for a moment, the weight of the fight ahead settling over them. But for the first time in weeks, there was a sense of unity—a shared determination to face the storm together.

James looked around at the people who had rallied to his side: his father, who had been distant but was now unwavering in his support; Lyra, who had risked everything to stand by him; and Theodore, a stranger just hours ago but now a crucial ally.

"Thank you," James said, his voice quiet but filled with sincerity. "I don't know how I'll ever repay any of you, but... thank you."

Lyra smiled warmly, her eyes glistening. "You don't have to repay us, James. Just focus on getting through this. We'll handle the rest."

Theodore closed his notebook, tucking it back into his briefcase. "Alright, let's take a break for now. James, get some rest. Pete, I'll follow up with you after your shift tonight. Lyra, I'll draft the subject access requests for you and James to review tomorrow."

As Theodore stood to leave, Pete clapped a hand on his shoulder. "Thank you, Theodore. Really. For everything."

Theodore nodded, his expression softening. "We'll get through this, Mr Smith. Together."

Lyra helped James to his bedroom to rest, leaving Pete and Theodore in the living room. The fight was only beginning, but for the first time, it felt like they had a chance. And that was enough to hold onto—for now.

****

CHAPTER 9 - Denials and Check Ins
Wednesday 7th May 2025

James sat in the corner of the Wolverhampton police station, the faint smell of disinfectant and damp paper lingering in the air. His knee bounced nervously as he stared at the clock on the wall, each tick dragging on like an eternity. Checking in for bail was becoming a routine he dreaded—a stark reminder that his life was still entangled in the mess Chloe and Manic had created.

What made it worse was that, although he lived in Pensnett and his local police station was Brierley Hill, he was being made to travel to Wolverhampton to check in due to "procedural requirements." The excuse felt flimsy at best, another layer of bureaucracy designed to remind him of how far his life had spiralled out of his control.

"Why do they do this?" James asked Theodore, confused why, even though he wasn't charged yet, his bail conditions felt like a punishment in themselves. He glanced at Theodore, who stood nearby, leaning against the wall with his arms crossed, the picture of calm authority.

Theodore adjusted his tie and sighed. "It's a tactic, James. They want to keep you on edge, make you feel the weight of the situation even before you've been charged. By dragging you all the way here instead of letting you check in at Brierley Hill, they're subtly asserting their control over you. It's petty, but it's effective."

James leaned back in his chair, letting out a frustrated breath. "Petty doesn't even cover it. I feel like I'm in some

Kafkaesque nightmare. And Chloe? She's probably sitting back, enjoying all of this. I mean, she lives in Brum, and probably hasn't had to lift a finger since she made the false accusations. Meanwhile, I'm jumping through hoops and being treated like a criminal for something I didn't do."

Theodore nodded, his expression grim. "Chloe's playing a dangerous game, and the system, unfortunately, allows for these kinds of manipulations. But that doesn't mean we're powerless. It's all about strategy, James. Keep your head down, follow the bail conditions, and let me handle the legal side. Now, you were suspended without pay, right?"

James nodded, his expression sour. "Yeah, they suspended me right after that ambush on air. No pay, no nothing, and they rejected my resignation because of the six-month notice period. I'm stuck, Theo. I can't even take another job because of their exclusivity clause. It's like they've thought of every way to keep me trapped."

Theodore frowned, his legal mind already turning over the situation. "Suspending you without pay technically means that you would have a hardship appearing here each week. Now, one little thing about conditional bail is that it must not impose undue hardship on the individual. Forcing you to travel from Pensnett to Wolverhampton every week without providing financial support could be grounds to challenge the conditions. What I can do is formally request a review of your bail conditions. Ironically, I prepared myself for just such an occasion..." he said, unclipping his briefcase and pulling out a neatly typed document. He handed it to James, who scanned the first few lines, noting the formal tone and meticulous detail.

"This is a request for variation of bail conditions," Theodore explained. "It outlines the undue hardship these conditions are causing you, particularly given your suspension without pay. I'll file it today. If the court agree, they might allow you to check in at Brierley Hill instead of trekking all the way here."

James stared at the document, a glimmer of hope breaking through his exhaustion. "Do you think it'll work?"

Theodore gave a small, reassuring smile. "It's a strong argument. The law's supposed to balance the interests of justice with fairness. Right now, these conditions are tipping the scales too far. If the magistrate is reasonable, they'll adjust them."

James nodded, a small flicker of relief in his otherwise bleak situation. It was then that James noticed in the case 3 large brown envelopes and a picture edging out from under one of them.

"What's that?" James asked, curious.

"Oh, I've also got other matters here to attend to," Theodore said with a shark like grin. "Being a concerned citizen and informing the police of a crime that is being committed."

James raised an eyebrow, leaning forward slightly in his seat. "A crime? What do you mean?"

Theodore tapped the corner of one of the brown envelopes, his grin widening. "Remember the little detail about the drug cache you mentioned at One Snow Hill? Well, I've printed off the photos your dad took on his phone, complete with photo metadata geodata and digital copies of the timestamps. These photos clearly show what appears to be a stash of cocaine and other substances stored in a broom closet on the third floor of the Manic Radio studios. With this evidence, I'm filing a formal report with the police."

James's eyes widened as he processed Theodore's words. "You're serious? You're actually reporting them?"

Theodore nodded, his expression turning serious. "Absolutely. This isn't just about you, James. If there's illegal activity going on at Manic Radio, it needs to be addressed. Not only does it strengthen your case by showing the environment you were subjected to, but it also shines a light on the culture of corruption and exploitation within the organisation. You may be called to provide a statement as you are an employee of Manic Radio, but rest assured, I'll be there to guide you through it. This is a chance to expose the rot at the core of the company—and, hopefully, to shift the narrative in your favour."

James felt a mix of apprehension and vindication. For months, he had been trapped in Manic's toxic web, feeling powerless against its sprawling influence. But now, with Theodore's calculated approach, it felt like there might be a way to fight back—not just for himself, but for everyone else who had been hurt or exploited by the company.

"I'm not sure how they'll react to this," James said, his voice tinged with nervousness. "Manic has a way of covering its tracks. They're not going to take this lying down."

Theodore nodded thoughtfully. "I don't expect them to. But the beauty of filing a report like this is that it creates a paper trail. Once the police are involved, it's harder for Manic to bury the evidence or intimidate witnesses without raising suspicion. And if they do try to retaliate, it only adds to the case against them. It's a calculated risk, but one worth taking."

Ping

James's phone buzzed on the table, drawing his attention. He picked it up and saw an email from Manic's Information Governance Team in Liverpool.

From: *Info.Gov@manicradio.group*

To: *jamie3443snetta@yahoo.co.uk*

Subject: *GDPR Request: MRG20250427*

Dear Mr Smith,

Thank you for your request under the General Data Protection Regulation (GDPR) dated 27th April 2025, in which you requested access to all data held about you by Manic Radio Group.

After reviewing your request, we regret to inform you that we are unable to provide the requested data at this time. Due to the sensitive nature of the ongoing internal investigation, we are invoking a temporary exemption under Article 23 of the GDPR, which allows organisations to restrict the rights of data subjects where necessary to safeguard the integrity of investigations, prevent interference, or protect the rights of others.

In addition, we are invoking a temporary exemption under Section 15(4) of the Data Protection Act 2018, which permits withholding personal data when disclosure would likely prejudice ongoing disciplinary or legal proceedings and also a temporary exemption from providing data that would compromise the legitimate business interests of Manic Radio Group.

We are also invoking a permanent exemption under the Data Protection Act 2018, Section 15(3), for data that includes trade secrets or commercially sensitive information. This exemption is applied to ensure the continued protection of proprietary processes and business operations within the Manic Radio Group.

Should you wish to challenge this decision, you may submit an appeal to our Information Governance Appeals Panel by writing to info.gov@manicradio.group, quoting your case reference MRG20250427. Please note that our appeals process may take up to 60 working days.

We appreciate your understanding and cooperation in this matter.

Kind regards,

Information Governance Team

Manic Radio Group

James stared at the email in disbelief, his grip tightening on the phone, and then noticed Theodore laughing, as if he was expecting this exact response.

Theodore leaned over, glancing at the email on James's phone. His laugh was sharp, almost triumphant, as he read through the legal jargon. "Oh, this is rich," he said, shaking his head. "They've just handed us another weapon to use against them."

James frowned, confused. "What do you mean? They're refusing to give me my data. Isn't that the end of it?"

Theodore tapped the phone screen with his index finger. "Not at all. What they've done here is invoke every possible exemption they could think of—most of which don't apply to your situation. It's overkill, and it's sloppy. By invoking Article 23 and the Data Protection Act exemptions, they're essentially admitting that they're withholding data because it's damaging to them. That's not going to fly with the Information Commissioner's Office. Now, I see they haven't even acknowledged that the ICO is the ultimate authority on whether these exemptions apply, which is a glaring oversight."

James watched as Theodore took his phone and forwarded the email that James had received to his own email address, and then pull a tablet from the briefcase, where the email appeared on the screen within seconds. Theodore tapped away, his face a mask of focused determination.

"What are you doing?" James asked, leaning over slightly to catch a glimpse of the screen.

Theodore didn't look up as he responded. "I had expected this, so I had drafted a copy of the email to the ICO ready to file as soon as we got a response from Manic. Their refusal to provide your data is a clear violation of GDPR's principles of transparency and accountability. By invoking such sweeping exemptions without providing detailed justifications, they're essentially asking for an ICO investigation. And we're going to give them one."

James watched as Theodore swiftly finalised the email, attaching the correspondence from Manic and highlighting the excessive and dubious nature of the exemptions. His words were precise and sharp, clearly laying out the case for why the ICO should intervene.

Ping

Theodore sent the email and turned back to James with a satisfied smile. "Done. The ICO will review this, and trust me, they don't take kindly to organisations abusing exemptions to avoid transparency. If the ICO rules in our favour, Manic will have no choice but to hand over the data—or face significant fines and sanctions. I've also copied in your MP, Mike Wood, as even though he's in opposition as a Conservative MP now, he might be able to raise questions about the broader implications of corporate abuses like this. Political pressure can sometimes work wonders in situations like these."

James nodded slowly, still trying to process the whirlwind of activity. "So… what happens now? Do we just wait for the ICO to respond?"

Theodore leaned back, his confidence radiating as he placed the tablet back in his briefcase. "Yes, but in the meantime, we keep moving forward. The ICO process can take weeks, but every step they take puts more pressure on Manic. And once we have that data—or even just confirmation that they've mishandled it—we'll have more ammunition for both your case and Lyra's."

James exhaled, a mixture of relief and apprehension washing over him. It felt like progress, but he couldn't shake the lingering fear that Manic would retaliate in ways he couldn't anticipate. "Thanks, Theo," he said quietly, his voice tinged with gratitude. "I don't know where I'd be without you and Lyra."

Theodore gave him a small, reassuring smile. "You're not alone in this, James. Remember that. They've built a fortress of manipulation and intimidation, but no fortress is impenetrable. Together, we'll find the cracks and bring the whole thing down."

****

Ping

Lyra was sitting on James's bed, having moved her clothes from the room she was renting in the Smith family home to James's room earlier that day, when she noticed an email pop up on her phone. She unlocked it, expecting another generic notification, but her heart sank as she saw the sender and subject line.

From: *Ian.Brant@bauermedia.co.uk*

To: *nottyly45@hotmail.co.uk*

Subject: *GDPR*

Dear Miss Nott,

We are writing in response to your recent correspondence regarding Bauer Media's handling of your data following the withdrawal of your job offer for the Hits Radio mid-morning presenter role.

Upon review of your inquiry and attached documentation, we attach copies of all correspondence and files received regarding yourself, with appropriate redactions where other identifiable individuals are referenced. Please note that some files have been withheld in line with data protection laws, specifically where disclosure would infringe upon the rights and freedoms of third parties, or where data is subject to legal privilege.

We have also noted your concerns regarding defamatory material allegedly shared by third parties. While we cannot comment on this matter without further substantiation, we advise you to seek independent legal counsel to address any concerns related to reputational harm.

The attached documentation includes:

Correspondence between Bauer Media's Talent Acquisition team and Manic Radio regarding your employment history and suitability for the role.

Internal notes from the Talent Acquisition process.

Media clippings and anonymous tips submitted to Bauer Media concerning your conduct during your tenure at Manic Radio.

Should you require further information or wish to appeal this disclosure, please contact Bauer Media's Data Protection Officer at dpo@bauermedia.co.uk.

We trust this addresses your concerns.

Kind regards,

Ian Brant

Assistant Compliance Officer

Bauer Media Group

Lyra scrolled down to the attachments, her hands trembling as she opened the first file. It was a heavily redacted email thread between Bauer and Manic, the tone of which made her stomach turn. Phrases like "potential reputational risk" and "unsuitable for a flagship role" jumped out at her, confirming her worst fears—that Manic had poisoned her prospects with targeted misinformation.

But then she noticed something interesting.

From: *[Redacted]@vibes.manicradio.co.uk*

To: *[Redacted]@bauermedia.co.uk*

Subject: *Hey Cousin - Quick Favour*

Hi L,

Hope you're doing well! I heard you're handling that presenter recruitment over at Hits—exciting stuff!

I just wanted to drop you a quick note about Lyra Nott, who I believe has applied for the mid-morning slot. I thought you should know that the bitch has snatched my ex-boyfriend [Redacted], who's also a presenter at Manic. She's been involved in some... questionable behaviour here, including a scandal involving drugs and inappropriate relationships. Trust me, she's not the kind of person you want associated with Bauer's brand.

Let me know if you need more info—I'd hate for Hits to get caught up in the fallout from her mess.

Take care,

K

P.S. See today's Daily Mail - it has images of Lyra in a studio with [Redacted], mid-way through a tryst. Thought you'd appreciate the heads-up.

Lyra knew that legally, Bauer had done what they believed was required by withdrawing the job offer, as it was standard in the industry for potential hires to be vetted for reputation risks, especially as Manic presenters were more likely to be risky to hire due to their frequent involvement in scandals, and so she knew that she had no leg to stand on regarding Bauer's decision to withdraw her offer. However, this email was a smoking gun—proof that Kylie had actively sabotaged her career by spreading lies and manipulating Bauer's perception of her.

Which meant that, although she couldn't sue Bauer, as they had acted within industry norms, she could absolutely take action against Kylie and her cousin as individuals, and as Kylie had used the Manic server to send the defamatory email, Manic Radio Group might also bear some liability for the actions of its employee.

Lyra leaned back against the wall, her mind racing as she processed the implications. This wasn't just a personal attack—it was a calculated move by Kylie to destroy her professionally and personally. But now, with the evidence sitting on her phone, Lyra had a weapon of her own.

The door opened in the ground floor bedroom, and Lyra saw James walk in, the two grey hairs having gone to three, and the dark circles under his eyes seemed even deeper than before. He gave her a faint smile as he closed the door behind him, his exhaustion palpable.

"Hey," Lyra said softly, putting her phone aside. "How did it go at the station?"

James shrugged, running a hand through his hair. "Theo filed for a bail variation. He's hoping the court will let me check in at Brierley Hill instead of trekking to Wolverhampton every week. And…" He hesitated, glancing at the phone in Lyra's hand. "I saw him filing something else. He's reporting the drug stash at One Snow Hill to the police."

Lyra sat up straighter, her eyebrows raising in surprise. "He's reporting it? Do you think it'll help?"

James gave a half-hearted laugh, leaning against the doorframe. "Honestly, I don't know. But Theo seems pretty confident. He's convinced it'll at least make Manic squirm. He says it's about creating a paper trail, making it harder for them to bury everything. You know, last night, when you were in your room and I was in here, I… I struggled to sleep. I... I kept dreaming that, when Clo had drugged me, she'd took me to her apartment, and encouraged Cody and Kylie to... well, let's just say that dream wasn't exactly pleasant," James said, his voice trailing off as he sank onto the bed beside Lyra. "I kept waking up, sweating, convinced it had actually happened... that they'd got their hands on me. I know it sounds corny, but I sleep better when you're holding me."

James then lay on the bed, and Lyra saw what he was wearing in the outline of his denim shorts as he was facing away from her.

"James... is... is that a..."

"Yeah... I... well, you know that dream, I... kind of needed to fill my arse when I woke up, as I... the memories of how in the dream Cody pounded me and made it full of his cock and cum... how I was his little anal slut who was made to beg for it... It just lingered when I woke up," James admitted, his voice trailing off with a mix of embarrassment and shame. He buried his face in his hands. "I couldn't shake it, Ly. It felt so real. I needed to do something to take the edge off, to remind myself that I had control over my body. So, I used your large dildo to pleasure my arse, to make me feel like I was reclaiming something that they had taken from me in the dream. It... it's not the only thing that I'm wearing."

James then took his t-shirt off, and Lyra saw he was wearing the same nipple clamps Kylie made him wear when he was under her control. Lyra's expression softened, a mix of sympathy and anger bubbling beneath the surface. She scooted closer to James, placing a hand gently on his back, her touch grounding and reassuring.

"James," she said softly, her voice steady but laced with emotion. "What you're feeling is valid. Dreams like that... they mess with your head, make you question what's real and what's not. But you have nothing to be ashamed of. What they did to you—what they put you through—it's not who you are. You're stronger than they ever gave you credit for, and reclaiming control, even in small ways, is a step forward."

James looked at her, his eyes glistening with unshed tears. "It doesn't feel like I'm strong, Lyra. It feels like I'm just... surviving. Barely holding it together. Help me take my jeans off as... well, you know the cock ring she made me wear... well, I... I had to put the alternative thing she made me wear on... I needed it... to remember my place in life... that I'm just a plaything."

Lyra watched as James unbuckled his belt and noticed he was in pain as he unzipped the front of his denim shorts. He hesitated for a moment, as if battling with the vulnerability of exposing himself, before finally unzipping them fully. Lyra's eyes softened with understanding as she reached out to help him slide the shorts down. Beneath them, James was wearing a chastity cage—an object which would prevent someone from physically arousing themselves or achieving full erections. Lyra's heart broke at the sight, her mind reeling with the implications of James choosing to wear it again. It wasn't just an object—it was a symbol of the control Kylie had once wielded over him, a relic of his torment that he was now using as a twisted form of self-punishment and coping.

"In... in the dream, she... she'd put it on me while Cody was using my arse... or while she or Chloe used a strap on, as I get erections easily, and they didn't want me enjoying it unless they said so… it was all about control, Ly. It always was."

James's voice trembled, his words laden with the weight of his trauma. Lyra reached out, her hand gently resting on his thigh, her touch firm yet comforting. Then she remembered that one of the items in one of James's unused draws that she had taken over was her own personal strap-on, something she had brought 7 years earlier when she had gone through a lesbian phase, and then later as an alternative to one of her dildos when she wanted to pleasure herself, and felt guilty, as she knew that if James discovered that she had one, that he'd likely spiral further into the mindset that he was only ever seen as a plaything, reinforcing his fears and insecurities about control and worth.

Lyra took a deep breath, her mind racing. She had to tread carefully. James was teetering on the edge, and any misstep could push him further into his trauma. She shifted her position, so she was eye level with him, her hand still resting gently on his thigh.

"James," she began softly, her voice steady and soothing, "do you trust me?"

James turned his head to meet Lyra's gaze, his eyes filled with vulnerability. He hesitated, his breathing shallow as he processed her question. After a moment, he nodded slowly.

"Yes," he whispered, his voice barely audible. "I trust you more than anyone, Lyra."

Lyra gave him a small, reassuring smile, her hand gently squeezing his thigh. "Good. When I was 19, I... I wasn't into blokes at the time, I hadn't met my ex, Si, I... I was in my second year at Uni... and I met this girl, Lucy."

James tilted his head slightly, his brows furrowing as he listened to Lyra's confession. He could see the mix of vulnerability and determination in her expression, and though he was still overwhelmed by his own turmoil, her willingness to open up felt like a small anchor in the storm of his thoughts.

"Lucy was... well, she was confident, bold, and very much not the kind of person I'd ever imagined myself with," Lyra continued, her voice soft but steady. "She introduced me to a lot of things—things I didn't even know I was curious about. One of them was, well... experimenting with control. It wasn't about dominance or power in a toxic way, but about trust. Letting someone else take the reins, knowing they'd respect your boundaries. That's when I bought... the strap-on."

James blinked, his cheeks flushing slightly at the admission. He wasn't entirely sure where Lyra was going with this, but he could sense that her words were chosen carefully, meant to reassure rather than overwhelm him.

"She also introduced me to BDSM. Now, she wasn't about pain or humiliation for the sake of it—it was about understanding limits, exploring vulnerability, and creating a space where trust was absolute. At first, I didn't get it. I thought it was all about control, but I realised it was more than that. It was about letting go, knowing that someone had your back. That's what real control is, James—not someone forcing it on you, but you choosing to give it because you trust the other person to respect you."

James's gaze softened, his breathing steadying as he listened. Lyra's words were like a lifeline, a bridge between the chaos in his mind and the reality of the present. She wasn't judging him or diminishing his feelings. Instead, she was sharing something deeply personal, showing him that control and vulnerability didn't have to be weapons—they could be choices.

Lyra reached out and gently brushed a stray strand of hair from James's face. "The thing is, we had what was called a safe word, which meant that at any moment, if either of us felt overwhelmed or wanted to stop, we'd say it, and we'd stop immediately. No questions, no hesitation. And before you ask, I usually ended up the top when we experimented because, well, Lucy liked the feeling of surrendering control, knowing she was safe. It was her way of healing from things in her past. But it was always mutual. It was never about one person having power over the other—it was about trust and respect."

James looked down, his fingers fidgeting with the hem of his t-shirt. "That's not what it was like with Kylie... well, at the start it was, before we went Insta official. At first, it was fun, like a game. But then... as soon as I joined Manic last October, the... the mutual aspect of it disappeared. Kylie started pushing boundaries, ignoring when I said no, and using things like the chastity cage and other stuff to control me, even outside of the bedroom. It wasn't about trust anymore. It was about power. And I didn't have any."

James's voice faltered as he spoke, his hands trembling slightly. Lyra stayed close, her presence steady and grounding, her heart aching for him as he bared his soul.

"That's not BDSM," Lyra said softly, her voice filled with conviction. "What Kylie did to you wasn't about trust or respect—it was abuse. She weaponised the things that are supposed to bring connection and turned them into tools for control and humiliation. That's not your fault, James. None of it is. Look, if you want, I'll show you what true trust and control look like—on your terms, with your consent, and with no pressure. It doesn't have to be now, or ever, if you're not ready. But I want you to understand that what you experienced isn't how it's supposed to be. I know the last three weeks, we've had sex and that it was vanilla sex, that I let you lead, let you decide when and how far we went. But if you ever want to explore something different, something that helps you heal instead of hurt, I want you to know I'm here for you. I... I need to confess one thing. In the second drawer is something that Lucy and I used to use when we were exploring those aspects of trust and control," Lyra admitted, her cheeks flushing. "I've kept it—not because I still use it on others, but it's useful as a dildo, as my bed at Si's house had bedposts and I could tie it to the posts and use it solo. It helped me feel in control when my life felt out of control. If you ever want to use it, not because of her or them, but because you choose to, I'll make sure it's something safe, something with boundaries. No pressure—just an option."

James hesitated, glancing towards the drawer and then back at Lyra. Her openness was disarming, her calm and gentle tone cutting through the haze of his shame and confusion. He could see that she wasn't offering to take control of him like Kylie had; she was offering a way for him to take back control for himself.

"I don't know, Ly," James said quietly, his voice cracking. "It's not like I hate the feeling... I mean, I... I've always been a bit submissive when it comes to them... Kylie, Toni Green, Chloe... Hayley... I'd get down on my knees and let them pound... let them pound me like the whore... I was. I'd... I'd enjoy it, enjoy the attention, even if it hurt— because at least they were paying attention to me. It's like, in those moments, I felt… needed. Like I had a purpose, even if that purpose was just to please them. Ly... can... can you... use it on me."

Lyra took a deep breath, carefully considering James's words. The vulnerability in his voice, the way his body language shifted between shame and longing for connection, spoke volumes about how deeply his trauma had affected him. She knew she needed to tread carefully, ensuring that this moment was about his healing, not about reliving his pain or reinforcing the dynamics that had hurt him.

****

Kylie had just finished her drivetime show on Manic Vibes West Midlands and was heading to the break area for a coffee before getting ready to do some voice-tracked sessions for Manic Urban, the brand within Manic which catered to a younger, more urban demographic when she saw in the corner of her eye out of the window that overlooked the Midland Metro blue flashing lights on the other side of Colmore Circus.

She knew that, being in Birmingham, it was likely that they were just responding to a typical city centre incident, but the sight of police vehicles always sent a shiver down her spine these days. Her mind raced to the growing storm surrounding James and the drug cache at One Snow Hill. She couldn't shake the feeling that something was brewing—something that could threaten her carefully constructed image.

Later that evening, as she finished work, she walked the few hundred yards down Upper Bull Street, past the City Big John's on Colmore Row, onto the Priory Queensway where the apartment building that Chloe and Cody lived and that she had moved into, when she saw 3 police officers standing outside the building. Their presence was a stark reminder that the world she had been trying to manipulate and control might be slipping through her fingers. As she approached the entrance, Kylie adjusted her coat, her heart pounding with a mix of paranoia and anger.

"Excuse me," one of the officers said, stepping forward to block her path. "Do you live in this building?"

"Yes," Kylie replied, forcing a polite smile. "What's going on?"

The officer's expression was unreadable when suddenly she heard "Kylie Morgan, you are under arrest on suspicion of theft, you do not have to say anything but it may harm your defence if you do not mention when questioned something which you later rely on in court. Anything you do say may be given in evidence."

Kylie's forced smile froze on her face as the officer's words sank in. Her mind raced, trying to process the situation. Theft? she thought, panic beginning to bubble beneath her carefully maintained exterior. She glanced around, hoping for some kind of escape route or explanation, but the officers stood firm, their presence leaving no room for negotiation.

Then she realised something - the laptop in her room in Cody and Chloe's apartment wasn't hers, it was James's, one he had done some of his personal remixes of current hit CHR songs on. She had taken control of it before James had left her, and not realised that he had the 'Find My on Mac' function Kylie's mind spun as the realisation struck her. She had been so caught up in her web of schemes and manipulations that she hadn't even considered the implications of keeping James's laptop. The 'Find My on Mac' function was a direct link to her, and now it was coming back to haunt her.

The officers escorted her towards a nearby police van, their grip firm but not overly rough. The reality of her arrest was setting in, and for the first time in years, Kylie felt the foundation of her carefully constructed persona start to crumble.

"Wait," she blurted, trying to regain some semblance of control. "This is a misunderstanding. That laptop—it was a gift! I didn't steal anything!"

One of the officers glanced at her, unimpressed. "You can explain that during questioning, Ms Morgan."

As she was guided into the van, Kylie's mind raced. She realised how precarious her situation had become. If James's laptop contained anything incriminating—files, emails, or even personal notes—it could be used as evidence against her. The control she had wielded so confidently over James, Chloe, and everyone else at Manic now felt like sand slipping through her fingers.

****

CHAPTER 10 - News
Thursday 8th May 2025

Pete was getting ready for work when the radio station he was listening to, Black Country Radio, turned to the news for the top-of-the-hour bulletin. He leaned in, tying his shoelaces, only half-listening until the newscaster's voice cut through the usual morning chatter with a headline that made Pete freeze mid-motion.

"In breaking news this morning, West Midlands Police have seized 2 tonnes of cocaine at Manic Radio Group's headquarters in Birmingham. Authorities have confirmed that the drugs were found in a supply closet on the third floor of the One Snow Hill studios during a late-night operation. Several arrests have been made in connection to the discovery, although police have not yet released the names of those involved. A spokesperson for Manic Radio Group has declined to comment, citing an ongoing investigation."

Pete chuckled, as the photos he had took a week and half earlier were clearly the catalyst for the raid. He shook his head, muttering under his breath, "So much for their squeaky-clean image." Standing upright, he headed over to the radio and turned it to 87.7FM, the Manic Goldies frequency for the West Midlands county, as he knew that the 10am network show, which was in its second hour, was a Birmingham produced programme hosted by Lily Mason, a sharp-witted and charismatic presenter known for her ability to handle even the most awkward on-air moments. As the station crackled to life, Pete couldn't help but wonder how Manic would spin the story, especially given how integral the Birmingham hub was to the company's operations.

Lily's voice came through the speakers, her usual upbeat tone slightly tinged with an edge of tension. "...yeah, today I'm presenting from home as the One Snow Hill studios are currently unavailable due to, well, unforeseen circumstances. I'm sure you've all heard the headlines by now. But don't worry, the show must go on, and I'm here to keep you entertained with the best classics. Coming up, we've got some Fleetwood Mac and Phil Collins to keep you company."

Pete smirked. "Presenting from home, eh? That's a clever way of saying the studio's crawling with police."

It was then that Pete noticed that, on his phone, was a text from his producer, Rachel Powell, who rarely messaged unless it was urgent. Pete unlocked his phone and read her text.

Rachel: *Morning, Pete. Heard the news? One Snow Hill's been raided. The bosses are scrambling to control the fallout. We've been asked to head to the Liverpool studios to do your drivetime show today. They're consolidating everything to avoid Birmingham while the investigation is ongoing. Car's outside to pick you up at noon. Let me know if you're good with that.*

Pete knew that, as Sarah had a home broadcasting setup, and he had access to remotely log into the Manic broadcasting system, he could easily do the show from home without the hassle of travelling to Liverpool. Furthermore, he knew that Manic Goldies WM had an OFCOM requirement to broadcast at least 8 hours of locally produced shows within the approved area, and Liverpool was not in the Midlands approved area.

Then he remembered that, technically, as the national new mid-morning and local Breakfast shows were Birmingham produced, as Lily was a Nuneaton native and, as she was broadcasting from home, she was theoretically fulfilling the local production requirements and that Alf and Lisa at Breakfast, the local duo who covered the region, would either have logged in remotely or would have been redirected to another Manic facility outside Birmingham to meet the regulatory requirements. Pete sighed, realising how adept the company had become at bending rules without breaking them outright.

He typed a quick reply to Rachel:

Pete: *Morning, Rach. Yep, I've heard the news. Absolute chaos, eh? Not sure Liverpool is the best call given OFCOM regs for local content. I've got the setup here at home and can log in remotely. Let me know if the bosses agree, but either way, I'll be ready.*

He hit send and grabbed his coffee, shaking his head at the surreal turn of events. A few minutes later, his phone buzzed with Rachel's response.

Rachel: *Ah, yeah, the OFCOM overlords. Lisa and Alf did their show from London this morning for some idiotic reason, so you're right—we're skating on thin ice as it is. Let me check with the higher-ups and get back to you. Hold tight."*

Pete chuckled, sipping his coffee. It didn't surprise him that the usual scramble to save face at Manic would include bending the rules as far as possible.

Heading over to the countertop where the kettle was in the Smith home, he decided that another cup of tea was in order. As the kettle began to boil, Pete's mind wandered to how James and Lyra were coping. The fallout from the police raid at One Snow Hill would undoubtedly stir the pot further, and knowing Manic, the executives were likely preparing to pin the blame on anyone but themselves.

His phone buzzed again with another text from Rachel.

Rachel: *Sorted. The bigwigs agreed you can do the show from home. Just keep it professional—no sly digs about the raid, yeah? They're in full damage-control mode and don't want any 'off-the-cuff' comments adding fuel to the fire. Log in by 3:30 to do some sound checks.*

Pete smirked. "Professional? Sure thing," he muttered, though he knew keeping his tongue in check might be a challenge.

Suddenly Lyra and James walked out of James's bedroom, and Pete could see the couple laughing at something on James's phone.

"What's up, son?" Pete said, confused why the two were so cheerful given the tense atmosphere of the morning. James grinned, holding up his phone as Lyra chuckled beside him.

"Dad, you're not going to believe this," James said, trying to stifle his laughter. "Hits and Capital are posting meme after meme about the raid at One Snow Hill. Look at this one—Capital tweeted a photo of a broom closet with the caption, 'Guess the Manic vibe was a little too strong. Hope they clean up their act soon!'"

Pete shook his head, unable to suppress a chuckle. "Hits and Capital piling on? That's rich. Manic always liked to act like they were untouchable."

Lyra chimed in, holding her own phone. "Hits went even further. They posted a mock playlist titled 'Snow Hill Classics' with songs like White Lines by Grandmaster Flash, Cocaine by Eric Clapton, and Under Pressure by Queen. Their followers are eating it up."

James burst out laughing, handing Pete the phone so he could see the tweet. "They've even got Every Breath You Take by The Police on there. Someone at Hits has been waiting for this moment. Even the BBC are memeing as though it were their first chance to poke fun at commercial radio. Look at this one," James continued, showing Pete a post from BBC Radio 1's Twitter account. It featured a screenshot of their playlist for the day with a cheeky caption: 'We promise our music's addictive, but not that kind of addictive. Over to you, Manic.'

Pete laughed harder than he had in weeks. "Well, I guess when your rivals smell blood in the water, they don't hold back. This is going to be a PR nightmare for Manic."

Lyra nodded, a mix of amusement and seriousness on her face. "Yeah, but honestly, they deserve every bit of this.

For too long, they've gotten away with all their shady practices. It's about time someone exposed them."

Pete's phone buzzed again, interrupting their laughter. This time it was an email from Cal Ellington, one of the regional managers at Manic. Pete opened it, already dreading the tone.

From: *cal.ellington@manicradio.group*

To: *AllDudleyStaff@manicradio.group, coverstaffuk@manicradio.group, freelancehosts@manicradio.group*

Subject: *URGENT - ONE SNOW HILL CLOSED UFN*

Dear All,

Due to unforeseen circumstances, the One Snow Hill studios are currently unavailable and will remain closed until further notice. This includes all offices, studios, and associated facilities.

We are currently working to minimise disruptions to our programming. All staff scheduled to work from the Birmingham hub will be contacted by their line managers to arrange alternative arrangements. This may include working remotely, relocating to one of our other hubs, or adjustments to your schedule.

Key Points:

Remote Broadcasting: Presenters with home setups should prepare to broadcast remotely. IT will be available for technical support as needed.

Alternative Studio Use: We are redirecting some operations to our Liverpool, Manchester, and London hubs. If you are required to travel, please consult with your line manager regarding transport and accommodation.

Public Relations: Due to increased media attention following recent events, all staff are reminded not to make public comments or social media posts regarding the situation. Direct any external inquiries to the PR team at comms@manicradio.group.

Security: Staff are reminded not to attempt access to the One Snow Hill building until further notice. Any questions regarding personal belongings left on-site should be directed to facilities@manicradio.group.

Thank you for your understanding and cooperation during this challenging time. We will provide updates as soon as we have more information.

Kind regards,

Cal Ellington

Regional Manager – Midlands

Manic Radio Group

What made Pete laugh, however, was that the management company that owned One Snow Hill, Union Investment Real Estate, had just sent another email which was completely open about why the Police had sealed off the premises.

Suddenly there was a knock on the door and Pete turned toward the door, his curiosity piqued. Lyra raised an eyebrow, while James, still holding his phone, frowned slightly. The knock came again, more insistent this time.

"I'll get it," Pete said, walking briskly to the front door. He opened it to find Chloe standing outside, Cody at the car that they had, with several boxes stacked in the back seat. Chloe stood with her arms crossed, her expression a mixture of defiance and frustration. Pete's jaw tightened at the sight of her—his estranged daughter, who had caused so much chaos, now appearing at his doorstep unannounced.

"What do you want, Chloe?" Pete asked, his voice cold but calm.

Chloe rolled her eyes and gestured toward the car. "Cody and I are moving back in. I want my room ready for once we've got back from the restaurant."

Pete stared at Chloe, his grip tightening on the doorframe. "Moving back in? Like hell you are," he said, his voice firm, though he kept his tone measured.

Chloe smirked, tilting her head. "It's still my home, Dad. You don't get to just change that because you're mad at me. Mum said—"

"Mum said nothing of the sort," Pete interrupted, his patience waning. "You've done enough damage, Chloe. Turning up here like nothing's happened? After what you've done to James? Unbelievable. Anyway, this is James's registered bail address, and his bail conditions require him to not be anywhere near you while he's waiting to be charged or not charged. So, no, Chloe, you're not moving back in here. Not now, not ever."

Chloe's grin widened. "Oh, I know his conditions of bail, Dad, and I'm moving in if you like it or not. That means you have to kick that cokehead out. After all, I'm pregnant with his son, your grandson, and you wouldn't want your precious grandchild to grow up without a roof over his head, would you?" Chloe's tone was smug, her words dripping with manipulation.

Pete's face hardened, his patience finally snapping. "Don't you dare try to guilt me into this, Chloe," he said, his voice steady but brimming with anger. "You've used and manipulated everyone around you long enough. If you think for one second I'm going to throw James out of this house—his own home—just to make room for you and your lies, you're delusional."

Chloe's smirk faltered, replaced by a flicker of uncertainty. "It's not a lie, Dad," she said, her voice losing some of its bravado. "James and I... we—"

Suddenly Pete heard Lyra chuckle at Chloe's statement about James being the father of Chloe's son, and

Lyra stepped into the hallway, her arms crossed and an amused smirk on her face. "Oh, Chloe," she said, her tone dripping with sarcasm, "you're still sticking to that story? You must really think we're all idiots."

Chloe's face flushed with anger, her smug expression replaced by a defensive glare. "What are you laughing at, Lyra?" she snapped. "This has nothing to do with you."

Lyra raised an eyebrow, unfazed by Chloe's outburst. "Oh, it has everything to do with me. You see, I've been spending quite a bit of time with James lately and let me tell you—he's not exactly been keeping secrets from me. Especially not about you."

Pete, sensing the tension building, interjected. "Lyra, what do you mean?" he asked, his voice sharp but curious.

Lyra turned to Pete, her expression softening slightly. "I mean, James has been upfront about everything Chloe's been doing—manipulating him, setting him up, and now trying to play the victim in all of this. And as for this 'baby,'" she said, turning her gaze back to Chloe, "well, let's just say James has some serious doubts about whether it's even his."

Chloe's eyes narrowed, her fists clenching at her sides. "You don't know what you're talking about," she hissed. "James and I—"

"James and you what, Chloe?" Lyra interrupted, her voice cutting through Chloe's protests like a knife. "Forced him into things he didn't want? Drugged him? Humiliated him? Oh, we all know what you and your little group of friends at Manic have been up to. Just like I know your husband is firing blanks, and that Liam is another of your regular fuck buddies. Anyway, I'm sure that Manic would know... with the Baby Bonus being on record, they've probably already taken a DNA sample from James under their so-called 'paternity assurance' initiative. So, let's not pretend there's any ambiguity here, Chloe. If you want to play the victim, you'd better be prepared for the truth to come out."

Pete noticed that Cody had suddenly pulled a phone from his pocket, and was asking for the Police to attend, saying that James had breached his bail by approaching Chloe, and that Chloe was fearing for her life. It was then Pete realised what the plan was. Chloe and Cody had orchestrated this entire scene to trigger a reaction, ensuring James would breach his bail conditions or at least make it appear so. Pete's mind raced as he pieced together their twisted strategy.

"James isn't even in the same room as her!" Pete barked, stepping into the doorway to block Chloe from entering further. "You're not dragging him into another one of your schemes, Chloe. You'd better think twice before trying this stunt."

Suddenly Pete found himself flying backwards as Chloe pushed past him, barging into the hallway with an air of triumph. He watched as she then screamed, accentuating the drama as he saw her walk into the living room where James was standing, and he knew that she was setting the scene to make it look like James had confronted her.

"James!" Chloe shouted, her voice trembling with feigned panic. "Stay back! Don't come near me!" She stumbled theatrically into the living room, clutching her stomach as if shielding her unborn child.

James, who had been standing by the sofa scrolling on his phone, looked up, confused and startled. "What the hell are you talking about, Chloe? I haven't even—"

****

An hour later, James found himself in an interview room, this time at Brierley Hill Police Station, being interrogated by two officers about breaching his bail conditions. The sterile walls of the interview room felt suffocating, and James's anxiety was palpable. He shifted uncomfortably in his seat, running a hand through his hair as the officers reviewed their notes.

"Mr. Smith," one of the officers began, her tone clipped and professional, "we have a report that you approached the complainant, Chloe Lane, at your residence earlier today. This would constitute a breach of your bail conditions, which explicitly forbid any contact with her."

James frowned, his frustration bubbling over, but he knew that he was going to keep quiet until Theodore arrived, as he knew that anything he said could be twisted against him. He leaned back in the uncomfortable chair, trying to remain calm, though his fists clenched under the table.

The door to the interview room opened, and Theodore Nott strode in, his sharp suit immaculate and his presence commanding. He carried a leather briefcase and a small, confident smirk that seemed to unsettle the officers.

"Gentlemen," Theodore said coolly, his gaze sweeping the room before settling on James. "Apologies for the delay. I understand my client has been accused of breaching his bail conditions. Now, I would like chance to confer with my client before we proceed further with this interview." Theodore's tone was calm but firm, leaving no room for argument.

The senior officer exchanged a glance with his colleague before nodding. "Very well, Mr Nott. You have ten minutes. We'll step outside."

As the officers exited, Theodore turned to James, his smirk fading into an expression of focused determination. "Alright, James," he said, pulling a notepad and pen from his briefcase. "Tell me exactly what happened. Don't leave anything out, no matter how small it seems."

James exhaled, his shoulders slumping as he recounted the events of the morning. "It started with Chloe showing up at the house unannounced, claiming she and Cody were moving back in. Dad told her no—said my bail conditions wouldn't allow it. Then Lyra called her out on her lies about the baby and the manipulation she's been pulling. That's when she lost it. She pushed past Dad, barged into the living room where I was, and started screaming like I was attacking her. I never even got close to her, Theo. I swear."

Theodore chuckled. "Well, I can tell you that the boxes in her car were empty, as I've just come from an online meeting with a contact of mine, a PI, who'd been following them. After you were hauled off and they gave a statement to the police, they headed... back to their Birmingham apartment. Seem's they're on bail themselves."

James's jaw dropped, his frustration turning into a mix of anger and disbelief. "They're on bail? For what? And they had the nerve to pull this stunt while they're under investigation themselves?"

Theodore smirked, a glint of satisfaction in his eyes. "Yes, they are. You remember how you reported that Kylie had your laptop, a Mac, and she was often at their apartment?" Theodore continued, flipping open his notebook. "Well, as the leaseholders, Chloe and Cody are sub-leasing a room to Kylie, and the laptop was in Cody and Chloe's bedroom. They're on bail for handling stolen property for that, as well as possession of a Class A drug."

James blinked, struggling to process Theodore's revelation. "Wait," he said slowly, leaning forward. "You're telling me Chloe and Cody were caught with my laptop and drugs? And they're still pulling these stunts?"

Theodore nodded, flipping a page in his notebook with a calm precision that only emphasised his confidence. "Indeed. The police discovered your laptop during a separate search of their apartment. When they ran the serial number, it flagged as belonging to you. That, combined with the drugs found in their possession, landed them in hot water. It appears that Chloe and Cody didn't anticipate the 'Find My Mac' function would lead to their doorstep."

James exhaled sharply, a mix of relief and incredulity washing over him. "So, they're on bail for my laptop and drugs, and they still had the gall to try and set me up today? They must be desperate. But why would the Police still haul me here for questioning if they know Chloe and Cody are already under investigation?"

Theodore tapped his pen thoughtfully against his notebook. "Procedure. Because your bail conditions are explicit about avoiding any contact with Chloe, the police are obligated to investigate any reported breaches, no matter how flimsy the evidence. I've already spoken with the Inspector, and they're not taking the report seriously, but they still have to follow protocol. That's why we're here, going through the motions."

James nodded, though his jaw tightened in frustration. "So, what now? Am I stuck here until they decide I didn't do anything wrong?"

Theodore leaned back in his chair, his confidence unwavering. "Not quite. I've already requested the body cam footage from the officers who responded at your house. If Chloe's performance was as theatrical as you say, it'll be easy to prove you didn't breach your conditions. I've also reminded the Inspector that Chloe and Cody are on bail themselves, which raises serious questions about their credibility as complainants."

James let out a shaky breath, a flicker of hope lighting up his otherwise grim mood. "You really think that'll be enough?"

Theodore gave him a reassuring nod. "It's more than enough... especially as the Inspector listens to your dad's show and is a big fan of it."

James couldn't help but chuckle at Theodore's confidence, though he still felt the weight of the morning's events pressing down on him. "Dad's show has fans in the police force? That's... surreal."

Theodore smirked. "Surreal, but useful. Never underestimate the power of a good reputation. Now, sit tight. Let's get this wrapped up."

The door to the interview room opened, and the two officers re-entered, their expressions a mix of professionalism and unease. The senior officer cleared his throat as he took his seat.

"Mr Nott, Mr Smith," the officer began, his tone noticeably more measured than before, "we've reviewed the initial report and spoken with the officers who attended the scene. Additionally, we've been made aware of some... complicating factors regarding the complainants. Given this, we're satisfied there's insufficient evidence to suggest Mr Smith breached his bail conditions."

James exhaled in relief, his shoulders relaxing for the first time that day. Theodore's smirk widened slightly, though he remained composed.

"Thank you, officer," Theodore said, his tone polite but firm. "I trust this will be the last time my client is dragged in for questioning over baseless claims?"

The officer nodded, clearly eager to wrap things up. "We'll ensure the report reflects our findings. Mr Smith, you're free to go. We apologise for any inconvenience caused."

As they left the station, James turned to Theodore, a mixture of gratitude and exhaustion in his voice. "Thanks, Theo. I don't know how you do it, but I'm glad you're on my side."

Theodore chuckled. "It's all about staying two steps ahead, James. Now, let's get you home. I think you've had enough drama for one day."

****

"And good evening West Midlands," Pete said as he sat in the bedroom that had, 10 years earlier, been converted into a home broadcasting studio by Sarah when she had, in 2014, left Smooth Radio a year after the station had gone from national to regional and established her production company. Pete leaned back in his chair, the soundboard glowing softly before him as the familiar jingle for Manic Goldies Drivetime faded out. Despite the chaos of the day, he kept his voice smooth and professional, a reassuring constant for his listeners.

"It's Thursday evening, and we've got some cracking tunes lined up for you, from Bowie to Blondie. Now, I know there's been a lot of chatter in the news about certain... events, and so we've got the news with Lucy Bowen."

Pete heard the pre-recorded pan-Central England news, as the studios were unavailable and so a pan-regional broadcast had been arranged from the Manchester hub, play out and knew that he had two minutes until he was back on air.

"Pete, Cal's emailed all Drive shows," Racheal said in his earpiece, as she was at her home in the West Midlands managing Pete's broadcast remotely, her voice calm but tinged with the urgency of the day's events, on the non-broadcast channel. There were two channels, Pete knew, that Racheal had access to, the broadcast channel that his listeners could hear and the internal one, where they could have private discussions without being heard on air.

"Let me guess," Pete said, adjusting his mic and leaning back in his chair. "We're supposed to keep pretending nothing's wrong?"

Racheal sighed. "Pretty much. Cal's message is clear—no mention of the raid, no allusions to anything remotely controversial. Just stick to the playlist and the usual chatter. They're in full damage-control mode."

Pete smirked, glancing at his show notes. "Figures. Well, let's keep it clean then. No cheeky comments about broom closets or 'snowy days', even though theoretically I'm not a Manic employee anymore since my contract was renewed under the freelancer model. Don't worry, Rach—I'll behave." He paused for a beat. "Though it's killing me not to make a crack about Cocaine by Clapton right now."

Rachel chuckled softly in his ear. "Save it for the pub later. You know Cal's got spies everywhere. Anyway, remember that the draw for the £500k Call is tomorrow. on the network evening show, so you need to promote that."

Pete nodded, his smirk fading into a more professional expression as the news update ended. He adjusted his headphones and leaned into the microphone, his voice smooth and reassuring as he segued back into the show.

"Thanks, Lucy. Well, folks, let's focus on the music tonight, shall we? Up next, we've got some Bowie to get you through the drive home, followed by a classic from Blondie. And don't forget, tomorrow night's the big £500k Money Drop draw on the evening show. To enter, just text Drop to 87106, texts are £3 or go to manicradioplays.co.uk. There is a free entry route, by phoning 0330 880 3601. It's a network competition across Manic Vibes, Manic Urban, Manic Classical, Manic Alt, Manic School Disco, Manic Dance, Manic Metal, Manic Goldies, Manic Rock, and Manic Soul—so the competition is definitely heating up! Lines close tomorrow at 7pm, and Dr Manic from Manic Dance will phone one lucky winner live on-air to make their dreams come true. Until then, keep it locked right here on Manic Goldies for all your classic favourites. Here's Heroes by David Bowie to get us started."

Pete knew that the track would be played out by the Network Centre in Speke, and so he leaned back, allowing himself a moment to reflect as the familiar opening chords of Heroes filled the airwaves. The day's chaos still lingered in his mind, but for now, his job was to keep things steady, even if the foundation beneath Manic was beginning to crack.

****

CHAPTER 11 - Pregnancy
Monday 12th May 2025

Lyra knew that she was late. It wasn't just her usual impeccable timekeeping that had slipped—it was something else, something more worrying. She and James had had their first round of unprotected sex a month ago, and her period was now two weeks late, officially well within the time that it was time to start asking questions she wasn't sure she wanted answered. Lyra sat on the edge of her bed, staring at the pregnancy test in her hand, the unopened box balanced precariously on her knee. The digital display was blank, waiting for her to gather the courage to take the next step.

Suddenly her phone rang and, looking at the caller ID, she declined the call from an unknown number. Lyra didn't have the bandwidth for yet another intrusive interruption from Manic, Chloe, or anyone else embroiled in the ongoing chaos. Right now, she needed a moment to focus on her own life—something that had felt increasingly out of her control since James had re-entered it.

She took a deep breath, placed the phone face down on the bedside table, and stood up, the pregnancy test still in hand. Her reflection in the wardrobe mirror showed a woman trying to mask her fear with determination. "Right," she muttered to herself, "it's just a test. No matter what happens, you can manage it."

A knock at the door made her jump, and Lyra turned to see James standing there, his hair slightly dishevelled and a worried crease in his brow. He was holding two mugs of tea, his usual attempt at diffusing tension.

"You alright?" he asked, stepping inside and placing the mugs on the dresser. "Look, if... if we're going to have a baby, then... will... would you consider m.."

Lyra watched as James sighed and hesitated, his words faltering as though he was too nervous to say what he was thinking. He ran a hand through his hair, the tension in his body obvious.

"Would I consider what, James?" Lyra asked gently, though her voice wavered with uncertainty. She wasn't sure if she was ready for whatever he was about to say—especially not with the pregnancy test still clutched in her hand.

She knew that if he asked her to marry him, even though they'd only been together a month, after she had pulled him out of the relationship with Kylie that he had been trapped in, she might just say yes. Not because she was sure they were ready, but because she wanted James to know he wasn't alone.

But the elephant in the room was that she would be number 5 of 5 women James had impregnated in the past 6 months, Kylie being one of the mothers of his children. The weight of that fact lingered between them, a stark reminder of the chaos that had consumed both their lives since they'd found each other again.

James hesitated, his hands fidgeting with the hem of his t-shirt. He finally blurted out, "Would you consider keeping it? The baby, I mean. If you are... if we are..." His voice trailed off, and he looked down, ashamed of how unprepared he sounded.

Lyra swallowed hard, her grip tightening on the pregnancy test. "James, I don't even know if I'm pregnant yet," she said softly, trying to keep her voice calm despite the storm of emotions swirling within her. "And if I am, we'll figure it out together. But let's not get ahead of ourselves, okay?"

Ping

Lyra looked on her phone to see an email had come through from a friend of hers who worked at Manic's Dundee hub who, like her, had been one of the few sane people within the chaos that the Manic ecosystem often created, one of the local HR officers at that hub. She opened the email cautiously, her heart racing as she skimmed the message.

From: *Patty454xluv@gmail.com*

To: *nottyly45@hotmail.co.uk*

Subject: *Thought you might want to see this*

Hey, Ly,

Was doing a bit of digging in the HR records and want a bit of goss? You know you mentioned some of the Brum lot was claiming your boyfriend was the fathers of their babies...

... well, the DNA tests on the system have some interesting things.

Kylie Morgan's baby daddy is... your boyfriend

Penny Carmichael's baby daddy is... your boyfriend

Zara Love and Chloe Smith's baby daddy... Liam Price.

So, Ly, looks like your hunk isn't quite as prolific as some of those rumours suggested, but he's still got some drama following him. Kylie and Penny? That's messy enough, but at least Chloe's and Zara's accusations are officially rubbish. Thought you'd want to know before someone else weaponizes this.

Take care,

Patty x

Lyra let out a breath she didn't realise she'd been holding, her emotions tangling into an unmanageable knot. James, who had been silently watching her read the email, noticed the subtle shift in her expression.

"Everything alright?" he asked, his voice laced with concern.

Lyra hesitated. Should she tell him now? The revelations in the email were bound to stir up a storm, but James deserved to know the truth—especially about Chloe's lies. She handed him her phone, watching his face closely as he read.

James frowned, his eyes scanning the message. His jaw tightened and Lyra could see how her boyfriend?

Hey... since when have I thought about James as my boyfriend?

Oh, come on Ly, you've been shagging him for a month, you're sharing a bedroom with him... hell, he's seen you naked and you're carrying his baby for God's sake. You never let Si sleep with you in the 3 years you two were together, and yet you're living with James after just a few weeks. Who are you kidding? He is your boyfriend—chaos and all.

Lyra snapped herself out of her thoughts as James lowered the phone, his expression a mixture of relief and frustration.

Then he lost it.

James's voice cracked as the rage poured out of him, his face reddening. "That fucking bitch of a sister! She's been lying through her teeth this whole time, dragging me through hell, making me out to be some kind of degenerate! And Zara too? What the hell is wrong with these people? Do they have nothing better to do than ruin lives?"

Lyra placed a calming hand on his arm, her voice steady but soft. "James, I know it's maddening, but this is actually good news. It means you're not tied to Chloe or Zara any longer. They can't use the baby claims to manipulate you anymore."

James shook his head, pacing the small room like a caged animal. "Good news? Ly, they've already done the damage! Chloe's been parading around acting like she's some saint carrying my child, and Zara's added fuel to that fire. Every bloody person at Manic probably thinks I'm some kind of... of..." His words trailed off, and he sat heavily on the edge of the bed, burying his face in his hands. "I can't escape this, Ly. No matter what we prove, the damage is done. Chloe raped me, claimed I was the father of her child, made me think that my soon to be nephew was the product of an incestuous relationship... And Zara? God knows what her motive was, other than stirring the pot. I mean, I know she was... that... you know, like me, the hub cum dump," James finished, his voice cracking under the weight of his emotions. "But why drag me into it? Why weaponize it against me?"

Lyra sat beside him, placing a comforting hand on his knee. "Because they're manipulators, James. People like Chloe and Zara thrive on control and chaos. They saw an opportunity to exploit your vulnerabilities, and they took it. But now we have the truth. And with the DNA results, they can't keep spinning their lies. It's over for them. You know one thing though... if I'm pregnant, then, even though I've left Manic thanks to my contract expiring, I'm still eligible for the Manic Baby Bonus, aren't I?" Lyra's tone was half-joking, an attempt to lighten the mood, but the bitter edge in her voice betrayed her true feelings. "What do you think of us playing the system and claiming that bonus to get back some of what Manic owes you? Think of it as poetic justice."

James let out a dry chuckle, though the pain in his expression lingered. "Honestly, Ly, part of me wants to take every penny they're offering and then some. But another part of me just wants to get as far away from Manic and their twisted schemes as possible. I'm sick of being tangled in their web. The annoying thing is that I'm still under contract until the end of October."

Lyra nodded, her mind racing as she considered James's predicament. She leaned back against the headboard, glancing at the pregnancy test still clenched in her hand. The thought of being tied to Manic Radio through a baby bonus felt both ironic and deeply unsettling. Yet, part of her agreed with James—it was tempting to take something back from the company that had taken so much from them.

"You're right, James," Lyra said softly. "The best thing we can do is focus on getting through this, together. Forget Manic and their twisted incentives. If I'm pregnant, this baby is ours, not theirs. We'll figure out how to make it work, no matter what. Anyway, you'll know that this one, unlike the others, is 100% your child. After all, Si and I split up back in January, and we only shared a bed but didn't have sex for the three years we were together. I'm not like Chloe or Zara, James, and I haven't had sex with anyone but you and Lucy, so there's no doubt about who the father is."

James glanced at Lyra, his eyes softening as her words sunk in. "I know, Ly. You're not like them. You've been the only person who's stuck by me through all of this. I just... I don't know how I'll ever make it up to you."

Lyra reached out, cupping his face gently in her hands. "You don't have to make anything up to me, James. We're in this together, remember? No more looking back—just forward. Now," she added, glancing at the pregnancy test, "I think it's time to find out if our future involves nappies and sleepless nights."

James let out a nervous laugh, the tension in the room momentarily lifting. "Right. Okay. Let's do this."

Lyra stood, clutching the test, and headed to the bathroom. James stayed behind, pacing nervously. The minutes felt like hours as he wrestled with a mixture of hope, fear, and uncertainty. When Lyra finally returned, her face was unreadable, the test clutched tightly in her hand.

"Well?" James asked, his voice barely above a whisper.

****

Chloe was sitting in the apartment she and Cody were leasing, as it was a day off from her Law with Criminology lectures, furious at the letter the management company had delivered to her door that morning. The letter informed Chloe and Cody that they were being evicted for breaching the terms of their lease, citing the possession of illegal substances and handling of stolen property as grounds for immediate termination of their tenancy. Chloe had crumpled the letter in her hand and thrown it across the room, where it now sat on the coffee table beside Cody, who was scrolling through his phone, oblivious to her anger.

"I'm going to sue these bastards," Chloe shouted as Kylie, who was painting her toe nails, looked up. "There's that many holes in the lease agreement that I could tie them in knots in court. Who do they think they're dealing with? They can't just throw us out without proper notice or a fair hearing. Cody, get Manic's lawyers on the phone, as they have access to far better resources than we do."

Cody looked up lazily, raising an eyebrow. "You really think Manic's lawyers are going to step in for this? After the police raid and everything going on, they're probably too busy covering their own arses."

"Ah, but Cody, my dear husband, it's in our contracts that we get unlimited legal advice and representation for any legal issues affecting our professional lives or anything that could impact our image as representatives of the company. Anyway, Kylie and I are pregnant women, so making us redundant or sacking us would be a PR disaster for them, and also a bit dodgy under the Employment Rights Act. They won't want to touch this with a bargepole. Besides, we've got a trump card: they still need to keep the 'family-friendly' image alive for the Baby Bonus campaign. Who better to front it than two glowing mums-to-be?"

Kylie rolled her eyes, blowing on her freshly painted toenails. "You're so deluded, Chloe. Manic's not going to care about you or me if it risks their reputation any further. If anything, they'll cut ties and spin some sob story about how we betrayed their trust. You're playing a dangerous game banking on their loyalty when they've already proven they'll sell anyone out to save themselves."

Chloe shot her a glare. "Who's the lawyer here? Me or you? I've read the fine print in the contracts, Kylie. They have a legal obligation to provide representation for us in any matter that could impact their business interests or reputation. Anyway, we all know that half of the staff at Manic's various hubs are in just as deep shit as we are. Each hub has its own drug problem, its own cum dump, its own secrets. Hell, the simultaneous raids across the hubs causing half of the presenters, producers, techs and management to be charged of drug-related offenses are proof enough that Manic isn't just a company—it's a sinking ship. They're not going to risk opening the floodgates by letting us go without a fight."

"So, you're saying that as long as we stay loud, pregnant, and legally threatening, they'll keep us on the payroll?" Kylie asked, her tone dripping with sarcasm as she picked up her coffee cup. "You're assuming-"

"Hey, if Dr Manic can stay at Manic even though he almost killed his co-host back in 2018 in their Manic Dance Halloween Prank," Chloe said, cutting Kylie off mid-sentence, "then yes, they'll keep us. Hell, Franz Prix killed his colleague and he's still doing the weekly show from Berlin. That's the kind of company we're dealing with. They value loyalty, even if it's toxic, and the façade of stability over actual accountability. As long as we play our cards right and keep up the appearance of the perfect Manic family, they'll have no choice but to keep us."

Kylie smirked, swirling her coffee. "You've thought this through, haven't you? I'll give you that. But what happens when the truth about our 'glowing mums-to-be' image comes out? The DNA tests won't stay buried forever, Chloe. Not when people like Lyra and James are fighting back."

Chloe narrowed her eyes, leaning forward. "The DNA tests won't mean a thing if we control the narrative. You see, they can't get the DNA information because of the Data Protection Act 2018, as its medical information. If Manic released it to James, then we can sue Manic for breaching confidentiality. As long as we spin the story right, James and Lyra will look like the bitter ones, trying to discredit innocent mothers-to-be. People love a good redemption story, especially when it's wrapped in a perfect, glowing, family-friendly package. We just have to play the game smarter than they do."

Ping

Chloe looked at the email on her phone and chuckled when she saw that the sender was one of Manic's Legal Team members:

From: *legal.support@manicradio.group*

To: *chloe.lane@vibes.manicradio.co.uk*

Subject: *Re: Eviction and Representation*

Dear Mrs Lane,

Thank you for reaching out regarding your current legal situation.

I have been assigned to your case and will be providing guidance regarding your tenancy and eviction notice. After reviewing your employment contract and the terms outlined in your tenancy agreement, I have noted several areas where we can challenge the landlord's actions.

Please be aware, however, that due to recent scrutiny surrounding Manic Radio Group and its employees, this case must be handled delicately to avoid further reputational damage. I advise against any public statements or confrontations with your landlord until we have thoroughly prepared our response.

I will schedule a meeting with you and Mr Lane at the Birmingham Hub tomorrow to discuss our next steps and strategy. In the meantime, please forward any correspondence or additional documentation related to this matter.

Kind regards,

Samantha Green

Deputy Assistant Head - Legal Support

Manic Radio Group

****

"Glass of wine, Lyra?" Pete asked her as he got home from work, the Smith family home continued to buzz with the residual tension from the day's events. Lyra hesitated, the pregnancy test result still fresh in her mind. Her instinct was to refuse, but she also didn't want to raise suspicion until she was ready to share her news.

"Not tonight, Pete," she said with a small smile, setting down her phone. "Sarah's scheduled me some time in her studio upstairs for James and I to record a podcast on her studio setup. We're thinking of calling it 'Broadcasting Boundaries', a series talking about the industry as a whole, not just Manic."

Pete raised an eyebrow, intrigued by Lyra's response. "Broadcasting Boundaries, eh? Sounds like a cathartic project for you both, especially given… well, everything. What's the first episode going to cover? Let me guess, 'How Not to Run a Radio Station'?"

Lyra chuckled softly, grateful for Pete's attempt to lighten the mood. "Something like that. We're thinking of starting with a discussion on toxic workplace cultures—drawing from our experiences but keeping it broad enough to not name names. We want it to feel like a safe space for people in the industry to share their stories without fear of backlash."

The next thing Lyra knew, Sarah came down the stairs, the positive pregnancy test in her hand, wrapped discreetly in a tissue. Lyra's heart sank as she realised, she'd forgotten to dispose of it properly, even though she had asked James to put it in the black wheelie bin.

Looking at James, she noticed he was snuggled into her, his hand automatically reaching for her stomach, completely besotted as the two had found out together that she was pregnant. James, for all his recent struggles and insecurities, had been utterly overwhelmed with emotion when the test revealed the truth. They had spent the last hour in a quiet bubble, discussing the future, their fears, and their hope for a fresh start away from the chaos of Manic. Now, though, with Sarah holding the test, their private moment was about to become very public.

"Lyra?" Sarah's voice was soft but tinged with concern as she descended the last step. "I found this upstairs. Is there something you'd like to tell me?"

Pete turned, wine glass in hand, his expression shifting from curiosity to surprise as he registered the test in Sarah's hand. Lyra flushed, her heart pounding as she exchanged a quick glance with James. He nodded, giving her an unspoken assurance that they were in this together.

"Well," Lyra began, her voice steady despite the nerves bubbling within her, "I was going to wait until we'd fully processed it ourselves, but since you've found out… yes, this idiot who's grinning like a Cheshire cat over here is going to be a dad, even though I'm the third one he's knocked up in the last six months. But," she added quickly, cutting off Pete's impending reaction with a raised hand, "before you start, let me clarify something. This isn't like the chaos with Chloe or Kylie."

"Wait, 3? I thought he'd got 2 other girls pregnant," Pete interjected, his voice tinged with confusion and concern. He looked between Lyra and James, clearly trying to process the news. "Is there something else we should know?"

Lyra sighed, deciding it was better to lay everything out in the open. "Yes, Pete, three. But before you start worrying, let me explain. Chloe and Zara's claims were false. We have the DNA tests to prove it. Kylie and Penny Carmichael? Well, they're legitimate, but James has been clear with me—and with them—that he'll do right by those children, even if the circumstances aren't ideal."

Pete's face darkened at the mention of Chloe. "So, Chloe lied? Again? And Zara too? I swear that girl has been nothing but trouble since she walked into Manic."

James nodded, his grin fading as the weight of the situation settled back on his shoulders. "Yeah, Dad. Chloe made everything worse, and Zara was just adding to the mess. But this—" He gestured toward Lyra, his voice softening. "This is different. This is real, and I'm going to do everything I can to make it right. Anyway, Lyra's not like Kylie, not plotting and manipulating. Which reminds me, I've got another meeting tomorrow."

Lyra knew what James was referring to, that he had joined Narcotics Anonymous as part of his attempt to heal and distance himself from the drug-fuelled chaos of Manic.

The irony of his sponsor being a former radio presenter who had lost everything to addiction was not lost on Lyra. She admired James's commitment to turning his life around, even as they both navigated the uncertainties of their new reality.

Sarah's expression softened as she absorbed the news, her maternal instincts kicking in. "Well," she said, her voice gentler now, "if you two are serious about this, then you'll need all the support you can get. A baby changes everything, you know. But if anyone can handle it, it's you, Lyra. And James," she added, turning to him with a knowing look, "you've got a lot of growing up to do. But I can see you're trying, and that's what matters."

Pete set his wine glass down, rubbing his temples as he processed the conversation. "So let me get this straight," he said, his tone a mix of incredulity and grudging acceptance. "My son has two confirmed kids on the way with two different women, plus a third baby here with Lyra. All while he's still under contract with Manic, battling them in court, and trying to rebuild his life. Did I miss anything?"

James chuckled nervously, scratching the back of his neck. "When you put it like that, Dad, it sounds… overwhelming."

"It is overwhelming," Pete said firmly, though his tone had softened. "But you're not doing this alone, son. You've got us. And Lyra," he added, looking at her with a rare warmth, "you've got us too. You've been through enough already, and if you're willing to stand by this idiot, then you're family."

Lyra felt a lump rise in her throat at Pete's words, her eyes misting slightly. "Thank you, Pete. That means a lot. It really does."

The tension in the room eased as Sarah took the pregnancy test from Lyra's hand and set it gently on the counter. "Right," she said, clapping her hands together. "Let's not make this into a pity party. There's a baby on the way, and that means there's planning to do. Have you thought about where you'll live? This house is already full, and you'll need your own space before the little one arrives."

Lyra hesitated, glancing at James. They hadn't even begun to think about practicalities, let alone discuss them. "We haven't really talked about it yet," she admitted. "Everything's been... so chaotic. But we'll figure it out. Together."

Pete nodded, his expression thoughtful. "You'll want somewhere close by, at least for the first few months. That way, we can help out when you need it. And James," he added, fixing his son with a serious look, "you'll need to make some tough decisions about your job. Manic's not exactly the place for a young family to thrive."

James sighed, running a hand through his hair. "I know, Dad. But I'm stuck there until October. I can't just walk away."

"Well," Sarah interjected, her voice calm but firm, "then you use the next few months to prepare for life after Manic. Focus on getting clean, staying out of trouble, and supporting Lyra. We'll deal with the rest as it comes."

The room fell into a comfortable silence as the weight of the conversation settled over them. For the first time in weeks, Lyra felt a flicker of hope amidst the chaos. They didn't have all the answers, but they had each other—and for now, that was enough.

James reached for her hand, squeezing it gently. "Whatever happens, Lyra," he said quietly, "we'll make it work. I promise."

She smiled, leaning her head against his shoulder. "We will, James. We will."

****

CHAPTER 12 - Dropped Charges
Wednesday 14th May 2025

James and Lyra were lying in James's single bed, their two bodies barely fitting on the narrow mattress. The room was dimly lit by the soft glow of the bedside lamp, its light casting a warm hue over the small space. Lyra rested her head on James's chest, listening to the steady rhythm of his heartbeat, her hand idly tracing patterns across his forearm. The intimacy between them was a quiet reprieve from the chaos that seemed to envelop their lives.

The quiet was broken by the soft buzz of Lyra's phone on the nightstand. She reached over, careful not to disturb James, and glanced at the screen. It was an email notification from Theodore. Her heart quickened as she opened it, scanning the contents.

From: *theodore.nott@nottsolicitors.co.uk*

To: *nottyly45@hotmail.co.uk, jamie3443snetta@yahoo.co.uk*

Subject: *Re: Update on Bail Conditions*

Dear Lyra and James,

I'm writing with some excellent news. The police have officially dropped all charges against you, James, due to insufficient evidence. The bodycam footage from the incident with Chloe, coupled with statements from Pete and Lyra, made it clear that the accusations against you were baseless.

Furthermore, I've had confirmation that Chloe and Cody are facing additional charges related to perverting the course of justice. The police are not taking kindly to their fabricated claims, especially given their own ongoing legal troubles.

James, this is a major victory, but it doesn't mean the fight is over. Manic Radio is still a toxic environment, and you'll need to decide how best to navigate the remaining months of your contract. However, this ruling gives us leverage if they attempt to retaliate or smear your name further.

Take a moment to celebrate this win. You've been through hell, and you deserve a break.

Let me know if you'd like to meet to discuss the next steps.

Yours,

Theo

P.S. Lyra, congratulations again on the pregnancy. If you need any legal advice regarding maternity rights, just let me know.

Lyra let out a small, relieved sigh, her shoulders relaxing as she read the email. She looked up at James, whose eyes were closed, his breathing slow and steady, but she knew he wasn't asleep. The tension in his posture betrayed him. She nudged him gently.

"James," she said softly, holding up her phone. "Theo's emailed. The charges have been dropped."

James's eyes opened, and he stared at her, his expression unreadable for a moment. Then, slowly, a wave of relief washed over his face. He exhaled deeply, his body sinking into the mattress as though a massive weight had been lifted.

"Dropped?" he repeated, as though he couldn't quite believe it.

Lyra nodded, handing him her phone so he could read the email for himself. As he scanned the message, his lips twitched into a faint smile, the first genuine one she'd seen in weeks.

"I don't... I don't even know what to say," James admitted, his voice hoarse. He set the phone down on the nightstand and turned to Lyra, his eyes glistening. "It's over. At least this part of it. I'm not a criminal. They can't use this against me anymore."

Lyra cupped his face in her hands, her thumbs brushing away the tears that had started to fall. "No, they can't," she said firmly. "And Chloe and Cody are finally facing the consequences of their actions. This is your chance to breathe, James. To start putting the pieces back together. You know, I was thinking... it's your mum's admin day, so she won't be using her broadcasting setup, will she?"

James blinked at her, processing the shift in conversation. "No, she usually keeps Wednesdays for paperwork and planning her shows. Why?"

Lyra's lips curved into a small, mischievous smile. "I was thinking we could record the first episode of Broadcasting Boundaries today. What better time than now, with this weight finally off your shoulders? It'd be a good way to start reclaiming your narrative."

James hesitated, glancing at the ceiling as he considered her suggestion. "You really think people would want to hear me talk about all this? After everything?"

Lyra reached for his hand, lacing her fingers with his. "Absolutely. James, your story isn't just about the chaos—it's about resilience. People need to hear that it's possible to fight back, even when it feels like the odds are stacked against you. And who better to tell that story than you?"

James smiled faintly, her words lifting his spirits. "Alright," he said, sitting up slightly. "Let's do it. But you're co-hosting with me. I'm not doing this alone."

Lyra laughed, leaning in to kiss his cheek. "Of course. It wouldn't be Broadcasting Boundaries without both of us."

An hour later, they were in Sarah's home studio, adjusting microphones and setting up the recording software. The room was a cosy space, filled with shelves of vinyl records and books on broadcasting history, a testament to Sarah's lifelong dedication to radio. Lyra sat at the desk, testing levels, while James paced behind her, still buzzing with nervous energy.

"Relax," Lyra said, glancing over her shoulder at him. "It's just the two of us talking. Think of it as a conversation, not a performance."

Before James could log in to the computer, he had a thought. "Ly, wouldn't your brother have something to say about this, as he's a lawyer, and... well, police are investigating Manic. Something like it being an open investigation and us needing to tread carefully?"

Lyra paused, her fingers hovering over the keyboard as she considered James's point. "Shit, I forgot about that." She frowned, her excitement dimming slightly. "You're right, James. Theo would probably advise us to be cautious about what we say, especially if it could interfere with the investigation or be used against us. Let me text him and check."

She pulled out her phone and quickly typed a message to Theo:

Lyra: *Hi Theo, quick question. James and I were thinking of recording the first episode of our podcast today, talking about workplace culture and resilience. Would discussing our experiences at Manic be a problem with the ongoing investigations? Don't want to mess anything up.*

Theo: *Hey Ly, good question. I'd hang fire at the moment, as the CPS would probably go ape at any public discussion that could be seen as prejudicial to ongoing investigations or future proceedings. You can still talk about toxic workplace culture in general, but steer clear of naming Manic or referencing specific incidents that are under scrutiny. Send me a copy of the script and I'll have one of my paralegals look over it to ensure you're on safe ground. Better to err on the side of caution for now.*

Lyra sighed as she read Theo's response, then turned to James. "He says we should hold off on talking about

Manic specifically. We can still do the podcast, but we need to keep it general—no direct references to anything currently under investigation."

James nodded; his expression thoughtful. "That makes sense. We don't want to accidentally sabotage anything. But we can still talk about broader issues, right? Toxic workplace cultures, resilience, and all that?"

Lyra smiled, nodding. "Exactly. We can frame it as a discussion about what we've learned, rather than pointing fingers. It's still our story, but we'll tell it in a way that doesn't jeopardise anything."

****

The interview room at Steelhouse Lane Police Station was sterile and impersonal, with grey walls and a single table surrounded by four chairs. Chloe Lane sat across from two police officers, her usual confident façade visibly cracking. Next to her was her solicitor from Manic, a 31 year old woman named Hermione Greengrass, one of their criminal law specialists who had been hastily assigned to represent her. Chloe's arms were crossed tightly over her chest, her gaze darting nervously around the room. Despite her usual bravado, the weight of the situation was beginning to sink in.

The police officer, a Detective Constable named DC Lance O'Shea, was looking at Chloe with the same neutral expression he had maintained throughout the interview. His notepad was open in front of him, his pen poised as if ready to strike. Next to him was a Detective Sergeant named DS Tom Jones, ironically not related to the DC or the famed Welsh singer that was the butt of karaoke jokes.

The DS was more imposing, his steely gaze fixed on Chloe as though he could see straight through her attempts at deflection.

The fact it was not an interview for her own case but that as a witness for a case against her own husband, Cody, meant that even though she had brought legal representation, the dynamics of the room were tense.

DC O'Shea leaned forward, breaking the silence. "Mrs Lane, thank you for attending today. As we've discussed, you're here as a witness in the ongoing investigation involving Mr Cody Lane. You are not currently under caution for this interview, but I remind you that any information you provide may be used in further proceedings."

Chloe chuckled, as she knew that she couldn't be compelled to provide any information that might incriminate herself or breach her rights, and she wasn't about to let the police manipulate her into saying anything she didn't want to. She glanced at her solicitor, Hermione Greengrass, who gave her a brief nod of reassurance.

DC O'Shea continued, his tone measured but firm. "Mrs Lane, we've reviewed evidence that includes communications between yourself and Mr Lane regarding items found at your shared residence. Specifically, we're referring to the stolen laptop and the presence of controlled substances. Can you clarify your knowledge of these items?"

"No comment," she said, as she recalled the strategy that had been put in place by Hermione during their pre-interview briefing, to basically say 'no comment' to everything, and then at the end offer a pre-prepared statement to avoid her words being twisted or incriminating herself. The reason for this, Hermione had told her, was so that it would irritate the police and their investigative process, ensuring that they couldn't use her own words against her without a strong rebuttal. Chloe smirked slightly as the detective continued, seemingly unfazed by her silence.

DS Jones interjected, his tone sharper than his colleague's. "Mrs Lane, I'd advise you to consider your position carefully. Refusing to comment may limit your opportunity to provide context or an explanation. We're giving you the chance to clarify your involvement, or lack thereof, in these matters."

Chloe's smirk widened slightly as she maintained her composure. "No comment," she repeated, her voice steady and confident.

Hermione glanced at her briefly, her expression impassive, before addressing the detectives. "My client has the legal right to refrain from answering questions that could incriminate her or lead to further legal complications. She will not be providing commentary at this time."

The DC exchanged a glance with his colleague, clearly unimpressed but bound by protocol. He leaned back in his chair, his pen tapping against the notepad. "Very well. Mrs Lane, we have reason to believe that Mr Lane's possession of the stolen laptop and the controlled substances was not incidental. Evidence suggests a level of coordination between the two of you. Do you wish to respond to that?"

Chloe maintained her mask of indifference, her mind racing as she considered the implications of their questions. After a brief pause, she uttered the same two words. "No comment."

DC O'Shea sighed audibly, clearly frustrated but careful to maintain his professional demeanour. He flipped through his notes, his gaze lingering on a particular page before speaking again.

"Mrs Lane," he began, his tone neutral but pointed, "it's worth noting that your continued refusal to cooperate may be seen as an unwillingness to clarify your role in these matters. While you're entitled to remain silent, the evidence we've gathered so far paints a concerning picture of your involvement."

Chloe remained silent, her smirk faltering slightly. She could feel Hermione's calm presence beside her, a steady anchor amidst the rising tension in the room.

"Fine," DC O'Shea said, closing his notebook with an audible snap. "If that's the approach you're taking, we'll proceed with the evidence we have. We'll conclude this interview and include your responses, or lack thereof, in our report. Any further contact will be through your legal representative."

Hermione nodded curtly. "We appreciate your time, Detectives. As you know, my client has exercised her rights within the bounds of the law. Now, would you like my client's pre-prepared statement regarding her husband's activities, considering that she wasn't given a choice to be a witness in-"

"With all due respect, Ms Greengrass," DS Tom Jones interrupted, his tone clipped, "we're fully aware of the rights afforded to Mrs Lane. If your client wishes to provide a statement, we'll accept it. However, given her stance throughout this interview, we'll treat it with the scrutiny it deserves."

Chloe watched as Hermione chuckled, knowing that the statement would throw Cody under the bus, and that she'd come out looking cooperative, at least to some extent. Hermione reached into her bag and pulled out a neatly typed statement, smiling. Chloe knew that, like herself, Hermione was an ambitious woman who would throw anyone under the bus if it meant advancing her career. Chloe had no illusions about Hermione's motivations but appreciated her ruthlessness—it was a trait they shared.

"My client's statement reads as follows," Hermione began, her tone smooth and calculated as she unfolded the paper and glanced at Chloe, who gave a subtle nod. She cleared her throat before continuing.

"I, Chloe Lane, wish to clarify my position regarding the ongoing investigation involving my husband, Cody Lane. While I have no direct involvement in the alleged activities under scrutiny, I was aware that certain items in our shared residence were not originally ours. Cody informed me that the laptop in question was borrowed from a colleague, though I later became suspicious of its legitimacy. Regarding the controlled substances found at our property, I categorically deny any knowledge of their presence or origin. I am prepared to fully cooperate with the authorities in any reasonable capacity that does not incriminate myself or violate my legal rights."

Hermione folded the statement neatly, handing it over to DC O'Shea. "As you can see, my client has addressed the concerns raised and maintains her position of non-involvement. This should satisfy your need for clarification."

DS Jones scrutinised the statement briefly before nodding curtly. "Thank you, Ms Greengrass. This will be added to our case file. Mrs Lane, you're free to go, but we may need to contact you again as the investigation progresses."

Chloe rose from her seat with a practiced grace, her confidence returning as she realised she had, for now, escaped unscathed. Hermione gathered her documents, her expression unreadable as she prepared to leave. As they exited the station, Chloe glanced at her solicitor.

"Think they bought it?" she asked, her tone laced with a mix of arrogance and curiosity.

Hermione smirked, adjusting the strap of her designer handbag. "They'll treat it with scepticism, but it'll muddy the waters enough to keep you out of immediate trouble. Cody, on the other hand? Well, let's just say you've positioned yourself nicely to come out ahead when the dust settles."

****

CHAPTER 13 – Deffo A Frat Party
Monday 19th May 2025

"Did you read Nott's Facebook post?" Pete heard one of the few Manic Vibes hosts who were still roaming the studios in the One Snow Hill hub. It was half past 12, and Pete was getting ready for his drivetime show on Manic Goldies. "That slut's up the duff like the rest of the whores here."

Pete knew that Lyra was no longer a Manic employee, but the toxic environment persisted even after her departure. The fact that she was dating his son meant that Pete was even more protective of Lyra, especially as she had been one of the few sane people that worked at Manic during her time at the company.

What he heard next enraged him even further. Another voice chimed in, dripping with derision. "Yeah, waste of a pussy. The frigid bitch wouldn't put out for anyone, yet she soils herself with the hub cum dump and gets preggers by him. She should have let a real man fuck her."

"Do you think she let the old fart fuck her too? Maybe Pete's been playing daddy in more ways than one."

Pete froze, his hand gripping the edge of the desk so tightly his knuckles turned white. He felt the heat rise in his face, his anger bubbling to the surface. It wasn't just the crude, disgusting language they were using—it was the casual way they demeaned and disrespected Lyra, his son James, and himself. The toxic culture at Manic had been festering for years, but this crossed a line he couldn't ignore.

The sound of disgusted laughter followed, echoing down the corridor. "Eww, Lucas, Pete and Nott? That's like something out of a bad porno. He'd probably have a heart attack before he even got his trousers off."

Pete knew that Lucas North, one of the trainee presenters Manic had hurriedly hired as several of their Vibes, Urban and Dance presenters had, in the past few weeks, been arrested and either put on remand or subject to strict bail conditions, was one of the newest batch of manipulative, self-serving personalities that Manic seemed to attract like flies to honey. It was an open secret that Lucas had no filter and thrived on shock value, which clearly extended beyond his on-air antics.

The irony that HR hadn't suspended anyone for their part in the toxic workplace culture but had instead doubled down on enabling it was not lost on Pete. The further irony in that some of the Goldies presenters who had been employed only a month and half earlier for the launch of the local Goldies Breakfast and Drive had resigned in protest of the toxic culture within Manic and the unethical decisions being made at the executive level, meaning that he along with the few remaining presenters were having to train the new batch of recruits while simultaneously dealing with the fallout from the toxic environment was enough to make Pete want to walk out the door himself. But he stayed—not for Manic, but for his listeners and for the hope that he could help create a space that still valued decency and professionalism, even if only on his own show.

Looking over to one of the former Greatest Hits Radio regional producers who had moved to Manic when they had been made redundant the previous October, Bauer having had decided to network the last remaining local shows on their Classic Hits stations, he could see the disgust on their face, the producer muttering under their breath, "This place is a cesspit." The producer, Alice Graham, was someone Pete respected immensely. She was a consummate professional, a rarity in the chaos of Manic, and Pete often relied on her to keep things running smoothly amidst the turmoil.

"Anyway," Lucas then said, and Pete knew that the conversation that the younger presenters were having wasn't going to get any better. "I banged that new slut that's the new cum dump. She's looser than any whore I've paid for. Me, Harry and Yousef fucked her at the same time and made the bitch squirt. What's with the whole hub cum dump thing anyway, Oscar?"

"Oh, it's just whoever's not in favour amongst us. Nott's boyfriend was the last hub cum dump, and we would fuck him any way we wanted, as he had to let us, or we'd make his life hell," Oscar said with a laugh, his voice dripping with malice. Pete knew that Oscar was one of the Manic Urban presenters who had joined back in January when Manic had purchased Drill FM, a national UK Drill, Urban and Grime station. Pete had heard from James that it wasn't only the Midlands hub that had a "cum dump", but all of the hubs, Exeter, London Olympic Park, Speke, Manchester, Huddersfield and Dundee all had their own version of this degrading practice.

At the Birmingham hub, Pete had heard rumours that one of the HR officers, Isla Granger, had now taken that position and even willingly allowing herself to be used by the toxic staff as a way to climb the ranks or gain favour in the hierarchy. Pete had thought such practices belonged in dystopian novels, not workplaces, and yet here they were, entrenched in the culture of Manic Radio.

The fact that, due to the staff shortages, the Vibes presenters had moved from their floor and the "B" studios to the same floor as Goldies, the "A" floor, whereas the Metal, Rock and Urban presenters, along with HR and technical, were still on the "C" floor of One Snow Hill's three Manic floors, level 3 as the official floorplan that the building management had issued called it, meant that Pete was forced to listen to these vile conversations more often than he cared to. The toxic environment was no longer something he could avoid by staying in his own corner of the building; it had seeped into every part of the hub.

On several occasions over the past week, Pete had considered moving down to the Rock floor, however the Rock and Metal presenters had a distinct lack of personal hygiene, and so the air down there often smelled like a mixture of sweat and stale beer. For someone like Pete, who prided himself on maintaining a clean and professional workspace, it wasn't much of an upgrade. That and they had finally added vinyl players Pete's Goldies studio as his Saturday show, the Football Phone-in for the West Midlands was one where he played actual 7 inch singles, 10 inch LPs and 12 inch LPs for some of his show's music, with it being a show where music between 1960 and 1999 was the focus.

"It's like The Menu in here," Pete muttered, referring to the 2022 film where the elite dined on twisted experiences designed by a sadistic chef, oblivious to the cruelty of their actions. The fact that, in the film, the chef ended up killing himself as well as his guests served as a grim metaphor for the self-destructive cycle Pete saw at Manic. The rot in the company culture didn't just harm the victims—it consumed everyone, including the perpetrators.

"I bet you wished you could go all On The Line with the Vibes lot," Tim Young, one of the former East Midlands Vibes hosts who moved to Manic Goldies East Midlands at the same time Pete had been swapped from Midlands Manic to Manic Goldies West Midlands to host Drivetime and, like Pete, had a reputation for professionalism, said, walking into the Goldies breakroom.

Pete chuckled despite himself, appreciating Tim's dark humour. On the Line, a 2022 Mel Gibson hostage film set in a radio station, where it had turned out to be a prank set up by Gibson's character's own team, had become a sort of running joke among older radio presenters as a fantasy of handling toxic workplace situations. Pete's humourless laugh betrayed the seriousness of his thoughts.

"If only, mate," Pete muttered. "Though, in this lot's case, it'd take more than a hostage situation to get them to see reason."

Tim grabbed a mug and poured himself a coffee, his expression mirroring Pete's frustration. "Honestly, I don't know how you stick it out here. I've been considering jumping ship. Got a mate at Boom Radio who says they're changing their line-up, even though I'll miss serving the East Midlands.

Pete knew that Tim, as someone who had lived in the East Midlands and lived and breathed all things Derby and Nottingham, would struggle with the idea of leaving his beloved East Midlands region behind. Pete could see the conflict in Tim's eyes, the way his passion for local radio clashed with the toxic reality of Manic.

"Boom Radio, eh?" Pete said, swirling his coffee. "I've heard good things about them. Proper radio for grown-ups, none of this TikTok influencer nonsense."

Tim nodded, his expression softening slightly. "Yeah, they actually value experience and professionalism. Hits also offered me a slot with Jo Russell and Sparky Colerangle on Hits East Midlands. They're still based out of City Link in Nottingham, so it'd be local for me. The only downside is their obsession with networking everything except breakfast. But honestly, even that seems better than the circus here."

Pete raised an eyebrow, considering Tim's options. "Hits might be a safer bet if you're looking for stability. They're not perfect, but at least they've got some semblance of professionalism. Boom's more niche, but if you're after freedom to play what you want and connect with listeners, they're hard to beat."

Tim sipped his coffee thoughtfully. "Yeah, I'm leaning towards Boom. Feels like the kind of place where I could actually enjoy radio again, you know?"

Pete smiled faintly. "I get that. At this point, I'm staying here because of the listeners. The older crowd who've stuck with me through all this madness—they deserve better than what Manic's become. It's funny how we've both worked for Woody Bones back in the 00s, you on Derby's and Nottingham's stations, and me on Dudley and then the Midlands stations he owned, and we've had our listeners grow up listening to our shows. That loyalty keeps me going, even when everything else is falling apart."

Tim nodded, a glimmer of nostalgia in his eyes. "Yeah, the listeners are what it's all about. I remember doing roadshows back in the day and seeing familiar faces at every stop. People who'd grown up listening to us, introducing their kids to our shows. That connection—it's rare, and it's why I haven't walked away yet. But even loyalty has its limits."

Pete sighed, glancing at the clock. It was 1 in the afternoon, and there was 3 hours until his show. "You know, I bumped into John Dalziel after he and Roisin finished their Hits West Midlands breakfast on Friday, and they were saying that Bauer was planning on expanding Hits with some more Rayo exclusive spinoffs to join Hits Pride and Hits Chilled."

The two knew that Rayo was Bauer's digital platform, which, like Manic Prime, offered free stations as well as subscription based ones. Both platforms had become central to their respective networks' strategies, allowing them to cater to niche audiences while maintaining the broader appeal of their flagship stations.

Tim raised an eyebrow, intrigued. "Rayo exclusive spinoffs? Like what? Hits Garage? Hits Country? They're already on Rayo as part of Kiss and Absolute, aren't they?"

"Yeah, he didn't say what stations were coming to Rayo, as its commercially sensitive information. But knowing Bauer, they'll probably lean into whatever trends are hot right now—maybe Hits Throwback for those nostalgic for the late '90s and early 2000s or Hits Viral for all the TikTok chart-toppers. Either way, it's smart. They're cornering every demographic without the chaos we deal with here. To be honest, apart from my footie phone in on a Saturday, and my DJ Strangelove community shows I do at home, feel like that Chef Slowik character in The Menu. I'm losing the love of the craft, mate. Every day feels like we're just serving up reheated leftovers, pandering to a crowd that doesn't even care about the quality. We're caught in this cycle of appeasing the suits in Speke while sacrificing what radio is supposed to be—authentic, personal, and meaningful."

Tim nodded, his brow furrowed. "You're not wrong. It's become about metrics, likes, and keeping up appearances rather than creating something people can genuinely connect with. It's no wonder you're feeling burned out. How's the DJ Strangelove stuff going, by the way? That still keeping the fire alive?"

Pete's expression softened at the mention of his side project. "Yeah, it's a lifeline, to be honest. Playing what I want, interacting with real communities—it reminds me of why I got into this business in the first place. No corporate nonsense, just pure radio. Even the name reminds me of the days when it was all about personality and connection, not algorithms and clickbait."

Tim smiled. "Sounds like a dream compared to this madhouse. Maybe that's where the future of radio lies—

independent, community-driven stuff. The big networks have lost the plot, chasing younger audiences who are already glued to streaming and social media. They're forgetting the people who actually listen to radio."

"Exactly," Pete said, his voice tinged with frustration. "The suits think throwing money at influencers and viral gimmicks will keep radio relevant, but they're alienating the core audience. The older generations, the people who grew up with us—they're loyal, but they won't stick around forever if we keep treating them like an afterthought. It's Ellen's last week, isn't it?"

Tim nodded, his expression sombre. "Yeah, Ellen's hanging up her headphones this Friday. She's moving to Dragon Radio to do a 2pm-4pm show. Funnily enough she's presenting it from home as to drive to Cardiff would be a 3 hour drive for her each way. She told me she's looking forward to working with a station that values experience and professionalism. Ellen's a legend, Pete. The industry's losing one of the good ones."

Pete sighed, running a hand through his greying hair. "Ellen's been a staple for so many years. She's one of those rare presenters who just gets it—who knows how to connect with listeners on a personal level. Manic's loss, Dragon's gain. Honestly, I can't blame her for jumping ship. She's been dealing with this toxic circus for far too long."

Tim chuckled bitterly. "She said something similar when I spoke to her last week. Called it 'escaping the asylum.' It's funny, isn't it? The people who've actually built this industry are the ones being pushed out, while the clowns and the sycophants get rewarded."

Suddenly a ruckus from down the hall came into the Goldies break room when Oscar, Lucas and their gang of technicians, producers and other support staff who had invaded over the past week burst in, their voices loud and obnoxious as they laughed and jeered about some crude joke that had clearly crossed the line. Pete could see that his own daughter, Chole, who had temporarily taken over the Manic Vibes West Midlands Drive show as Kylie Morgan had been arrested again, this time instead of drugs and theft, she had been arrested for coercive behaviour and sexual assault against James. Chloe had joined in their laughter, clearly thriving on the chaos and attention. Pete's stomach turned as he watched his daughter indulge in the same toxic behaviour that had driven so many others out of the industry.

He saw Isla Granger walk in, dressed in what could be described as the most humiliating outfit Pete had ever seen in a professional setting. Isla, the HR officer supposedly tasked with maintaining workplace professionalism, strutted in wearing a neon crop top emblazoned with "Hub Queen" and a pair of shorts that left little to the imagination. Coupled with the high heeled boots that screamed prostitute and the sort of makeup that belonged on a night out rather than in an office, it was a stark reminder of just how far Manic had fallen. She walked over to Lucas, who had sat down and unzipped his shorts, his erection sticking up like a red rag to a bull. Pete turned away in disgust, his stomach churning. The scene in front of him was not only unprofessional but utterly dehumanising. This wasn't just a toxic workplace—it was a breeding ground for exploitation, degradation, and unchecked power. He felt a surge of anger that threatened to boil over, but he forced himself to keep calm.

The fact Isla was a HR officer, and she was engaging in such disgraceful behaviour sent Pete's anger skyrocketing. She was meant to protect employees and uphold standards, not degrade herself and the workplace further. Pete clenched his fists and took a deep breath, steadying himself as he debated whether to step in or let the scene implode on its own.

"Really?" Alice piped up, and Pete noticed that she had put her notes for Tim and Ellen's East Midlands drive show down on the table that was next to the sofa she was sat on, the Goldies breakroom more of a kitchen and living room than a standard office lounge. Her voice cut through the cacophony like a whip. "Is this what we've come to? Turning the workplace into some cheap stag do? And you, Isla, HR of all people—aren't you supposed to be setting an example instead of joining in this degrading circus?"

The room went silent for a moment, the stunned expression on the younger presenters' faces almost comical. Isla paused mid-strut, her exaggerated confidence faltering as she registered the disgust in Alice's tone. Lucas zipped up his shorts hurriedly, his bravado replaced by an awkward, sheepish look.

"What's your problem, Alice?" Lucas sneered, trying to regain control of the situation. "Can't handle a bit of fun? Maybe if you loosened up, you wouldn't be stuck in Goldies babysitting the oldies."

Alice's gaze was icy as she rose from her seat. "Fun? This isn't fun, Lucas. It's workplace harassment disguised as banter, and it's poisoning the entire culture here. You think this makes you look cool? All it does is show how little respect you have for anyone—including yourselves."

The tension in the room was palpable as Lucas opened his mouth to respond, but Pete cut him off. "She's right," Pete said, his voice firm and steady. "This place has turned into a joke, and it's because of people like you. You treat this hub like a frat house, and you think you're untouchable. But let me tell you something—your so-called 'fun' is driving good people away, ruining lives, and dragging Manic's reputation even further into the mud."

Chloe, who had been leaning against the counter with a smug grin, rolled her eyes. "Oh, come on, Dad. Don't be so dramatic. It's just a laugh. Anyway, I noticed your Dido LP laying in your studio. It'd be a pity if something... happened to it."

The chuckles from the Vibes crew about a Dido LP, which Pete had brought back in 2010 when Dudley FM had been absorbed, like the rest of the Bones network, by Breeze Media. Even though the Bones network had moved to the RCS suite in 2005, starting with Selector and NexGen, with GSelector being introduced in 2006, and Zetta in the early 2010s at the Bones and then later Breeze Media stations to replace the Selector and NexGen systems, Pete had always kept a small collection of vinyl in Studio A1, the Manic Goldies West Midlands studio, where Alf Tomlinson and Lisa Jenkins did their Goldies Breakfast for the same area, and he did his Drive show, and there was an understanding between the trio of Goldies presenters that the records there were for the two shows that the records could be used, as Alf also presented "Alf's Sunday Night Future Goldies", a show which aired tracks from the late 1990s and early 2000s which would be classed in a few years as part of the classic hit repertoire, and he occasionally included vinyl tracks in his set to add authenticity to the sound.

Pete was particularly attached to that specific Dido LP as the sleeve of it had been personally signed by Dido herself, along with Eminem, when they had performed in London in 2000, the duo having done a Stan performance at the latter's concert during his UK tour. There were other signed LP sleeves that he had in his possession, both white label ones where they had been supplied to Dudley FM as part of the usual promotional materials and commercial releases he had bought over the years, many of them featuring autographs from artists he had met during his long career in radio. The one that was usually next to it on the shelf that he had in his studio, which reminded him of his Dudley FM days even more, was that of Wolverhampton's Beverley Knight's Prodigal Sista, also signed by her in 1998 when the station had hosted her for an exclusive live session. These records were more than just vinyl—they were cherished memories, symbols of a time when radio was about personal connection and real passion for music.

Pete knew that only Manic and Hits Radio had hosts that, on one of their major brands, played vinyl records on air, him and Alf for Manic Goldies, and Stephanie Hirst on Hits Radio, who like Pete had gone through the ranks, with Pete starting at Dudley FM as a mascot at 13, his role being that of someone who dressed up in a Dudley Bug costume and appeared at local events before becoming a tea boy at 16, and then a runner at 18, before moving to presenting at 21, and Stephanie, who had started as a helper at Radio Aire before climbing the ladder. Pete was proud of the authenticity he brought to his show with the vinyl. He wasn't about to let anyone disrespect his collection, least of all his own daughter.

Pete took a step closer to Chloe, his tone measured but firm. "That Dido LP means a lot more to me than you'll ever understand, Chloe. It represents a time when radio was about connection, passion, and respect for the craft—things this place has completely lost sight of. You can laugh, you can joke, but you won't touch that record. Ever. You've already made fake accusations against your brother, raped him, assaulted him and stole from him, you've done enough damage to this family and to people I care about. You won't cross that line, Chloe. Not here, not now, not ever."

Chloe's smirk faltered for a brief moment, but she quickly recovered, crossing her arms defensively. "Oh, please, Dad. You're acting like I burned the Mona Lisa. It's just an old record."

"It's not just an old record," Pete snapped, his voice rising. "It's part of my history, my integrity, and my love for this industry—something you wouldn't understand because you're too busy tearing people down and playing games. You've chosen this toxic path, Chloe, but I won't let you drag me or anyone else down with you."

The room fell silent as Pete's words hung in the air. Even Lucas and Oscar, who had been chuckling moments earlier, looked uneasy. Alice gave Pete a small, approving nod, her respect for him growing in the face of his unwavering stance.

"Alright, old man, next you'll be doing a William Foster and pulling a gun on a McDonalds worker when you get sacked," Isla said with a snicker, referring to the infamous character from *Falling Down*. Her tone was dripping with mockery, but her attempt at humour landed flat in the tense atmosphere of the room.

Pete turned to Isla, his expression a mixture of exasperation and disgust. "Isla, you're meant to uphold workplace standards, not degrade them further with your antics and cheap jokes. Comparing me to a violent man in a movie because I care about professionalism and respect? That's not clever; it's pathetic."

Isla opened her mouth to retort but seemed to think better of it, retreating slightly as Pete's words struck home.

Tim leaned against the counter, arms crossed, smirking slightly as he observed the scene. "Looks like you lot might finally have met someone who's not afraid to call out your nonsense."

Lucas glared at Tim but didn't respond. The bravado that had filled the room earlier had all but evaporated, leaving an awkward silence in its wake. Pete used the moment to take a step back and regain his composure, breathing deeply to steady himself.

"Listen," Pete began, his voice calm but resolute, "this is more than just a toxic workplace. It's a reflection of everything wrong with what this industry has become—an obsession with image and metrics over content and integrity. If Manic wants to keep spiralling into chaos, that's on them, but I refuse to let this hub become a cesspit on my watch."

****

CHAPTER 14 - Mixing OFCOM, Meetings & Beats
Monday 26th May 2025

James was sitting on the edge of his bed, headphones plugged into his phone as he tuned into Capital Midlands' mid-morning show. He was half-listening, his thoughts drifting, when a notification lit up his screen—a tweet that stopped him cold.

@Ofcom: *An investigation has been launched by Ofcom into allegations of widespread workplace misconduct, harassment, and regulatory breaches at Manic Radio Group. Our primary concern is ensuring compliance with broadcasting standards and the safeguarding of all employees. Further updates will follow.*

James stared at the tweet, his mind racing. The dam had finally broken. After months of chaos, arrests, and whispered rumours, Ofcom had stepped in. It wasn't a question of if this would impact Manic—it was a question of how much and how soon.

Sighing as he looked at the notification on his phone, he knew that he was due to leave for another Narcotics Anonymous meeting in an hour, he looked at the parcel that had arrived the previous day from Amazon that his dad had brought, a new MacBook Pro, which, unlike the one of his that was currently being held in evidence by West Midlands Police as part of their investigation into Chloe and Cody, was pristine, untouched by the chaos that had consumed his life. The MacBook was a fresh start—a tool for rebuilding, for reclaiming control over his narrative, for launching the projects he and Lyra had been discussing.

He unwrapped the parcel and set up the device, his fingers hesitant as he typed in his name and email address during the setup process. His thoughts returned to the Ofcom investigation. He'd been through the wringer at Manic, seen its darkest corners, and experienced its toxic culture firsthand. Part of him felt vindicated that the regulator was finally stepping in, but another part was anxious. He couldn't shake the feeling that this was just the beginning of a storm that could sweep through everyone connected to Manic—including him.

James knew that his mixes that he had made of tracks synced with both his iCloud and OneDrive, as which meant that most of his work wasn't lost despite the chaos surrounding Manic and his personal life. He knew, however, that he had to reinstall some of the apps that had been central to his work—Ableton Live for producing mixes, Serato DJ Pro for live sets, and Audacity for quick edits.

As he waited for the downloads to complete, his phone buzzed with a message from Lyra, who had gone to her native Crewe for the day to see her parents, and then was going to drop into Wolverhampton to see Theodore, Ellie, his wife, and Clarice, her niece. The fact that she was spending the time with her family pleased James, as, despite the chaos in their lives at the moment, doing something normal was a small but important step in reclaiming a sense of stability. He smiled faintly as he opened her message.

Lyra: *Hey, just letting you know I've made it to my parents' house. Mum's already trying to feed me the entire contents of the fridge. Guess who I had a phone call from as I was pulling into my parent's street?*

James smiled, typing a quick reply as he leaned back against the headboard.

James: *My money's on either OFCOM or Manic.*

Lyra's response was almost instant.

Lyra: *Yep, Manic. They're offering a job again. Desperate or what?*

James let out a short, disbelieving laugh, shaking his head. It was almost comical how predictable Manic had become in their desperation. Offering Lyra her job back, after everything she'd endured, was not only insulting but a glaring sign of just how dire the situation must have been inside One Snow Hill.

James: *What did you say?*

Lyra: *I told them where to stick it, obviously. Then they revealed it was a Network show on Goldies... presenting remotely.*

James raised an eyebrow at her response. A Network show on Goldies? He knew how much Lyra had loved live radio, and Goldies was one of the last bastions of classic broadcasting. The offer was tempting on paper—far removed from the chaos of Manic's "hub culture" and with the potential for creative freedom. But he also knew that any connection to Manic, no matter how remote, carried risks.

James: *Remote or not, sounds like they're trying to buy your silence. You okay?*

Lyra: *I'm fine. Just pissed off they think I'd jump back in after everything. They even threw in the Baby Bonus as a sweetener, as if THAT would tempt me.* 😒

James rolled his eyes. The infamous "Baby Bonus" scheme had become a sick joke within Manic. Offering financial incentives to new parents in exchange for "family-friendly" PR was just another way the company tried to gloss over its failings.

James: *Classic Manic. 'Forget the trauma, here's some cash and a microphone.' You're better than them, Ly. Always have been.*

Lyra: *Thanks, love. How's your day going?*

James glanced around the room at his newly set-up MacBook, the half-empty coffee mug on his bedside table, and the faint buzz of Serato's installation progress.

James: *Just about to head to a meeting. To be honest, I think that its helping me, as I'm not alone, that I'm getting clean and reclaiming control over my life. But it's slow, Ly. Some days I feel like I'm making progress, and others... well, you know how it is."*

Lyra: *You're doing brilliantly, James. Don't forget that. Recovery isn't linear. Just keep going. I'm so proud of you.* 🖤

James smiled at the message, her words giving him a small boost of confidence. He replied quickly before closing the conversation.

James: *Thanks, Ly. Call me later? I miss your voice already.* 🖤

Lyra: *Always. Speak soon. xx*

Setting his phone aside, James turned his attention back to the MacBook, the familiar Serato DJ Pro interface finally loading onto the screen. He plugged in his headphones and opened a recent mix he'd been working on, tweaking transitions and adjusting beats. The act of mixing music was therapeutic—a moment of control in an otherwise chaotic life.

****

The community centre in Brierley Hill was quiet when James arrived for his Narcotics Anonymous meeting. The late afternoon sun cast a warm glow over the modest brick building, a stark contrast to the turmoil inside his mind. As he stepped inside, the familiar scent of coffee and the murmur of low conversation greeted him. The room was filled with a mix of faces—some familiar, others new—all here for the same reason: to share their struggles and seek solace in solidarity.

James knew that he had been 'on the wagon' as some people would describe it, since the end of the previous month, when Chloe had drugged him, the same day he had tried to get back on his media studies course at Wolverhampton but had been told that he was not welcome due to Manic putting in a bad word, despite him, when he had attended, being on course for a 2:1, as well as attending every session and submitting all assignments on time. The irony of being driven to drugs by the chaos of his own workplace wasn't lost on James, and neither was the bitter truth that his life was still tangled in the fallout.

The meeting began with the usual introductions. Each attendee took a turn, sharing their name and their reason for being there. James listened attentively, finding a strange sense of comfort in the shared experiences. When his turn came, he stood, his voice steady but low.

"Hi, I'm James," he began, the room offering a collective "Hi, James" in response. "I've been clean for a month. I... well, technically I'm still employed by them, even though I've been suspended by Manic Radio, and I used to use cocaine."

James paused, taking a deep breath. He could feel the weight of the room's attention, but it wasn't judgmental—it was supportive, understanding.

"It all started three days into working for Manic, back at the end of October. My sister's then boyfriend, now husband, got me hooked on it during a night at home, when she brought him over and I brought my then girlfriend over. A couple of days later, I was taking 5 to 6 lines a night just to keep up with the chaos of working at Manic. It felt like everyone was doing it, and if you weren't, you'd fall behind. I became... I don't know, dependent, I guess. It felt like the only way to survive there."

James glanced around the room, his hands fidgeting nervously. The supportive nods from others encouraged him to continue.

"Then on New Years Eve, my then girlfriend and I were doing a live show on Manic, and I think that she sabotaged me, by giving me the wrong scripts and prompts, and... well, my parents kicked me out. Over the next four months I was degraded, sexually abused, even raped, and forced to take cocaine as if it were water. I thought I was keeping it together, but I wasn't. And then, mid-April, while I was pre-recording a show for Manic Urban, I... I was used again, but instead of being ignored by people, someone actually stood up for me. That moment, it was like a switch flipped. Lyra, my dad's close friend and colleague, walked in and saw everything. She didn't turn away. She didn't pretend not to notice. She stood up to the person who was... exploiting me and told me I didn't have to live like that anymore."

James took another deep breath, his voice growing steadier. "It wasn't immediate. I didn't suddenly decide to quit everything the next day. But that moment gave me hope. Lyra's been my anchor ever since. She's helped me see that I can rebuild my life, that I don't have to be the person I became at Manic. I've been clean since the end of April, and honestly, it's the hardest thing I've ever done. Some days, I feel like I'm just barely holding on, but I'm still here."

James paused, looking at the faces around the room. The understanding in their eyes gave him strength to finish.

"I'm here because I don't want to go back to that place—not just the drugs, but the person I was when I used them. I want to be better."

The room remained silent for a moment after James finished speaking. The silence wasn't uncomfortable—it was reflective, understanding. Then, as if on cue, a round of soft applause rippled through the group, not as a celebration, but as a show of support.

The meeting continued, and James found himself relaxing into the shared rhythm of storytelling, advice, and camaraderie. The group leader, a woman named Sandra with a calm voice and years of sobriety under her belt, shared words of encouragement after each story, weaving a thread of hope through the room.

It was then a latecomer walked in to the room, and James had to do a double take as he recognised as one of his torturers who had been an administration person at Manic's Dudley, then Birmingham's, hub, Kyle Lawrence, a 24 year old who James remembered had had a habit of coercing junior staff into compromising situations under the guise of camaraderie. Seeing Kyle brought a rush of emotions—anger, fear, and a flicker of disbelief. James shifted uncomfortably in his seat, his heart pounding as Kyle took a seat near the back, avoiding eye contact with anyone in the room.

The group leader, Sandra, paused briefly to acknowledge the new arrival. "Welcome," she said warmly, before continuing with the session. Kyle nodded, his expression guarded, and James couldn't help but notice the subtle signs of someone who wasn't entirely comfortable in their own skin.

As the session wrapped up, Sandra invited anyone who needed to speak privately to stay behind. James stayed seated, unsure if he was ready to face Kyle. Part of him wanted to leave immediately, but another part—the stronger part—wanted answers. Why was Kyle here? Was this an attempt to seek redemption, or was it something else?

As the room emptied, Kyle approached James with one of those grins that James recognised all too well—a grin that masked manipulation and malice.

"Reevesy, I've got a message from Kylie for you," Kyle said, a grin on his face as smug as ever. James felt his stomach churn. Kylie Morgan, his former girlfriend turned tormentor, was the last person he wanted to hear about, let alone from Kyle, one of her loyal lackeys. The group leader, Sandra, hovered nearby, subtly observing the interaction.

James crossed his arms, his voice steady but cold. "Whatever Kylie has to say, I don't want to hear it."

Kyle smirked, leaning in slightly as if to whisper, but his voice was loud enough to carry. "She just wanted me to remind you that no matter how far you run, you'll always be tied to her. You might think you're escaping, but trust me, Reevesy, she's always a step ahead. Pay her £50,000 or she'll abort your baby."

James felt the blood drain from his face, his pulse pounding in his ears. He clenched his fists, forcing himself to stay seated as the urge to lash out bubbled just beneath the surface. Sandra, sensing the tension, stepped closer, her calm presence a quiet reminder to stay grounded.

"You've got some nerve, Kyle," James said, his voice low and measured despite the fury threatening to erupt. "Kylie's got nothing over me anymore. Whatever game she's playing, I'm not a part of it. Anyway, its over 24 weeks, so she couldn't legally terminate even if she wanted to. Anyway, my lawyer told me that if she tried to contact me, even though she's under investigation by the police, she'd be breaching the terms of her bail conditions. So, if you're delivering her threats, Kyle, you're putting yourself in the firing line, too."

Kyle's grin faltered for a moment, replaced by a flicker of unease. He straightened up, his bravado slipping as he realised James wasn't the same broken man he'd tormented at Manic. Sandra stepped closer, her calm but firm voice cutting through the tension.

"This is a safe space," she said evenly, looking at Kyle. "We're here to support each other, not to bring threats or intimidation. If you have something constructive to say, you're welcome to stay. If not, I suggest you leave."

Kyle hesitated, his gaze darting between Sandra and James. After a tense moment, he raised his hands in mock surrender, backing away. "Fine, I'm leaving. But don't think this is over, Reevesy. Kylie doesn't forget."

With that, he turned and walked out of the room, leaving James sitting in a swirl of emotions. Sandra placed a reassuring hand on his shoulder, her steady presence a small comfort in the storm.

"You handled that well," she said softly. "If he causes any more trouble, let us know. We can make sure this space remains safe for everyone."

James nodded, his jaw tight as he tried to process what had just happened. "Thanks, Sandra. I didn't expect... him."

Sandra gave him a gentle smile. "Unfortunately, people like that often carry their baggage into places meant for healing. But you're stronger than you realise, James. Don't let him derail your progress."

James took a deep breath, nodding again as he stood to leave. "I won't. Thanks again."

****

James knew that he was going to be on a sticky wicket, as he was technically still under suspension by Manic, and therefore he shouldn't be accessing his work user area while on his personal devices, but as he had access via some shortcuts that he'd saved in his OneDrive on the MacBook which had synced to his new MacBook Pro, he couldn't resist the temptation to log in and see if there were any updates or files he might need for his ongoing projects. It wasn't about defying Manic's suspension; it was about trying to regain some semblance of control over his career and life amidst the chaos.

That, and some of the mixes he had made of popular songs, such as Tom Grennan's Tom Grennan's Remind Me and Rita Ora's Praising You, were projects he had spent hours perfecting, and they were sitting there, unfinished, on his Manic account. It was more than just music to James—it was therapy, a way to channel his creativity and find solace amidst the turmoil. Logging in felt like reclaiming a small piece of himself, even if it came with a risk.

Clicking on the one track he had been working on, a mashup of Sunchyme by Dario G and links that Hits Radio's Stephanie Hirst had done on her Belters show, a satirical project where he had mixed Stephanie's playful banter seamlessly with the uplifting beats of Sunchyme, James felt a sense of satisfaction as he pressed play. It wasn't a professional commission, or something destined for air—it was just something for him, a reminder of the joy he used to find in creating. The mix was unfinished, but it was raw, fun, and authentic, something that had been sorely missing in his life since the chaos of Manic had taken over.

One of his other mixes, a remix of Fleur East's Favourite Thing, a track that had only reached 80 in the UK Charts, mashed up with Roman Kemp's Capital Breakfast links, he had to chuckle to how, if the Bauer and Global executives ever heard it, they'd likely either applaud his creativity or send a strongly worded cease-and-desist. But to James, these projects were reminders of a time when his passion for radio and music was uncomplicated—before contracts, legal battles, and betrayals had turned it all into a minefield. He saved the updated mixes to his personal drive, careful not to leave any traces on the work systems.

Loading up his emails, he chuckled at how, in the past 24 hours, there were several all-staff emails sent to the various distribution lists that circulated around Manic. Each subject line seemed more absurd than the last:

"Mandatory TikTok Strategy Meeting – Attendance Required"

"Workplace Culture Workshops: Let's Build A Better Manic"

"Workplace Benefits - What You Are Entitled To"

James snorted, shaking his head at the irony. "Building a better Manic?" he muttered to himself. "That ship sailed the moment they let the frat boys take over." Scanning the emails, he noticed that there were some that were forwarded to him and not from the original distribution lists. Selecting all of the emails on the internal Outlook system that were in his inbox, he decided to forward them to his personal email address, so he could then see which ones would be best to forward to Theodore for the ongoing legal proceedings. James knew that forwarding internal emails could be considered a breach of Manic's policies, but the potential evidence they contained regarding the company's toxic culture, double standards, and mismanagement was too important to ignore. If anything, it was a way to fight back against the system that had nearly destroyed him.

Flicking over to his personal email, he waited for the forwarded email to arrive. As it was one large mail, James knew that it would take several minutes for it to download onto his MacBook, especially as, unlike the streets surrounding his family's Pensnett home which had Full Fibre, his street, Bird Street, was only on the older fibre-to-the-cabinet infrastructure.

He leaned back in his chair, stretching his arms above his head. The sound of the kettle boiling from the kitchen, which was on the same floor as his bedroom, which had at one stage been the dining room of the 1930s built former council house, a pre-war property which had been part of the Upper Pensnett housing estate before being sold off by Dudley Council in the 1980s. James remembered his parents telling him stories about how they had saved up to buy it in the mid-1990s, converting the dining room into an extra bedroom to allow for the third bedroom upstairs to be converted to a soundproof studio for Sarah's work, initially, and then when Covid came around and Manic mandated that its staff work from home unless broadcasting live, for Pete's work as well.

James smiled faintly, remembering those stories as he waited for the emails to load. It was one of the few comforting constants in his chaotic life: this house, filled with the sounds of his parents' shared passion for radio and the occasional distant hum of a kettle or clink of a mug. It was home, even amidst the turmoil.

An hour passed with no email coming through. James refreshed his inbox repeatedly, feeling a mix of frustration and apprehension. He knew the forwarded email, given its size, might take longer to process, especially with the outdated internet infrastructure in his neighbourhood. But a nagging feeling gnawed at the back of his mind—what if Manic's IT systems had flagged the forwarding attempt?

Flicking back to the open session on the work systems that he had access to, an idea came to mind - what if he could log into Zetta2Go, as it was half past 3, and mess up Chloe and Kylie's Manic Vibes West Midlands show. He knew the two were due on air soon, and if he rearranged some of the elements in the system, it might disrupt their carefully planned playlist or create chaos during their show. James hesitated, his finger hovering over the mouse. It would be petty, but part of him felt an undeniable temptation to hit back at the people who had tormented him for so long.

Typing his credentials in, he noticed that they still worked, and that he had access to the live playlist for Manic Vibes West Midlands. The temptation grew as he saw Kylie and Chloe's show lined up with tracks carefully curated to fit the usual high-energy, commercial vibe. He gritted his teeth, remembering how Kylie had manipulated him and how Chloe had framed him for crimes he didn't commit. The thought of throwing a wrench into their perfect on-air image felt like poetic justice.

Deleting some of the pre-recorded links the two had done, James grinned as the sueges that had been carefully crafted by both their producer, Lily Jenkins, and the network team at Speke to create a seamless flow of high-energy music were now thrown into disarray. In their place, James dragged in obscure tracks—some of them throwbacks to the 1990s and 2000s, and a few of his own mixes that had been finished, such as a mix of Eminem's Houdini that still contained the explicit lyrics. The thought of Chloe and Kylie scrambling to explain a sudden blast of expletives on air brought a mischievous smile to James's face. It wasn't professional, but it was deeply satisfying.

That, and it would make OFCOM have even more to investigate, adding fuel to their scrutiny of Manic Radio's already fragile reputation, especially as explicit language during the peak shows were a major breach of broadcasting standards. OFCOM would have no choice but to take notice, adding yet another layer of chaos to Manic's crumbling infrastructure. James knew it was risky—if they traced the tampering back to him, it could land him in even hotter water. But the catharsis of disrupting Kylie and Chloe's show, even momentarily, outweighed the potential fallout.

As James finalised the changes, he leaned back in his chair, feeling a rush of adrenaline. He logged out of Zetta2Go and cleared his browser history for good measure, ensuring there were no traces of his meddling.

Going to the main, public, Manic Radio website, he logged in to the radio player it used as it was nearly time for the West Midlands Drive show to begin. James put on his headphones, his heart racing in anticipation as the clock struck 4:00 p.m. and the station's jingle played, signalling the start of Chloe and Kylie's show. He couldn't wait to hear the chaos unfold.

****

CHAPTER 15 - Under Siege
Monday 26th May 2025

Chloe chuckled to herself, basking in the irony of her rapid promotion. Less than five months ago, she'd been handed the unenviable Saturday night dance slot on Manic Vibes, a graveyard shift often overlooked by the network's loyal fanbase. Now, here she was—fronting Drive, one of the most coveted slots in commercial radio.

"Not bad for a Smith," she muttered, twirling a pen idly between her fingers as she stared at the rundown for today's show. Her co-host Kylie Morgan was running late, as usual, leaving Chloe to enjoy a rare moment of quiet in the chaos that was Manic's Birmingham hub.

As 4pm struck, and the sweeper for the drive time show came on, but unlike the normal one which was upbeat and said "It's now time for the craziest Midlands drivetime show", it was one of the Manic Goldies West Midlands sweepers that played instead: a nostalgic, laid-back jingle announcing, "Driving home with the greatest hits of the '60s, '70s, '80s and '90s—this is Goldies Drivetime with Pete Smith, on FM, on DAB, online and ad-free on the Manic Prime app."

Chloe's face twisted in confusion as the unexpected jingle echoed through her headphones. She shot a glare towards Lily, who was sitting in Kylie's seat. Chloe knew where Kylie was, as she'd said to the younger girl that she wanted some time with the hub cum dump, and so it was up to Chloe to salvage the situation. She scrambled for the mic fader, muttering curses under her breath.

"Alright, Midlands, it's Chloe here, holding the fort while Kylie's running late, must be that traffic on the Fort Parkway. First up, it's the news with my dear husband and all round good looking Cody Lane," Chloe improvised, her voice laced with false cheer as she glanced toward the control room, where technicians scrambled to figure out what had gone wrong. The studio was buzzing with tension, but Chloe kept her game face on, masking her frustration as the news bed music faded in.

Chloe knew that Cody's bulletin for the Midlands area was live, unlike the other areas, such as the Stoke, East Midlands, Northamptonshire and the Goldies stations, which had pre-recorded bulletins from Cody played out in their respective slots. She tapped the desk impatiently as Cody's smooth voice filled the airwaves, delivering a carefully crafted blend of local news, entertainment, and travel updates.

As the bulletin ended, Chloe quickly faded Cody out and looked at her script, which she knew first was to promote another new competition, the "Manic Cash Dash", a giveaway that promised a hefty £150,000 prize to one lucky listener each day, as long as they could answer a series of questions live on air within 60 seconds. It was the kind of high-energy, attention-grabbing content Manic Vibes loved to push, and Chloe was ready to milk it for all it was worth.

"Right folks, we're live here on Manic Vibes West Midlands, your hottest mix of newest hits, chart toppers and the best throwbacks from the '90s to today! And guess what, Midlands? It's time for our brand-new competition—Manic Cash Dash! Fancy winning

£150,000? All you need to do is answer as many questions as you can in 60 seconds. If you think you've got what it takes, go to www.manicradioplays.co.uk, or by texting DASH to our usual 87106. Texts are £3.50 a go, but entering online is free, and lines close at 1pm tomorrow, when Sue and Kyle are doing their mid-afternoon show, so get entering now for your chance to win big!" Chloe's voice was bright and polished, masking her simmering frustration over the earlier jingle mishap. "It's a Manic network competition, and entrants must be 16 or over. Terms and conditions can be found on the website as well as by texting 'INFO' to 87106—texts charged at standard network rate. Let's get the Midlands buzzing with Cash Dash energy!"

Chloe looked at her screens, which, on one, had GSelector on it and the other had Zetta, the two main RCS software that Manic used for its broadcasting system, and noticed that she had another minute to fill, having sped through the Cash Dash promotion faster than anticipated. She leaned into the mic with a smooth recovery.

"Alright, let's keep the vibes rolling while we wait for Kylie to join us—hopefully she's not stuck on the Fort Parkway too long. We're live and across the Midlands from Central Birmingham, and later I'll be telling you about the newest experience coming to Birmingham City Centre, the Manic Live exhibit, but first, it's a throwback to 2003, when Tom Fletcher of McFly fame joined forces with Busted to create this absolute banger—here's Crashed the Wedding!"

The familiar pop-punk intro filled the studio, and Chloe exhaled, grateful for the quick save. The chaos in the control room was finally starting to settle as technicians frantically worked to resolve the earlier playlist mix-up. Chloe shot a glance toward Lily, who was glaring at the monitor, her face a mix of frustration and disbelief.

"Can someone explain why we're playing Goldies jingles?" Chloe hissed, her voice low enough to avoid being picked up on the mic. "We're not running a retirement home show!"

Lily shrugged, clearly just as baffled. "Not sure. The system says everything's fine on our end, but it's like someone's been tampering with the Zetta playlist remotely."

Chloe frowned. "Who the hell would do that? And why? Unless..." Her mind drifted to James. He still had access to some systems, and if anyone had a reason to mess with their show, it was him.

"Check the audit log," Chloe snapped. "I want to know who's behind this."

Lily nodded, her fingers flying across the keyboard to pull up the system logs. Meanwhile, Chloe composed herself, preparing to deliver the next link as the track faded out.

"That was Crashed the Wedding by Busted, taking us all the way back to 2003!" Chloe's voice was as upbeat as ever, but there was a slight edge to her tone. "Now, if you're planning a wedding or just love a good party, stay tuned—we'll be talking about some Midlands hotspots later in the show. But first, here's something brand new from Dua Lipa—this is Dance the Night."

Instead, Eminem's Houdini, a 2024 single from his twelfth studio album, The Death of Slim Shady (Coup de Grâce), blared through the speakers. Unedited. Explicit. Complete with all the language that would send Ofcom into a frenzy.

The explicit track continued to blast through the Midlands airwaves, its unfiltered language a direct violation of broadcasting standards. Chloe's face drained of colour as the realisation hit her—this wasn't just a minor mistake; it was a catastrophic breach that could result in serious consequences for the station and for her.

Chloe scrambled, her hands darting to the soundboard to kill the track. Her brain raced, adrenaline spiking as the unfiltered lyrics continued to play out. This wasn't just a technical hiccup—this was sabotage. Her fingers finally found the "off" button, cutting the music mid-verse.

Dead air. The golden sin of radio.

Lily, who had been frantically typing on her laptop, looked up in horror. "What the hell was that? Houdini? That's not even in the approved library!"

Chloe, her cheeks flushed with anger, slammed her palm on the desk. "That bastard. It's James. It has to be. No one else would dare pull something like this. I'm going to fucking kill him!"

"Little shitbag tried to ruin my show?" Kylie said as she walked in, clearly having missed the initial chaos but instantly aware something was off. She plopped her handbag on the desk and raised an eyebrow at the silence in the studio. It was then that Chloe and Kylie noticed something.

The On Air light was on.

Their microphones were still live.

They were going out across the entire Midlands, their voices carrying through homes, cars, and workplaces.

Chloe froze mid-rant, her eyes widening in horror as the realisation hit her. Kylie's mouth was still open, mid-sentence, before she clamped it shut, her face turning pale. For a few seconds, they both sat in stunned silence, the weight of their mistake sinking in. The dead air had been bad enough, but now their explicit reactions had just made things exponentially worse.

And then the WhatsApp screen, which contained both written messages as well as voice notes from listeners started going mad, as if a bomb had gone off. Messages and voice notes poured in, each more chaotic than the last. Chloe and Kylie could see the notifications piling up on the studio screen:

"Did Chloe just threaten someone on air?!"

"Kylie swearing live—are you guys okay? This is unhinged!"

"This is better than a reality show. Keep it coming!"

The laughter and mockery from listeners were bad enough, but the professional repercussions began to dawn on Chloe. This wasn't just a blip—it was a disaster. Ofcom would be on them like a hawk, the press would pick it up within minutes, and her career could be over before she could even spin the next track.

"Lily, get this sorted!" Chloe hissed, jabbing a finger toward the frantic producer, who was already typing furiously on her laptop.

"I'm trying," Lily snapped. "But someone's tampered with the Zetta logs. There's no trace of how Houdini got in there or how the microphones stayed live."

Kylie slumped into her chair, burying her head in her hands. "We're screwed. Totally screwed. What the hell are we gonna do?"

Chloe, ever the schemer, straightened up and forced herself to think. Damage control. That was her only option. She leaned into the mic, her voice dripping with feigned calmness.

"Apologies, Midlands. We seem to be experiencing some technical difficulties today. Rest assured, we're working to resolve the issue, and we'll be back with your favourite tunes in no time. Anyway, here's Wow by Kylie to save the day!"

Chloe hit play on the next track, Kylie Minogue's "Wow", letting the bright, upbeat tune fill the airwaves as she ripped off her headphones and glared at Kylie and Lily.

"That should buy us a few minutes," Chloe hissed, her composure cracking. "Lily, I need a full rundown of what happened—now. Who's behind this?"

Lily shook her head, panic evident on her face. "I'm telling you, someone's tampered with the system remotely. The audit logs are wiped clean. This isn't just a mistake; someone planned this."

Kylie groaned, kicking her chair back. "Of course they did. Who has access? You know who—James. He's the only one bitter enough to try something this dumb."

Chloe's jaw clenched. "He's on suspension; how would he even get in? Unless..." Her voice trailed off as she connected the dots. "He must still have remote access to Zetta2Go or the server backups. I'll bet my Baby Bonus he did this."

Kylie grabbed her phone, furiously tapping out a message. "I'll sort this out. If James thinks he can mess with us and get away with it, he's got another thing coming."

Chloe glanced at the clock. The show was only ten minutes in, and their meltdown had already created a storm they couldn't hope to contain. Kylie's fury was palpable, but Chloe forced herself to focus. This was salvageable—at least in her mind. But the damage was already done, and she knew the fallout would be immediate and brutal.

It was then one tweet from Hits Radio which made her temper worse.

@hitsradiowestmids: *You ok, @manicvibeswestmids? That bit of audio wasn't very family-friendly. Need a hand with your playlist? We've got a few Belters ready for you. #OopsOnAir* 🎤 🎧

Of course, Chloe noticed, it wasn't just Hits which had taken the opportunity to mock Manic Vibes' disastrous broadcast as Capital, who, like Manic, had a regional drive show, also decided to weigh in:

@CapitalBham: *Manic Vibes keeping it explicit today—guess they're redefining 'drive-time drama.' Need some clean, high-energy bangers? We've got you covered. #BroadcastingChaos* 🎧 😂

Chloe's face burned with embarrassment as she glared at the notifications pouring in. The rival stations weren't just poking fun—they were revelling in Manic's very public meltdown. The fact that OFCOM was also investigating them for workplace misconduct and regulatory breaches only added to the humiliation. Manic Vibes had become the laughing stock of the industry, and Chloe's name was now firmly attached to the disaster.

Lily looked up from her laptop, her face pale. "Chloe, it's worse than we thought. Listeners are sharing clips of the live meltdown on Twitter, TikTok, and everywhere else. It's already trending."

Chloe's stomach churned. "Trending? What do you mean trending?"

Lily turned her screen to show the hashtag #ManicMeltdown, which was quickly climbing on Twitter alongside related phrases like #ExplicitDrive. The clips were brutal—raw audio of the explicit Eminem track, Chloe's live rant, and even snippets of her and Kylie's oblivious chatter as their mics stayed on.

Kylie groaned, sinking further into her chair. "Great. Just great. What now? Do we grovel on air? Apologise and hope for the best?"

Chloe gritted her teeth, her mind racing. "No. We play this off as a technical issue and keep it vague. We stick to the party line: 'unexpected technical difficulties.' We do not admit fault or give anyone more ammunition."

"And what about James?" Kylie snapped. "If he's behind this, we need to make sure he pays. Let's call HR. They'll know what to do."

"HR?!" Chloe barked a bitter laugh. "You mean Isla Granger? The same HR officer who spends more time having us fuck her because she's the hub cum dump thanks to falling out of favour of us."

Kylie groaned, her frustration boiling over. "Fine, not HR then. What about IT? Surely they can trace the tampering back to James or whoever's responsible."

Lily interjected, her tone cautious. "IT's already swamped dealing with the Ofcom investigation fallout and Legal's trying to cover up anything that could make the regulators dig deeper. If we escalate this now, it might just add fuel to the fire. Besides, if we can't prove it was James without a shadow of a doubt, we'll look like we're grasping at straws. Anyway, you're still doing your law studies, Chloe, aren't you?"

Chloe snapped her attention to Lily, her frustration momentarily replaced by indignation. "Of course, I'm still studying law! What does that have to do with anything?"

Lily hesitated, then shrugged. "I just meant you'd understand the importance of evidence. Without proof, accusing James publicly could backfire. Anyway, he's already in enough trouble with his suspension. If this was him, he's digging his own grave."

Chloe's lips thinned, but she forced herself to nod. Lily had a point, however much it grated her. Publicly going after James without hard evidence could shift the narrative from Manic's technical disaster to Chloe's personal vendetta. And with the #ManicMeltdown hashtag still climbing, she couldn't afford any more missteps.

"Alright," Chloe conceded, her voice clipped. "But IT better figure this out fast. If it is James, I'll make sure he never works in radio again."

"Yeah, because our careers are in such a great place right now," Kylie muttered, slumping further into her chair.

Chloe ignored her, her focus shifting back to the show. The current track, Wow by Kylie Minogue, was winding down, and she needed to regain control of the broadcast before it spiralled further. Adjusting her mic, she plastered on a bright, fake smile and leaned forward.

"Alright, Midlands, thanks for bearing with us through some unexpected technical difficulties. Technology, eh? Always keeping us on our toes! But we're back on track and ready to bring you more of the music you love. Coming up, we've got the latest from Harry Styles and a special giveaway you won't want to miss! First though, I mentioned earlier the new Manic Live exhibit. From July, you can come to our new attraction at the Resorts World centre at the NEC, where you can see what makes Manic... well, Manic, from what our studios look like, to meeting Kylie, Toni Green and even Kyle and Sue. Tickets can be brought via www.manicradioexperiences.co.uk, and don't forget that for every ticket purchased in June, you'll be entered into a draw to win exclusive backstage passes to

July's House of Manic Dance, the Manic Dance live show this July from the bp pulse Arena at the NEC, with live DJ sets from Dr Manic himself, as well as Calvin Harris, Fedde Le Grand, Armand Van Helden and David Guetta. It's going to be the biggest night of the summer, and you won't want to miss it!" Chloe finished her plug, her voice brimming with forced enthusiasm.

As the intro to Harry Styles' As It Was began to play, Chloe noticed it wasn't the regular version, but a slower one when suddenly, twenty seconds in, heavy dubstep beats kicked in, completely obliterating the mellow vibe of Harry Styles' As It Was. The sudden shift left Chloe momentarily frozen, staring at the console in disbelief. The dubstep remix was loud, chaotic, and entirely unapproved—yet another sabotage on what was supposed to be a flawless drivetime show.

And then she remembered that James had made such a dubstep version of the mellow Harry Styles' track, blending his melodic vocals with jarring beats and explosive drops as a Manic Dance special for one of the shows that he was tasked with hosting earlier in the year before his suspension. Chloe's frustration boiled over as the unorthodox remix pounded through the studio monitors.

Looking at the screen which had the social media dashboard, Chloe noticed a mixture of messages that ranged from mocking to outright disbelief flooding the station's Twitter and Instagram feeds.

@BrummieBeats: *Did Harry Styles join a rave or something? What even is this remix?* 😂 *#ManicMeltdown"*

@MidlandsMum85: *Trying to enjoy Harry Styles on the school run, and BAM—dubstep attack. Thanks, Manic. #RadioFail*

@EDM4Life: *Okay, that Styles dubstep mix is fire, but what's going on at Manic? Total chaos! #ManicMeltdown*

@HitsRadioWestMids: *Manic's playlist is as unpredictable as their workplace culture. Need a steady beat? We've got you covered.* 🎧 *#OopsOnAir*

What made Chloe laugh was that although the playout was controlled by the network centre in Speke, with the tracks coming from there, she could see her colleagues in the Manic Vibes East Midlands studio expressing similar frustrations and confusion over their monitors. Turning to see what was happening with the Manic Vibes Stoke and Cheshire studio, she could see the two newbies that had took over a couple of weeks from the previous host, who was currently in custody, who ironically had replaced Lyra Nott who had been the drive host there before leaving Manic altogether, both looking utterly bewildered. It was clear this sabotage wasn't confined to her show—it was network-wide.

Chloe reached for the intercom to the network desk at Speke, her anger palpable. "Speke, what the hell is going on? We're playing dubstep Harry Styles, Goldies jingles, and God knows what else. Who's in charge of the system right now?"

The voice of one of the Speke network operators crackled back, a mixture of exhaustion and irritation. "We don't know. The system's been compromised, and we're working to regain control. But it looks like someone's accessing Zetta remotely—again."

"AGAIN?" Chloe yelled, her voice echoing through the studio. "How the hell does this keep happening? Isn't IT supposed to stop this sort of thing?"

"Working on it," came the clipped reply. "We've locked out several accounts, but whoever's behind this knows what they're doing. Just sit tight and ride it out for now."

Chloe slammed the intercom button off, her fists clenched. "Ride it out?" she muttered through gritted teeth. "We're the laughing stock of British radio, and they want us to just sit tight?"

Kylie, who had been scrolling through Twitter with increasing despair, looked up. "It's trending again. #ManicMeltdown is at number two in the UK right now. Even some of the artists we've played are commenting."

Chloe blinked. "What do you mean?"

Kylie held up her phone, showing a tweet from Harry Styles' official account:

@Harry_Styles: Didn't know I had a dubstep remix—love the creativity, Manic Radio. 😉 #ManicMeltdown

Chloe's eyes widened as she stared at the tweet, unsure whether to laugh, cry, or scream. Harry Styles, of all people, had acknowledged the chaos, and while his comment seemed cheeky and light-hearted, the implications were anything but. The tweet would only amplify the spotlight on Manic's disaster, drawing even more attention from fans, media, and regulators alike.

Kylie groaned, dropping her phone onto the desk. "That's it. We're done for. Harry-freaking-Styles just turned our meltdown into a meme. This'll be on Have I Got News for You by Friday."

The laughter echoing from the control room wasn't helping Chloe's mood. She turned to Lily, who was feverishly typing away, her face a mask of concentration.

"Lily, any updates?" Chloe demanded, her tone sharp.

Lily didn't look up. "Still trying to trace the source. Whoever's doing this knows how to cover their tracks. IT says it might take hours to figure it out—if we're lucky."

Kylie, scrolling through more Twitter updates, let out an exasperated sigh. "Speke better be sorting this. If not, I'm going to march down there myself and start unplugging cables."

Chloe ignored Kylie's outburst, her mind racing. The fallout from this was going to be massive. OFCOM was already investigating Manic, and now this public disaster would only strengthen their case. Sponsors would start pulling out, listeners would switch to rival stations, and their reputations—what was left of them—would be in tatters.

****

CHAPTER 16 - A Reckoning on Memory Lane
Thursday 10th July 2025

It had been a month and a half since OFCOM announced their investigation into Manic Radio's operations. The findings were damning, highlighting systemic workplace misconduct, multiple breaches of broadcasting standards, and a corporate culture that prioritised profits and cliques over professionalism and ethics. The report's release had sent shockwaves through the industry, and Manic was now facing the fallout.

Pete Smith sat in the Goldies studio, the dimly lit room a stark contrast to the bright chaos playing out across the airwaves. The OFCOM findings were dominating the news cycle, with every major station and media outlet dissecting the report's details. Manic's once-bold claims of being the most innovative broadcaster in the UK were now little more than a punchline.

Pete adjusted his headphones, glancing at the rundown Alice had handed him earlier. Today's show was supposed to be a celebration of '80s classics, but Pete couldn't help but weave commentary on the current state of the industry into his links.

Looking at the clock, it was a few minutes to four, the start of his drivetime show, with the classic Goldies jingle signalling his handover from the network show to his localised West Midlands broadcast. Pete straightened up in his chair, cleared his throat, and leaned into the mic.

"Good afternoon, West Midlands," he began, his voice steady but tinged with a seriousness that his listeners rarely heard. "It's Pete Smith here on Goldies Drivetime, bringing you the greatest hits of the '60s, '70s, '80s, and '90s. But before we dive into today's playlist of classics, I'd like to talk about something that's been making waves—not just in our industry, but across the country."

He paused, letting the silence linger for a moment. It was a deliberate move, giving his words more weight.

"When I started as a presenter in 1994 on Dudley FM, yes, 31 years ago this summer, radio was a different beast. It was about connection, about community. About being a voice in the room, a companion to people driving home or cooking dinner, or even just looking for a laugh or a good tune. Back then, we knew our listeners by name; they weren't just metrics on a spreadsheet.

"Back then, Dudley FM was one of a small number of radio stations owned by Woody Bones, a man who had built a network of local stations that cared about their communities. Dudley FM had a heart, a soul. It wasn't perfect, but it was real. We had to struggle, struggle against our neighbours and rival, Wolverhampton FM, Capital Radio's BRMB, GWR's Beacon Radio, and against Lucy Kildare's West Midlands network, comprising of several local stations in the Midlands. Now, in reality, Lucy Kildare's network and Woody Bone's network wasn't rivals in the traditional sense, as the two were in-laws, Woody's wife being Lucy Kildare's sister, so there was an unspoken agreement to keep their stations complementary rather than competitive. But there was a healthy sense of rivalry when it came to talent and innovation. We wanted to outdo each other not because of corporate pressure, but because we genuinely cared about delivering something exceptional to our listeners. That's what made radio special—it was personal, it was authentic."

Pete took a deep breath, leaning back slightly in his chair. His fingers played idly with the edge of the desk as he continued.

"Then in 2005, the Bones and Kildare networks merged, as Woody Bones was losing money on his stations, despite their loyal listenership, and Lucy Kildare's empire was feeling the pressure of competition from larger conglomerates like GWR and Chrysalis. The merger made sense on paper—create a unified network with local roots but the resources to compete across the West Midlands. There was only 2 stations in the Midlands that became Midlands Manic that wasn't Bones or Kildare stations, Wolverhampton FM, which Breeze had brought in 2005, and one that covered Sandwell, which Woody brought in 2006 when the owners, Calvin Pennyworth and Lawrence Thomas, decided to retire and sell their station. That merger brought with it opportunities but also challenges. It introduced new voices, new technology, and new ideas. But even then, there was a sense that the heart of local radio was being chipped away, bit by bit."

Pete paused, letting the memory linger in his mind before returning to his listeners. His tone grew sombre.

"And then GWR and Capital merged in 2008 to form Global Radio, and everything changed. Local stations became regional hubs, regional hubs became national networks, and the voices that had built radio into what it was were replaced by algorithms and celebrity presenters. It was the era of networking, of consolidation, and while there were advantages—more polished production, broader reach—it came at a cost. Local voices, the lifeblood of our industry, began to disappear.

"Beacon FM, BRMB, and its 3 sibling stations, Heart 106, Wyvern FM and Mercia FM, they all were forced to be sold off to another company, which was Orion Media, in 2009, due to competition rules, and then Orion became part of Bauer in 2016. The Bones-Kildare Network got sold in 2010 by Woody Bones to Breeze Media, a small media group similar in size to Orion Media."

Pete then sighed as he saw the network mandated track, the theme tune to Fame, a 1982 pop classic, queued up as his next song. The irony wasn't lost on him—a song about ambition and dreams, set to play in a world where the dreams of many local presenters had been stifled by corporate bureaucracy.

He decided to finish his reflection before the track began.

"And now, we find ourselves here, in 2025, amidst an industry reckoning. You see, even though I host this show, I'm not directly employed by Manic. I'm what we call a freelance presenter, contracted to deliver a service. That change came about last year when my contract, because we have them renewed annually, something that the radio industry does as a standard practice, was altered to reflect a new reality. The days of being a station employee, part of a close-knit team, were replaced by the gig economy model—just another freelancer with a microphone. For me, this shift was manageable. I've been in the game long enough to adapt. But for others? For the younger presenters trying to carve out careers, for the producers and engineers who once had stable jobs? It's a different story."

Pete leaned closer to the microphone, his voice steady but weighted with emotion.

"If anyone remembers last year, another station, Bauer's Absolute Radio, declined to renew the contract of a legend, one who, like me, is known for being on the airwaves and from the West Midlands. That legend, Frank Skinner, whose voice had been synonymous with Saturdays on Absolute Radio, was suddenly gone."

Pete paused, letting the moment linger, the weight of his words hanging in the air like the final notes of a symphony. The silence was deliberate, a moment for his listeners to absorb the gravity of his reflection.

"Frank Skinner," Pete continued, "wasn't just a presenter—he was an institution. A voice that bridged generations, a man who could make you laugh, make you think, and make you feel connected to something bigger than yourself. And yet, despite his contributions, despite the loyalty he inspired in listeners, his time on Absolute ended not with a fanfare but with a whisper. His departure was a stark reminder of the transient nature of this industry and how even the most cherished voices can be silenced by the relentless march of corporate strategy."

Pete glanced at the clock. It was time to bring his reflection back to the present, to the story dominating the headlines, and to the reckoning that was now at Manic's doorstep. But he still had a final point to make before transitioning to the music. He leaned into the microphone, his voice resolute but tinged with weariness.

"In my career, I've had the privilege to be on air against and alongside Graham Torrington, Les Ross, Jeremy Kyle, Ed Doolan, Nigel Freshman, Jo Russell, John Dalziel, and Stephanie Hirst. Each of them brought something unique to radio—be it humour, gravitas, or sheer authenticity. They understood that radio is more than just a job; it's a responsibility, a privilege to be welcomed into someone's home, car, or workplace. And yet, as I sit here in 2025, it's hard not to wonder if the values they, and so many others, held dear have been drowned out by metrics, branding, and profit margins."

Pete's hand hovered over the button to play the next track, but he wasn't done yet. The words that followed were heavier, tinged with a deep sadness for what had been lost and a flicker of hope for what might still be salvaged.

"The OFCOM report on Manic Radio lays bare what happens when an industry loses sight of its purpose. It's not just about the technical failings or the gross misconduct—although those are damning enough. It's about the culture. The culture that allowed toxic behaviour to thrive, that prioritised clicks and quick wins over integrity and community. And make no mistake, this reckoning isn't just about Manic. It's about all of us in radio, across every station, network, and format. It's about asking ourselves what we want this medium to be—not just today, but for the future."

Pete's voice softened as he added a personal note, one he hoped would resonate with his listeners.

"I'll tell you this: I didn't stay in this industry for the fame, the money, or even the music—although I do love the music. I stayed because of you. Because of the listeners who've stuck with me through the years, who've called in to share stories, who've laughed with me, argued with me, and sometimes cried with me. You're the reason I do this. And as long as there's a place for real voices and real stories, I'll be here. Anyway, here's Irena Cara's Fame to keep things moving along this afternoon."

Pete hit the button, and the upbeat anthem burst into life, filling the studio with its iconic energy. For a few moments, the music carried the weight of his words, a poignant counterbalance to his heartfelt monologue.

As the track played, Pete leaned back in his chair, his eyes scanning the studio. Alice stood in the doorway, her expression a mix of admiration and concern. She gave him a small nod, the unspoken acknowledgment of a shared understanding. Pete returned the gesture, his mind still racing with thoughts of the day's show and the industry at large.

Looking at his screen which had the WhatsApp and text messages, Pete noticed that several listeners had texted in, which, for a station whose focus was on the 35-65 age demographic, was not uncommon. However, the tone of the messages today was markedly different—less about song requests or shoutouts and more about Pete's monologue.

Jean from Dudley: *Pete, your words just now brought tears to my eyes. You're right—radio used to mean something, and you're one of the few left who still cares. Thank you for staying true."*

Dave in Hereford: *Spot on, Pete. The OFCOM report is a wake-up call for the industry. Radio needs voices like yours now more than ever. Don't let them take that away.*

The messages kept coming, each one a testament to the connection Pete had cultivated over the years. Despite the chaos engulfing Manic Radio, moments like these reminded Pete why he had stayed. He typed a quick reply to Jean and Dave, thanking them for their kind words, before leaning back into the chair and mentally preparing for the next segment.

By the time Fame faded out, Pete's focus had shifted back to the show. He leaned into the mic, his tone lighter now, but still carrying the gravitas of his earlier reflection.

"Thanks for sticking with me, West Midlands. That was Irena Cara's Fame—a song that reminds us of ambition, dreams, and, let's be honest, the rollercoaster ride of life. Now, let's go down memory lane. In 2005, a young woman named Beverley Knight came into the studio at Dudley FM. She was promoting her new album Affirmation, and I'll tell you what, folks—she absolutely blew us away. Beverley grew up right here in the Midlands, a true Black Country girl who never forgot her roots. And today, we're playing one of her early hits, a track which is one of the hidden gems, which... is going to, instead of the normal computer based play, I'm going to play it in a minute from the original vinyl record she signed for me back in 1998 when she visited Dudley FM. It's called Down for the One, a groovy number that takes us right back to the late '90s when Beverley was already showing the world what she could do. Before that, while I'm going to get the vinyl, I'm going to ask my producer, the wonderful Alice Graham, to share a little something with you. Alice, you used to work for Free Radio 80's and Absolute 80s before joining us at Goldies, and you've seen your fair share of changes in the industry too. Care to share some of your thoughts on what's happening now?"

Pete let Alice talk while he stood up and headed for the shelving unit that was in Studio A1, where the physical records that he and his Breakfast colleagues on Manic Goldies West Midlands had as part of their various broadcasts were stored. As he flipped through the records, Pete found the worn yet cherished vinyl sleeve of Beverley Knight's Down for the One. The corners were slightly dog-eared, but the bold, vibrant artwork and Beverley's signature across the cover gave it a timeless charm. He smiled to himself, remembering the day Beverley had visited Dudley FM and signed the record. She had been warm, down-to-earth, and full of passion for her craft—a reminder of what music and radio were supposed to be about.

Alice's voice came through the speakers in the studio as she spoke to the listeners.

"Thanks, Pete. You know, working in radio for as long as I have, I've seen the industry change in ways I never thought possible. When I was at Free Radio 80s, it was all about nostalgia—the songs, the memories, the connection to a simpler time. Then moving to Absolute 80s, I saw how you could take that nostalgia and repackage it for a digital audience, creating something that felt both modern and timeless. But even then, the focus was always on the music and the listeners. It wasn't about who had the most viral TikTok or the flashiest influencer campaign.

"What's happening now, though... it's hard to watch. The OFCOM report didn't just highlight Manic's failings—it put a spotlight on an industry that's losing its way. We're so busy chasing trends and analytics that we've forgotten why people tune in to radio in the first place. It's not for gimmicks or chaos. It's for connection, for authenticity. And that's what stations like Goldies, and presenters like Pete, still offer—a genuine link to something real."

Pete returned to his chair, placing the vinyl on the turntable as Alice wrapped up her thoughts.

"Thanks, Alice," Pete said as he adjusted his headphones. "You've hit the nail on the head. And that's why we're here—to remind everyone that amidst all the noise, there's still a place for the real, the heartfelt, and the timeless. Now, as promised, here's a true gem from a Midlands icon. From Wolverhampton's very own Beverley Knight, this is Down for the One, spinning straight from the vinyl."

As Pete gently lowered the needle onto the vinyl, a soft crackle filled the airwaves, a nostalgic prelude to the rich, soulful rhythm of Down for the One. The unmistakable voice of Beverley Knight followed, its smooth vibrancy echoing through the studio. Pete leaned back in his chair, a small smile tugging at his lips as the track played. The sound of the vinyl wasn't just music—it was a memory, a connection to a time when radio and music were deeply intertwined with authenticity.

As the song played, Pete glanced over at Alice, who had slipped into the producer's chair. She gave him a thumbs-up, her expression one of quiet pride. They both knew this moment wasn't just about filling airtime; it was about reminding their listeners—and themselves—of what radio could be.

When the song ended, Pete leaned back into the mic, his voice warm with genuine enthusiasm. "That was Beverley Knight with Down for the One, straight from the vinyl, folks. You don't hear it like that every day. Beverley, if you're listening—and I know you sometimes do—thank you for giving us music that still resonates, years later."

He paused, letting the sentiment hang in the air before continuing. "Now, I promised earlier to take you down memory lane, and I've got a few more stories to share. But before that, let's check in with your traffic updates and see how the Midlands roads are looking. Alice, over to you."

Alice nodded, her voice steady as she took over the mic. "Thanks, Pete. It's just gone quarter past four, and here's what's happening on the roads. The M6 northbound is still seeing delays near Junction 10A, so if you're heading towards Stafford, expect some hold-ups. The Distressway is congested because the Lichfield Road is shut, and surprise surprise, there's congestion in Worcester because the bridge over the Severn is still undergoing repair works. If you're in Birmingham, there's heavy traffic around the Queensway Tunnel, as usual. In Coventry, the A46 at Toll Barr Island is moving slowly, so if you're heading towards Warwick, you might want to plan an alternative route. And for those in Wolverhampton, there's been an incident on the A4124, causing some tailbacks near the Wednesfield Road junction. That's your update for now—back to you, Pete."

Pete nodded his thanks to Alice, his expression relaxed but contemplative as he leaned back into the mic. "Cheers,

Alice. Sounds like a typical Thursday on the Midlands roads, with congestion here, there and everywhere. West Midlands Railway have announced that there are cancellations on Cross City South due to an incident at Selly Oak, so if you're commuting by train, best check your travel apps for updates. And don't forget, folks—whatever the traffic or travel woes, you've got us here at Goldies to keep you company. Up next is Wham, but not their two time Number 1 Christmas track, Last Christmas—it's too early, Colin in Kenilworth, its only July. Instead, we've got George Michael's 1984 single from the album Make It Big, yes, its Careless Whisper. Following that, I'll dive into your requests, so keep them coming. Whether you're at home, in the car, or stuck in the middle of the chaos on the M6, we're here to soundtrack your Thursday afternoon."

Pete watched as Zetta queued up Careless Whisper, letting the smooth saxophone intro fill the studio as he sipped his tea, a small smile playing on his lips. The track was a perfect follow-up to Beverley Knight's soulfulness—a reminder of music's power to create moments of calm amidst the hustle and bustle of life.

As the song played, Pete reflected on the contrast between his show and the rest of Manic's crumbling empire. His programme was a rare pocket of authenticity, untainted by the toxicity highlighted in the OFCOM report. He knew it wasn't perfect—no station could be—but it felt good to hold onto a slice of what radio was meant to be.

****

CHAPTER 17 - The Podcast That Broke the Radio
Friday 18th July 2025

Lyra was reading The Guardian's website when the first media reviews of Broadcasting Boundaries, the podcast that she and James had launched just three days earlier, began rolling in. The headline on the Media & Tech section read:

"The Podcast That Broke the Radio: How Two Ex-Manic Insiders Exposed a Network's Decay"

Her stomach fluttered with equal parts nerves and excitement as she clicked on the article. The subheading was equally bold:

"Lyra Nott and James Smith, two former presenters caught in the chaos of Manic Radio, are unmasking the industry in a raw, unapologetic podcast that could redefine audio storytelling."

James shuffled into the room, still groggy from a rare long lie-in, wearing an oversized hoodie and clutching a mug of coffee. "You're up early. What's got you so... focused?" he asked, his voice still rough from sleep.

Lyra glanced up, her eyes sparkling with a mix of pride and disbelief. "The Guardian just called us the podcast that broke the radio."

James blinked, momentarily stunned, before flopping onto the sofa beside her to peer at the screen. "No way. Let me see that."

The pair read the article together, the words bringing a mix of validation and apprehension.

"Broadcasting Boundaries is not just a tell-all—it's a masterclass in candid storytelling. Nott and Smith don't hold back, weaving their personal experiences with wider industry analysis. The two former Manic Radio presenters new podcast launches with revelations of a Baby Bonus, a scheme where female Manic Radio presenters and producers can claim either a £32,000 up front, or £2k annual, bonus just for having children, with the caveat that they present the network's 'family-friendly' image in carefully curated social media posts and avoid discussing topics that could tarnish the company's public persona. This practice, among other shocking revelations, paints a damning picture of a network spiralling into self-destruction.

"A whistle-blower from Manic Radio—who remains anonymous for their safety—has told The Guardian that the Baby Bonus scheme was not only a gross manipulation of personal lives for corporate gain but also a means to distract from deeper systemic issues. 'It was all a façade,' the whistleblower said. 'While the public saw family-friendly smiles and glossy Instagram posts, behind the scenes was a culture of coercion, exploitation, and cover-ups.'"

James let out a low whistle as he finished reading the section aloud. "They're really laying it out there, aren't they?"

Lyra nodded, her expression a mixture of satisfaction and apprehension. "Yeah, but this is exactly what we wanted—to shine a light on what's been happening. It's not just about us; it's about everyone who's been crushed under that machine."

James leaned back against the sofa, sipping his coffee thoughtfully. "Do you think this is going to change anything? Or is it just another media flash in the pan?"

Lyra shrugged, her gaze drifting to the window where sunlight streamed through the curtains. "I don't know. But if enough people hear this, if it puts pressure on OFCOM, on Manic's sponsors, then maybe. We've started something, James, and it's bigger than us now."

The article continued with more excerpts from their podcast, highlighting the raw honesty that had captured listeners' attention. The launch episodes of Broadcasting Boundaries had shot to the top of podcast charts, fuelled by their willingness to speak openly about their experiences and expose the inner workings of Manic Radio.

"Smith's confession of enduring systemic abuse at the hands of Manic Radio colleagues is a stark reminder of how unchecked power and toxic cultures can thrive in corporate environments. Meanwhile, Nott's revelations about workplace manipulation, particularly through coercive social media policies and forced compliance with branding, highlight the wider issues plaguing the industry."

James put down his coffee, his jaw tightening. "Reading it all like this... It feels heavier, doesn't it?"

Lyra reached over, squeezing his hand gently. "It does. But we're finally being heard. People are listening, James. This is how we fight back."

Turning to the GB News website, Lyra noticed a headline which made her smile, the right leaning paper calling upon the Labour Government to "tighten regulations on corporate practices in media companies." The article, surprisingly critical of Manic Radio, read:

"Broadcasting Boundaries has done more than expose a crumbling empire—it's ignited a necessary conversation about the dark underbelly of corporate media. The Labour government, under Prime Minister Kier Starmer, must act decisively to ensure that what happened at Manic Radio cannot happen again. Stronger workplace protections and stricter OFCOM oversight are essential. Reform Leader Nigel Farage said in an interview to GB News that '...this podcast is a wake-up call. What we've heard from Nott and Smith isn't just about one company; it's about an entire industry that's lost its way. We need accountability, and we need it now. OFCOM must grow a backbone, and the government must ensure media conglomerates don't become unchecked empires where abuse thrives.'"

Lyra snorted. "Nigel Farage, a champion of accountability? That's rich."

James chuckled, shaking his head. "If Farage is getting involved, you know this is hitting nerves in all the right places. Though I'd rather not have him as our unofficial spokesperson."

"Oh, this is a good one," Lyra then said as she read the article. "Even Tommy Robinson has something to say about it in the GB News article."

James groaned, setting his coffee mug down with exaggerated caution. "Oh no. If Tommy Robinson's chiming in, we've officially hit the point where everyone wants to co-opt this for their agenda. What did he say?"

Lyra scrolled down, smirking as she read aloud. "'This podcast reveals the true rot at the heart of our media elite. While the mainstream have been distracted by woke nonsense, hardworking Brits like Nott and Smith have been silenced and exploited. It's time we take back our airwaves.'" She snorted. "Yeah, because that's exactly what we were going for."

James threw a cushion at her, mock-offended. "Hardworking Brits? Wasn't he the one calling radio a 'dying art' a few years ago? Now we're his poster children?"

Lyra dodged the cushion, laughing. "Hey, at least we're uniting people across the political spectrum. Who knew exposing workplace abuse could bring Farage and Robinson into agreement?"

James sighed, shaking his head. "This is exactly why I'm nervous. The focus is supposed to be on the people hurt by all this, not on giving soundbites to Farage and Robinson."

Lyra leaned forward, her expression softening. "James, we can't control how people react. What we can control is the story we tell. And so far, it's resonating with people who matter—the ones who've been through this, who've seen it, and who want it to stop."

He nodded, exhaling slowly. "You're right. It's just… surreal, isn't it? Seeing our stories out there, being dissected by everyone from The Guardian to GB News. I mean, Tommy Robinson quoting us? That's… not what I pictured when we started this."

"Same here," Lyra admitted, closing her laptop. "But you know what? Let them talk. Every article, every soundbite—it's putting more pressure on Manic and OFCOM. That's the goal."

James stretched, a slight smirk tugging at the corner of his mouth. "I just hope Robinson doesn't ask us to be guests on his next rant. Can you imagine?"

Lyra laughed, shaking her head. "Pass. But speaking of appearances, Hits emailed… well, JD and Roisin off Hits Radio Breakfast want us on their show to talk about the podcast."

James sat up straighter, his eyebrows rising in surprise. "Hits? As in Hits Radio? They're actually reaching out to us?"

Lyra nodded, a small smile playing on her lips. "Yep. There again JD and Roisin are Hits West Midlands, our patch, so it's in their interest to keep the story local. They've invited us to do an interview next week. It's not the national show, but still—it's Hits. They must see the impact this is having."

James leaned back, a thoughtful look crossing his face. "That's... big. I mean, Hits Radio is Bauer, and Bauer's been poking fun at Manic for weeks now. This could be another chance to highlight the issues—but also to reach people who might not usually listen to podcasts. And then there's Elliot Holman and Matilda Newthorpe on their Stoke and Cheshire breakfast too, which is their Hits version of your old Stoke and Cheshire drivetime slot. You mentioned you haven't seen them in ages, since Northern Vibes was based in Stoke and Signal 1 was based up there too."

"Yeah, I used to often bump into Elliot and Matilda when we were all Stoke-based, especially during crossover shifts," Lyra said, her voice tinged with nostalgia. "They're good people. Funnily enough Elliot was the first person who gave me advice when I was told I was joining Northern Vibes nearly 7 years ago. He said that no matter what the station people were on, that friendships between hosts at different companies were what made the industry worth staying in. He wasn't wrong." Lyra smiled fondly. "Matilda and I used to joke about how often we'd end up promoting the same events, despite being on competing stations. It's weird to think about those days now, given everything that's happened. You know she's a mum herself, so I might ask her for some guidance for 7 months' time, when our little one arrives. I might drop down to 54 Hagley Road one of the days, see if she's free for a coffee and a chat. It'd be nice to reconnect, especially now we're out of the chaos and can talk openly about everything."

James nodded, his expression softening. "That sounds like a good idea. It's easy to forget that not everyone in radio is part of the problem. There are good people—people who care about the craft and the connections it creates. It'd be nice to build bridges again."

Ping

Lyra noticed that it was James's phone that had gone off in their shared bedroom that was originally James's, and that she had moved into 3 months ago. "Your phone's going mad," she said, gesturing towards the door. "Might want to grab that."

James groaned, rolling off the sofa with exaggerated effort. "If it's another message from Chloe or someone from Manic, I swear…" he grumbled as he trudged to the bedroom.

When he returned, his face was a mix of amusement and mild confusion. "I am officially... fired."

Lyra's eyebrows shot up. "Fired? How? You're on suspension!"

James flopped back onto the sofa, holding up his phone to show her the email.

"**From**: *charlotte.mcdonald@manicradio.group*

To: *jamie3443snetta@yahoo.co.uk*

Subject: *Termination of Contract – Manic Radio Group*

Dear Mr Smith,

We regret to inform you that your contract with Manic Radio Group has been terminated, effective immediately. This decision has been made following a thorough review of your recent conduct, including your suspension, and the subsequent public statements made via the Broadcasting Boundaries podcast.

While we respect your right to free speech, we must emphasise that your actions have brought the company into disrepute and caused significant disruption to ongoing operations. We consider this a breach of the terms outlined in your employment agreement, specifically clauses regarding confidentiality and public conduct.

As such, you are no longer authorised to access any Manic Radio systems, premises, or resources. We request that you return any company property in your possession, including equipment, by no later than 5 p.m. on Monday 21st July 2025.

Please note that your final payment, including any remaining holiday pay, will be processed in the next payroll cycle. Should you have any questions, you may contact the HR department directly.

We wish you the best in your future endeavours.

Regards, Charlotte McDonald HR Manager, Manic Radio Group"

Lyra blinked, processing the email. "Wow. And the irony that they're under investigation by the Police for human trafficking, drugs, facilitating

Lyra blinked, processing the email. "Wow. And the irony that they're under investigation by the Police for human trafficking, drugs, facilitating sexual abuse, and workplace harassment, and you're the one who's brought the company into disrepute." Lyra shook her head in disbelief, handing the phone back to James. "They really don't have a clue, do they?"

James smirked, though there was a faint edge of bitterness in his eyes. "If this is their attempt to silence me, they're about six months too late. Besides, what are they going to do—call OFCOM and complain about my conduct while they're the subject of a criminal investigation? Oh, and Theo emailed too."

Lyra leaned forward, curiosity sparking in her eyes. "What did Theo say? Please tell me it's something good."

James tapped on his phone, opening the email from Theodore Nott, Lyra's brother and their legal ally through the chaos. He read it aloud, his voice a mix of amusement and vindication:

From: *theodore.nott@nottsolicitors.co.uk*

To: *jamie3443snetta@yahoo.co.uk*

Subject: *Re: Update on Police Cases*

James,

I hope this email finds you well—or at least better than those fools at Manic HQ. First off, congratulations on the podcast's success. You and Lyra are making waves in ways most people can only dream of.

Now, onto the fun part. The cases of the Crown versus your sister, your ex, Manic and several others are being investigated by the CPS, which is why I haven't updated you much on the criminal side. The civil claim you wanted to make against them, however, is on hold until the criminal proceedings are further along, but I can confidently say that you have a strong case. The OFCOM findings, coupled with the podcast's impact, have created a perfect storm that makes your claims nearly impossible for them to refute.

Interestingly, I've received some preliminary correspondence from their legal team. They seem rattled—not that they'd ever admit it outright. They're trying to deflect and downplay, of course, but their tone suggests they're more concerned about damage control than actual defence. Classic move from a corporation on the ropes.

The CPS say that they intend to set a date at the Magistrates soon for the initial trial. It's a standard thing, but they'll bump it to the Crown Court, which means there will be more waiting, as the CPS and Crown Courts are overwhelmed right now. But when it does get to trial, they'll face not only the charges from you but those from the other victims and whistleblowers who have come forward. It's shaping up to be one of the biggest media scandals in years. Honestly, it's like watching a slow-motion car crash, and they're still pressing the accelerator.

Keep your head up, James. You're winning this, even if it doesn't feel like it right now.

Best,

Theodore Nott LLB (Oxon), JP

Nott Solicitors"

James let out a low whistle after finishing the email, a flicker of hope crossing his face. "Theo really knows how to make a courtroom drama sound like an episode of Top Gear, doesn't he?"

Lyra chuckled, leaning back against the sofa. "Honestly, I can't wait to see Manic's legal team squirm. It's like they're trying to defend the Titanic after it's already hit the iceberg. And with everything in the public eye now, they can't spin this in their favour."

James nodded, his expression turning serious. "Still, it's going to be a long road. Criminal cases, civil claims… I just want this to be over, Ly. For both of us. For everyone who's been hurt."

Lyra reached for his hand, intertwining her fingers with his. "It will be. And when it is, we'll still be here, stronger than ever. Besides, we've already done the hardest part—speaking out."

James gave her a small smile, the warmth in her words easing the tension in his chest. "Yeah, you're right. It's just surreal, you know? Being at the centre of all this."

"Surreal, but necessary," Lyra said firmly. "And speaking of necessary, we should start planning the next episodes of Broadcasting Boundaries. We've got momentum now, and we need to keep the pressure on. That, and we need to start looking for paying jobs, not just me doing my community shows for the Bones Network of community stations. I mean, working for Woody is great, but community radio doesn't exactly pay the bills, and now you're a free agent, you can see if other stations would want your services."

"I don't think Hits or Capital would touch me with a bargepole," James interjected, smirking ruefully. "Not after everything that's come out about Manic. They probably see me as damaged goods—or worse, a whistleblower who might turn on them next."

Lyra rolled her eyes. "That's their loss. You're one of the best presenters I've ever worked with, well, minus the Reevesy persona and the whole 'Manic lifestyle' phase. But seriously, you've got talent, James. Real talent. You know Ibiza anthems and EDM/Club tracks like the back of your hand. There's always a market for specialists who know their stuff."

James chuckled. "Well, can I let you into a secret, Ly?"

Lyra raised an eyebrow, intrigued. "Oh, do tell. What's this big secret of yours, Mr Smith?"

James leaned back, crossing his arms with a small, conspiratorial smile. "Before I went to Uni, during my gap year, after Covid, I... may have... well, spent a few months in the Balearics working as a DJ in Ibiza," James finished, his grin widening as Lyra's jaw dropped.

"You what?" she exclaimed, swatting him playfully on the arm. "You've been holding out on me, Ibiza Boy? All this time we've been talking about club mixes and EDM, and you've never once mentioned this?"

James laughed, holding up his hands in mock defence. "It wasn't exactly a career highlight, Ly. I wasn't headlining

Amnesia or anything. It was more... low-key. A couple of beach bars, a few underground clubs, and one very memorable night playing at a villa party for a group of slightly unhinged Swedish tourists."

Lyra shook her head, a mixture of disbelief and amusement on her face. "I can't believe you never told me. This is gold, James! Why didn't you mention it before?"

"I guess it didn't seem relevant," he said with a shrug. "I mean, it was the winter of 2021, summer of 2022. I did the normal stuff there, waiting, doing DJ sets, doing cleaning and other odd jobs. It was more survival than career building. Plus, back then, I never imagined it would come up. I was just a kid figuring things out. Although one gig paid me over £20k in one night."

Lyra's eyes widened, and she let out a low whistle. "£20,000 in one night? James, you're sitting on a treasure trove of stories, and you've been holding out on me this whole time. That's more than most people make in a year working nine-to-five!"

James shrugged, looking slightly sheepish. "It wasn't exactly the norm. That night was a fluke. The guy running the villa party was this Arab billionaire, and I think he was just throwing money around to impress people. Half the guests probably didn't even notice I was there, but the ones who did were really into it. They asked for everything from classic house tracks to remixes of Adele songs. It was insane. At the end of the night, he handed me this envelope stuffed with cash and said, 'For your vibes.' I didn't know whether to laugh or cry."

Lyra burst out laughing, shaking her head. "For your vibes? That's brilliant. Honestly, James, it's no wonder that you can afford the best mixing apps on your MacBook, if you were banking £20k in a single night back in the day! You've been a secret high roller this whole time, and here I was, thinking you were just scraping by on student loans and odd jobs."

James chuckled, rubbing the back of his neck. "Trust me, that money didn't last long. Ibiza isn't exactly cheap, especially when you're living there for months. Rent, food, equipment—it all adds up. But yeah, it was a wild time. Maybe too wild. It's part of why I was so drawn to Manic and the whole Ibiza Headbangers vibe. It reminded me of those days… but with less Swedish tourists and more corporate chaos. There was one celeb I did a set for there, my final week on the Island."

Lyra leaned in, eyes sparkling with curiosity. "A celeb, huh? Don't tell me—someone completely unexpected, like Alan Sugar raving to your beats?"

James smirked, shaking his head. "Not quite. Think someone who Manic plays often, an Albanian pop star who's taken the world by storm. She along with Callum Turner and a few other music and film stars were filming a project on the island and decided to host a private wrap party. You might have heard of her—Dua Lipa."

Lyra's eyes widened, and she let out an incredulous laugh. "Dua Lipa? You DJed for Dua freaking Lipa? And you're just casually dropping this now, like it's no big deal?"

James shrugged with a sheepish grin. "It's not like I had a deep conversation with her or anything. She was polite, though—complimented my set and even asked for a couple of specific tracks. It was surreal, but honestly, at the time, I was just trying not to mess up. The pressure was insane. It's ironic, as she and Turner are a thing now, so she probably wouldn't even remember the DJ from that one random villa party in Ibiza."

Lyra shook her head, still laughing. "James, you're unbelievable. Here I am thinking I know everything about you, and now I find out you were not only raking it in as a secret DJ but also rubbing shoulders with global superstars."

"To be fair, their booked DJ had come down with Covid, and apparently someone had recommended me from one of the beach bars I worked at. It was all very last minute and chaotic," James added, grinning. "But yeah, that night... well, it's a memory I'll never forget. Got a few photos with her, Turner, Ronaldo and a few other A listers who'd been to the party. But I never posted them anywhere. I guess I didn't want to seem like one of those people who brags about their 'connections' when really, it was just luck. Want to see the pics?"

Lyra's jaw practically hit the floor. "Do I want to see them? James, are you seriously asking me that? Of course I want to see them! You've been sitting on what could've been a legendary Instagram flex, and you never thought to show me?"

James laughed, pulling out his phone and scrolling through his gallery. "Alright, alright, give me a second. I think they're still in my cloud storage somewhere. I didn't want to delete them, but like I said, I didn't really share them with anyone."

Lyra leaned in, her curiosity building as James flipped through folders. "You're killing me with this suspense, James. Come on, show me the goods!"

After a few moments, James found what he was looking for and handed the phone to Lyra. On the screen was a series of photos: James looking slightly out of his depth but grinning ear to ear, standing next to Dua Lipa in a sleek black dress, Callum Turner holding a drink and giving a thumbs-up, and even Cristiano Ronaldo posing with a group of guests under the villa's fairy-lit canopy. She then saw what looked to be a different party with Alicia Keys, a few DJs, and James in a waiters uniform holding a tray of drinks, clearly multitasking between gigs.

Lyra's jaw dropped further as she swiped through the pictures. "James! These are incredible! You're out here with Dua Lipa, Ronaldo, and Alicia Keys, and you just... forgot to mention it?"

James chuckled, scratching the back of his neck. "I didn't forget, per se. I guess I just never thought it was relevant. I mean, yeah, it was a cool experience, but it's not like I'm still mingling with celebs. It was one chaotic summer that feels like a lifetime ago. Anyway, for some, I had to sign NDAs because they were doing things that... well, let's just say they weren't exactly PG. I figured it was better to keep my head down and enjoy the moment rather than risk making waves."

Lyra stared at him, still processing everything. "You DJed for Dua Lipa, took photos with Ronaldo, and signed NDAs for A-lister parties... James, you've been living a secret double life, and I'm not sure whether to be impressed or annoyed that you kept this from me!"

James laughed, leaning back against the sofa. "I wasn't keeping it from you, Ly. I just... didn't think it mattered anymore. I mean, it's not like it's relevant to the podcast or what we're doing now."

****

CHAPTER 18 - Catharsis
Monday 21st July 2025

Walking out of the Bauer offices at 54 Hagley Road, James had to admit that the meeting had gone far better than expected. He'd spent the past hour with the Hits West Midlands team—JD and Roisin—discussing the next steps after his and Lyra's explosive podcast. The invitation to appear on their breakfast show had felt like a lifeline, a rare opportunity to share his side of the story on a major platform without the Manic branding looming over him.

That they'd, after doing an interview on the Hits Radio West Midlands show gone across to the other Hits Radio studio there, the Staffordshire and Cheshire, what used to be Signal 1 until the April 2024 rebrand of Bauer's Hits Network portfolio from their heritage names to align with their "Hits Radio" branding, had been a nostalgic yet surreal experience for James. He'd once walked similar halls when he was still part of Manic, competing for listener loyalty. But today, as he crossed over to meet Elliot Holman and Matilda Newthorpe at the Stoke and Cheshire studio, there was no rivalry—just camaraderie and mutual respect.

"See, I told you Elliot and Matilda were great folks, and that they'd be welcoming," Lyra said, giving James a gentle nudge as they left the studio of the latter pair. "I mean, they've been holding the fort in this patch long before Hits became, well, Hits. Matilda's advice on balancing work and life is going to be so helpful for when our little one arrives."

James smiled, his heart warming at Lyra's enthusiasm. "Yeah, they were brilliant. And it's weird—being in those studios felt so different from the chaos at Manic. It's like... they actually care about the craft, you know? Dad said yesterday that he misses the old days when JD was on at Wyvern, after he'd cleared his name from that Mercia scandal a couple of years earlier, back in 2008, some competition fixing nonsense back in 2008, something about a rigged prize draw that wasn't his fault but almost cost him his career."

James's voice trailed off as he thought about the stark contrast between the environments. The Bauer studios, even amidst the hustle and bustle of commercial radio, exuded a sense of professionalism and genuine camaraderie that had long been absent at Manic. It was refreshing and oddly comforting—a reminder of what radio could and should be.

Lyra smiled knowingly. "Your dad's got a point. JD's a legend. The fact that he bounced back after that Mercia drama and built such a solid career says a lot about him. And honestly, seeing you in that studio today... it made me think that you had potential, and that had you not been on Manic, but had gone to Global or Bauer, you might have had a very different career. A smoother one, maybe, without all the chaos. But then again, we wouldn't have Broadcasting Boundaries, and let's face it, you've made more impact in the past week than most people do in their whole careers."

James chuckled softly, looking down at the pavement as they walked towards the Edgbaston Village metro stop, the terminus of the Edgbaston Village tram line. "You're not wrong, Ly," he said, his voice thoughtful. "It's weird, isn't it? All that chaos at Manic—it was horrible, but it led to this. The podcast, the attention, the chance to actually be effective. And being in that studio today... It felt like a glimpse of what might be possible. A fresh start."

Lyra nodded, her hand slipping into his as they walked. "It's a fresh start for both of us. Hits, Elliot and Matilda, JD and Roisin—they're showing us that not everyone in radio has lost the plot. There's still integrity out there, still a love for what we do. And you've still got so much to give, James. Whether it's radio, podcasts, or something completely different, you're not done."

James smiled, squeezing her hand gently. "And neither are you. Seriously, Ly, the way you handled yourself in that interview—it was amazing. You've got this natural presence, this authenticity that people connect with. If anyone's got a bright future ahead, it's you. Especially after what Elliot and Matilda said to you after they went off air."

Lyra blushed, laughing softly. "Oh, you mean when Elliot said I had the 'voice for radio and the backbone to take on the world'? Or when Matilda told me I'd be a 'brilliant mentor for the next generation of presenters'? That was... unexpected. But it felt good, you know? Like maybe all the chaos and crap we've been through wasn't for nothing."

James grinned. "Exactly. And they're right. You've got that mix of experience and authenticity that's rare these days. You don't just do the job—you live it. That's why people like Elliot and Matilda respect you. And that's why you're going to thrive, no matter what."

They reached the Edgbaston Village tram stop, the sleek metro line glinting in the morning sunlight, it being only quarter to 11 and the city was already bustling with energy. They boarded the tram heading towards the city centre, finding a quiet corner to sit and reflect on the morning's events. The rhythmic hum of the tram was a comforting backdrop to their conversation.

James glanced out of the window, watching the buildings of Edgbaston give way to Broad Street, the nightlife district of Birmingham looking unlike its pre-COVID self, with modern bars and venues replacing some of the older establishments. His thoughts wandered to what life might have been like if he had never joined Manic—if he'd gone straight into a network like Hits or even stayed in community radio.

"I can't believe how much has changed," James said quietly, almost to himself. "Not just in radio, but in the city, in everything. It feels like... like we're on the other side of something, Ly. Like the chaos is finally behind us."

Lyra tilted her head, studying him for a moment. "It's not fully behind us yet," she said gently. "There's still the court cases, the civil claims, everything with Chloe and Kylie... but you're right. It feels like we're finally moving forward. Like we've got control again."

James nodded, a small smile tugging at his lips. "And it's weird, but... I'm excited about what's next. For the first time in ages, I'm not dreading tomorrow. I'm looking forward to it."

Lyra leaned her head against his shoulder, her voice soft. "Me too. And you know what? No matter what happens, we've got this. Together."

"The next stop is... Brindleyplace..." the automated tram voice announced, breaking their moment of reflection. Lyra smiled as she stood up, as they had just under 5 hours until their next appointment, Capital Birmingham's Tom and Claire on their afternoon drive show. The opportunity to speak on Capital, even after everything that had happened, was a chance to reach a younger audience and solidify their message about resilience and standing up to toxic workplace cultures.

"I'm surprised BBC WM or one of the BBC's national stations haven't called us yet," James remarked as they stepped off the tram at Brindleyplace, the area bustling with professionals and tourists. "You'd think they'd want to weigh in on all of this, especially with how much OFCOM's report has shaken things up."

Lyra chuckled as they strolled along the canal, her eyes scanning the familiar Birmingham skyline. "Give them time. The BBC moves at its own pace. Besides, they're probably strategizing how to address the OFCOM findings without coming across as too critical of Manic while subtly reinforcing their own reputation for 'integrity and balance.'"

James smirked. "Ah, classic BBC. Subtle digs wrapped in neutrality. They'll probably frame it as an exploration of the 'changing dynamics in radio.'"

Lyra grinned. "With a panel of media experts, of course. Can't forget that."

As they reached a café overlooking the water, Lyra pointed to a quiet table outside. "Let's grab a coffee before we head to Capital. We've got time, and honestly, I could use a caffeine boost."

Settling into their seats, James pulled out his phone, scrolling through notifications and messages. The response to their morning interviews was already rolling in—tweets, WhatsApp messages, and even a few emails from former colleagues and listeners. One message stood out, bringing a mix of surprise and gratitude.

"It's from Nigel Freshman," James said, his voice tinged with awe. "I remember Dad once saying how the Fresh and Jo breakfast show on Beacon was his biggest competition when he and Mum worked together for a week on Dudley FM once. He said that Nigel was a broadcasting legend, someone who could effortlessly connect with his audience while still holding his own against the larger stations."

"Wait, I thought your mum was a Wolverhampton FM presenter back then?" Lyra interrupted, raising an eyebrow. "Or was she moonlighting on Dudley FM too?"

James laughed, shaking his head. "She was one of Wolverhampton's heavyweights, used to do their football phone in back in the late '90s and early 2000s against Dad on Dudley FM. For a week when I was only 2, Woody Bones had had to beg Wolverhampton FM to loan them mum as the two breakfast hosts back then, Lisa and Colin Hargreaves, had eloped to Gretna Green and gotten married on a whim, leaving Dudley FM without a breakfast team. Of course, Dad said that Woody dropped it on him the Saturday before that he and Mum were teaming up for a week, and that my granddad, Alan Reeves, mum's dad, would be babysitting us. He told me once that they'd had to be up for 4am to do the 5 minute drive from home to The Waterfront, ready for 6am, and that first morning together was chaos because Mum wasn't used to Dudley's setup, which apparently included a temperamental coffee machine that nearly caused a mutiny." James grinned, his voice filled with affection for the anecdote. "It didn't help that they were networked between Dudley and Walsall because the Walsall crew had defected to Beacon."

Lyra laughed, shaking her head in disbelief. "Sounds like classic local radio chaos. I can't imagine your dad and mum teaming up under those circumstances. Must've been like walking a tightrope with no safety net."

James grinned, leaning back in his chair. "Dad always said it was one of the most memorable weeks of his career. Mum kept him on his toes, though. Apparently, the listeners were all "Team Sarah" all week and hoping that Mum would continue permanently take over the show. But, of course, once Lisa and Colin came back from their whirlwind Gretna Green escapade, things went back to normal." James laughed, his eyes lighting up as he recalled the story. "Dad said he was secretly relieved because Mum had such a strong personality on air that she overshadowed him at times. He was glad to go back to being the 'king' of Dudley FM."

Lyra chuckled, stirring her coffee. "Your parents were like the Ross and Rachel of local radio—full of drama, but everyone loved them together."

James nodded, his expression turning thoughtful. "It's funny, isn't it? How those stories from the past feel so different from what we've been through. Back then, it was about the love of radio, even when things went sideways. Now it's... well, you've seen it. Metrics, branding, and chaos."

Lyra reached across the table, squeezing his hand. "And yet here we are, trying to bring some of that authenticity back. Your dad would be proud, James. Both your parents would."

James smiled, his eyes softening. "Thanks, Ly. That means a lot."

Their conversation was interrupted by a notification on Lyra's phone. She glanced at it and her eyes widened slightly. "Well, speak of the devil. The Beeb just emailed. They want us on tomorrow's breakfast show to talk about the podcast and the OFCOM findings. Not on WM though..."

James raised an eyebrow, leaning forward in curiosity. "Not WM? Where, then? Midlands Today?"

Lyra shook her head, a sly grin forming on her lips. "Nope. The Today programme. National Radio 4. They want us in London tomorrow morning."

James blinked in surprise, leaning back in his chair as the weight of the news sank in. "The Today programme? As in, the most respected breakfast slot in the country? Wow. That's... huge."

Lyra nodded, her grin widening. "Yeah, no pressure or anything. Just us, in front of millions of listeners, dissecting the implosion of one of the biggest radio networks in the UK. Casual."

James let out a low whistle, shaking his head in disbelief. "First Hits, then Capital, and now the Today programme. We're really making waves, aren't we?"

Lyra's expression turned serious, though the excitement still glimmered in her eyes. "We are. And it's not just about us anymore, James. This is a chance to highlight everything—Manic's culture, the systemic issues in radio, the people who've been hurt. If we do this right, we could spark real change. Anyway, did you hear about the Manic Classical host, Edmund Leatherhurst and his producer, Arabella Hargrove?"

James shook his head, intrigued. "No, what happened with them? Manic Classical always seemed like the last bastion of sanity in that madhouse."

"It's just come up on Radio Today that they both resigned on air, mid show. Something to do with an email Manic is sending staff, which they, as classical hosts and therefore the 'only bastion of highbrow content' in their words, found condescending and offensive," Lyra explained, her tone tinged with disbelief. "Apparently, Edmund said something along the lines of, 'Ladies and gentlemen, Arabella and I have decided this will be our final broadcast on Manic Classical. This is not a decision we take lightly but given the patronising tone of an email we've just received from management—an email instructing us on how to better represent the 'Manic brand' while staying 'relevant to modern audiences'—we feel it is impossible to continue with integrity. Arabella and I thank you for your loyalty, and we encourage you to support broadcasters who respect their audiences as much as they respect their staff.' And then they played Beethoven's Symphony No. 9 and walked out. Now, considering he's 49 and ex Radio 3, and she's 82 and has been in radio for half a century, that's a pretty bold way to go out," Lyra said, shaking her head in awe. "It's like they decided, 'If we're going down, we're going down with a symphonic mic drop.'"

James burst out laughing, a genuine, belly-shaking laugh that felt like a release of all the tension he'd been carrying. "You're telling me they walked out to Ode to Joy? That's... I mean, that's legendary. That's the radio equivalent of flipping the table and striding off into the sunset. They were the last two there, wasn't they, as the rest of them had resigned slowly over the past 2 and half months when the story about the "Baby Bonus" broke and the OFCOM investigation started heating up. I mean, they were holding out, but I guess even they hit their limit. Dad said the Goldies lot at Huddersfield were having to cover shifts on Classical between doing their own local drives or breakfast shifts. That's a lot to juggle, even for the best presenters," James said, shaking his head. "I wonder how Manic's going to spin this one. It's like the wheels are falling off faster than they can patch them up."

Lyra chuckled, leaning back in her chair and swirling the last of her coffee. "You know what they'll do. Same as always. Spin some PR nonsense about 'restructuring' or 'refining their vision' for Manic Classical. Meanwhile, the listeners will be left wondering why Beethoven sounds so angry all of a sudden."

James smirked. "They'll probably start looping AI-generated presenters with canned intros like, 'This is Manic Classical, the sound of sophistication.' All while playing the same four pieces of Mozart on repeat because no one left knows how to curate a proper playlist. That or they'll just use a voiceover artist who works cheap to churn out pre-recorded links between tracks. 'Here's another timeless classic on Manic Classical, your destination for culture.' Meanwhile, they're Googling 'top ten classical songs for relaxing' to fill the gaps."

Lyra laughed, shaking her head. "You joke, but I wouldn't be surprised if that's their backup plan. Honestly, I feel for the listeners. They signed up for a station that respected their love of classical music, not some slapped-together algorithm pretending to care about culture. Even Magic Classical, Bauer's own classical substation on Rayo, would be a better option at this point. You know, the old Scala Radio team that got rebranded last year when Magic Chilled got flipped to Hits Chilled and Magic Classical took its spot? That lot had the right idea. Keep it simple, keep it classy, and let the music do the talking."

James nodded, the humour fading slightly as he considered Lyra's point. "It's just sad, isn't it? Watching something that once had so much potential fall apart because the people running it cared more about metrics and image than the actual content. Edmund and Arabella were pros—they deserved better. The listeners deserved better."

Lyra reached across the table, resting her hand on his. "But that's why we're doing this, James. To call it out. To make sure people know there's still a way back from all this chaos. Broadcasting Boundaries isn't just our story—it's theirs too."

James smiled, the determination in her voice reminding him why they'd started this journey in the first place. "You're right. And if Edmund and Arabella walking out to Beethoven isn't a rallying cry, I don't know what is."

Lyra grinned. "Ode to Joy as a protest anthem—who would've thought? But seriously, if there's one thing this industry has taught us, it's that the people who care, the ones who stick it out even when it's hard, they're the ones who make it worthwhile."

James raised his coffee cup in a mock toast. "To the survivors of the Manic madness. And to whatever comes next."

Lyra clinked her empty cup against his with a soft laugh. "To what comes next. Because whatever it is, it's going to be ours—not theirs."

As they stood to leave, the city of Birmingham bustling around them, James felt a flicker of hope amidst the chaos. For the first time in years, the future didn't feel like something to fear—it felt like something to fight for. And with Lyra by his side, he knew they could face whatever came their way.

Tomorrow would bring new challenges, new opportunities, and maybe even new revelations on national radio. But for now, they had a moment of calm—a brief pause before the next chapter in their story began.

****

Books by Thomas Brant

Broadcasting Boundaries Series
Broadcasting Boundaries

Broadcasting Chaos

www.ingramcontent.com/pod-product-compliance
Ingram Content Group UK Ltd.
Pitfield, Milton Keynes, MK11 3LW, UK
UKHW032236230125
454132UK00004B/78